Pride & Pressure

A Classics Retold Romance

C.J. Owens

Author Note

The characters in this book are Christian; in fact, one of them is a pastor of a nondenominational church. It is not the intent of the author to convert or try and persuade anyone to become Christian by reading this book. This is still a love story like any other you would find in a contemporary romance novel. Criticizing the hypocrisy of so-called "Sunday Christians" is part of the story, however, so if you are not okay with that, this is not the book for you. If you have any type of religion/church-based trauma, this is also not the book for you. All that being said, this book is written for all romance readers, regardless of what you do or do not believe in.

Potential Additional Triggers: Dom/Sub/BDSM, anxiety, parental loss, body shaming, and suicide (mentioned).

Playlist

"Insecurities" – Jess Glynne

"If You Want Love" – NF

"No Mercy" – Austin Giorgio

"Bad Habits" – Nation Haven

"Dangerous Woman" – Ariana Grande

"Trust in You" – Lauren Daigle

"Tell Me Like It Is" – Warren Zeiders

"Am I Okay?" – Megan Moroney

"Alone With You" – Bryce Savage

"Tell Your Heart to Beat Again" – Danny Gokey

"The Good Ones" – Gabby Barrett

"Thank God" – Kane Brown & Katelyn Brown

<u>Dedication</u>

To all those who feel like giving up on love, don't.
There's someone out there just waiting for you to propose.

"Happiness in marriage is entirely a matter of chance. If the dispositions of the parties are ever so well known to each other or ever so similar before-hand, it does not advance their felicity in the least. They always continue to grow sufficiently unlike afterwards to have their share of vexation; and it is better to know as little as possible of the defects of the person with whom you are to pass your life."

-Charlotte Lucas, *Pride and Prejudice*

Contents

Chapter 1
Charlotte

I am far too old to be in a club at one in the morning. Unintelligible lyrics scream in my ears while pounding beats accost my senses. My personal space is being invaded on all sides by wriggling and gyrating strangers. I would much rather be at home, on the couch, reading a book with my cats on my lap.

At least once a month, Lizzy convinces me to try clubbing one more time and, like a fool, I give in. She's five years younger than me and still enjoys this type of thing. Given my lack of success on dating apps, I find myself resorting to club visits for any kind of male attention. I'm just that pathetic.

A couple in serious dance mode bump into me and I almost fall over. Everywhere I turn, people are slinging sweat and shaking body parts. I steady myself by grabbing onto Lizzy's extended hand. She's trying to tell me something, but no matter how loud she gets, her voice is just a whisper in this chaotic sound experience. I point to the bar which is far away from the DJ. She nods and follows me, grasping my hand so we don't lose each other in this sea of energetic bodies.

"I was trying to tell you that guy was checking you out!" Lizzy's voice is now unnaturally loud away from the dance floor. I glance behind her and spot a blonde guy a few feet away who's definitely giving me a slow once over. The dark-haired guy next to him appears disgruntled, almost disgusted by everyone in the club. Lizzy stares at him longingly and starts fanning herself with her hand. "His friend is so hot."

"If you say so. He looks a little nauseous." I lean my back against the bar, careful to suck in my stomach and angle my body in a flattering manner.

"I wonder if we should go talk to them," Lizzy says, one foot already stepping in their direction.

"You always told me that making the first move makes you look desperate," I remind her. I'm not above approaching a guy first; in fact, that's usually how handle these situations. However, it would be nice to be the one getting asked out instead of the doing the asking myself.

"Fine." Lizzy pouts and glances towards the back of the club. "I wonder what's taking Jane so long." Jane, Lizzy's sister, had abandoned us to use the bathroom ages ago.

"She's probably fidgeting with her makeup or something," I suggest. I couldn't care less where Jane is. She's tolerable in small bursts, so the longer she's gone, the better.

"Oh my God, Charlotte! Look!" Eyes wide, Lizzy jerks her head to the side. Blondie and his sickly companion are walking our way. Before I can fully panic, they're standing in front of us.

"Evening, ladies," blondie says, a broad smile on his handsome face. The friend says nothing.

"More like morning," I subtly correct him with a laugh.

"I suppose you're right," he admits, running his hand through his short, wavy blonde hair. "I'm Charlie, Charlie Bingley. This is my friend, Darcy." He gestures to the grim-faced man next to him.

"I'm Charlotte Lucas. This is Lizzy Bennett." I nod towards Lizzy who is doing her very best to seem nonchalant though nervous energy radiating off of her. She's trying desperately to match Darcy's weird vibe to get his attention. He's not even looking at us. Instead, he's looking past us, almost through us, to the busy bar behind us.

"This is our first time at this club. Do you come here often?" His cliché line makes me cringe internally; however, I refuse to be deterred.

"About once a month or so. It's the least crowded one we've been to, if you can believe that." I gesture towards the mob of people moving behind him.

"Ah. Darcy just moved here about a week ago and I forced him to explore the city. I'm much more of an extrovert than he is," Charlie says, laughing at his friend's expense.

"You don't say?" Part of me wonders if Charlie often makes people do things against their will. That doesn't speak very highly to his character. I sort of feel bad for Darcy at this point.

"I hope you don't find this too forward, but..." Charlie leaves his sentence unfinished and stares to my left. I turn my head to find out what has caught his attention and my heart sinks: its Jane.

"Don't mind me!" Jane says, inserting herself into our conversation. "Sorry I was gone so long. There was a major line," she explains to Lizzy and I.

All of Charlie's attention is now on her instead of me because of course it is. I'm an elephant next to Jane's perfect, sample sized body with her bountiful cleavage. What man would want a size twelve woman with a giant ass and paradoxically small boobs over her? Not to mention her makeup skills are top tier, whereas I flinch at the very thought of an eyeliner pencil near my eyes. My plainness is never more obvious than when we go out with her. I had begged Lizzy not to invite Jane, but she insisted, and now I've lost any chance I may have had with Charlie.

"I'm Jane!" She extends her hand to Charlie and, instead of shaking it, he kisses it like a chivalrous knight. Yep, I'm done. She wins. She always wins.

Sighing deeply, I release my stomach muscles and shake my head. Guys I've dated in the past claimed to love my intelligence, my compassion, and my sense of humor, but at the end of the day, it always came down to a lack of physical attraction. Despite their constant rejection, I refuse to change my appearance to make a man happy. If they are that shallow, I don't want to be with them anyway.

"I'm Charlie Bingley. So nice to meet you," he says, his voice smooth as silk. That's not the greeting I got. I inhale slowly and count to ten. It's fine. It's fine. It's fine.

"Would you like to dance?" He gestures toward the crowded dance floor.

"Sure!" Jane giggles and allows him to lead her away into the mass of gyrating bodies. Darcy is left behind, looking dismayed and annoyed. He huffs and starts to turn away.

"Wait," Lizzy begins, "is Darcy your first name or your last name?" She wants to play hard to get so bad. Unfortunately, she's so bad at it. I shake my head as her eyes flick to me for assistance.

Surprisingly, he answers. "It's my last name," he explains in a monotone voice.

"Not many people go by their last name," I chime in. "Is your first name really weird?" The moment I ask the question, I regret it. I really want to help Lizzy out and be her wing woman. Unfortunately for her, I'm quite bad at it. It doesn't help that my ego has entirely been deflated by the Charlie and Jane situation. I just want to leave and pretend that never happened.

"My first name is Fitzwilliam. It's a family name and not all that common anymore." He sighs as he speaks, as if each word causes him immeasurable pain. He's clearly annoyed with us and would like to leave just as much as I do. Lizzy is undaunted.

"I think that's a cool name. I'm named after my grandmother." She smiles sweetly at his sour expression.

"Fascinating." Sarcasm drips from his voice in a way that makes my skin crawl.

"Well, it's late. We better go." I nudge Lizzy toward the exit as her eyes linger on Darcy.

"It was so nice to meet you, Mr. Darcy," Lizzy says, fluttering her eyelashes at him.

"Indeed." He frowns and watches us with a judgmental glare as we leave the club.

"He's awful," I tell Lizzy as we wait for our Uber to arrive. "Don't even think about it."

"Too late!" She's already searching for him on Instagram, Facebook, Twitter, and who knows what else. Lizzy has a habit of dating "bad boys," and despite how often they break her heart, she keeps going back for more punishment.

"Suit yourself." I shrug my shoulders.

"Sorry about Jane," Lizzy says, glancing up at me with sympathetic eyes. I hold up a hand to stop her apology.

"I told you not to invite her," my tone more scathing than I intended. "On a good day, I'm a 7. Next to Jane? I'm a 3."

"Don't be so hard on yourself. You're beautiful!" She compliments me, though it feels hollow and unwarranted.

"I almost had a chance with Charlie. I was so close!" It doesn't matter that I wasn't really feeling a connection to him yet; that takes time and a completely different atmosphere. I groan as I sit down on the bus stop bench. Placing my face in my hands, I sigh deeply. "I know it's not your fault and I shouldn't be taking out my anger on you. I'm just so damn frustrated!"

"I get that," Lizzy says, sitting down next to me and patting my back to comfort me. "We won't bring her next time, I promise." She lays her head on my shoulder.

"Thanks," I say, unclenching my fist and rubbing my fingers over the indentions in my palm from my nails.

"Besides, you need a man who's interested in you for more than just your looks. Charlie was too shallow."

"You're right," I nod in agreement. "Finding a guy at a club is pointless, yet, I keep coming back."

"You need something more substantial than just a one-night stand."

"You mean because I'm so old and I don't have a lot of time left?" I'm only half-serious in my jest. My age is a touchy subject when it comes to matters of the heart.

"Thirty isn't old! That's not what I meant." She stands up and waves down our Uber. "I meant you deserve better than a guy who's looking to get laid and leave. We both do," she resumes once we're in the car.

"It would be so nice to already just have someone and be in the comfortable part of a relationship without all the awkward dating and getting to know each other crap. Dating is the worst." I lean back against the seat and close my eyes. Streetlights flicker across my eyelids as we drive through town. I want to dissolve into the darkness, exist outside of space and time, and fade away from reality for just a moment.

When Lizzy begged and pleaded for me to come out with her one more time, I knew it would end badly, and yet I couldn't disappoint her. Unlike me, she still believes love is out there, which makes sense since she's younger than me and hasn't had her heart broken into shreds. Her endless optimism is both annoying and endearing. I want to love again, I truly do. I want to have a marriage like my parents, a permanent bond, a faithful companion to care for me and spend my days with. I mean, there's always my cats, but I can't even claim them as dependents on my taxes, so I'm not sure they count.

The ride is over too soon and we trudge up the stairs to our apartment door. Lizzy steps out of her heels and places them carefully on the shoe rack by the door. I sling mine off to the side where they clunk against the TV stand.

We say good night and head to our separate bedrooms, both too tired to talk anymore about our disastrous night. Turning on my lamp, I'm pleased to find Cleo and Tony purring in a contented ball on my pillow. Cleo opens her eyes slowly and yawns, revealing her ferocious teeth. Tony stretches in his sleep and rolls over.

"Hi, pretty kitty," I whisper as I pet her soft head. "At least I can always rely on you and Tony to love me." She jumps from the bed and hops in her cat bed where she proceeds to make biscuits.

As I clamber into bed, Tony smushes himself against my face before curling against my chest. When I asked God for a loving man after Brad destroyed my heart two years ago, he sent me Tony, and I am forever grateful.

Chapter 2
William

There's nothing like the high I get from sharing the word of God with my congregants. However, that high was dulled today since, throughout my sermon, all I could think about was my impending meeting with my boss, Cat De Bourgh. Despite my distracted focus, the congregants still praise me for an excellent message as I make my way down the aisle and to my office.

"Another excellent sermon, Reverend Collins!" Mrs. Johnson says, grasping my hand firmly in her own as I walk by.

"Thank you," I respond politely as she releases me from her sweaty palms.

"How do you always know just want to say?" Mr. Hughes places his hand on my shoulder with a look of disbelief on his face. "I really needed to hear that message today."

"I'm just a humble messenger," I reply. I try very hard to not let the praise get to me and give me a big head. Pride is a sin, after all.

After countless more congregants seek me out to thank me or get my advice on something, I finally make it to my office, a quiet place all my own within the walls of this mega sanctuary.

"It's about time." Cat's voice resounds as she dramatically turns around in my desk chair to reveal herself like the villain in a Bond movie. The chain from her glasses to her neck sways as she shakes her head at my tardiness.

"It couldn't be helped." I shrug my shoulders. It's odd to be on this side of my own desk, but she's is the boss, so I guess it makes sense in this situation.

"I've been speaking with the board and there's an issue we need to have rectified." She places her elbows on the desk and rests her double chin on her hands. "You are thirty years of age and unmarried, correct?"

"Correct?" I raise an eyebrow at her passive aggressive tone. Where is this going?

"It's time to fix that." Her eyes take on a malicious gleam.

"My age or marital status?" My response is only partially sarcastic.

"Don't be childish, William. Its time you got married. It's unseemly for a man of your age to be unmarried. You are the head pastor of this church. You are a role model. You need to set an example for all the married couples in the church. This is part of your job."

"What are you suggesting?" Despite my approaching apprehension, I maintain a calm, detached attitude.

"Here is a list of approved church members." She hands me a list of about ten names. "Choose one of them to marry."

"You want me to marry one of these women?" I want to tell her she can't be serious, but with Cat, it's always serious. I give the list of names a cursory glance.

"Yes. You have one year." She stands up abruptly and begins to leave my office.

"Wait." My request makes her halt. "One year to get married? That's not enough time to get to know someone and decide if you want to marry them," I protest.

"If you are not married in a year's time, consider that your resignation." Cat doesn't wait for my response before sneering and exiting my office. The congregants may think I'm the one in charge, but with a 51% share in the Hilltop board, Cat's the true boss around here. It's her way or no way.

I sit down at my desk and lay my head in my hands. This is preposterous! What woman would agree to such a ludicrous proposition? What if I date someone for a few months and she's not the one? Then I have even less time to find someone who is!

Then again, does it even matter if I love her? Cat doesn't seem to think so. To her, my future marriage is just another part of Hilltop's perfect image. I can only imagine the amount of press my wedding would create. From Cat's perspective, it's all about business. A married preacher appeals to more families and gives the appearance of permanence and stability. Honestly, it's impressive it took her this long to drop the ultimatum.

However, not only must I get married, but I have to marry a church member, which, while it looks good on paper, is the worst part of this whole situation. There are two reasons why I don't date the women in my congregation. First of all, it's incredibly awkward. Second of all, my romantic proclivities don't exactly match my day job. The idea of repressing my sexual desires for the rest of my life to marry a *suitable* woman fills me with dread and a little bit of nausea.

The chances of finding a woman on the list who happens to accept my darker nature is slim to none. I pick up Cat's list and quickly read over the names. Fortunately, all of the women on the list are young and beautiful. Well, if I'm going to have boring sex the rest of my life, at least she'll be nice to look at.

At the top of the alphabetically arranged list is Elizabeth Bennett. I run my finger over her name. If I had to choose a woman from the church to be tied down to forever, she would be the one. I've spent many a Sunday glancing at her in the front row with her parents and sisters. The way her brown eyes light up when she leads the children in their weekly lesson shows that she has what it takes to take on the role of "pastor's wife."

Cat has conveniently put each woman's phone number next to their name. I add Elizabeth's number to my contacts and send her a message inviting her to dinner with me this Friday. Now all I have to do is wait. I'm a very patient man.

***

Despite my insistence that I pick her up for our date, Elizabeth told me to meet her at the restaurant instead. My foot taps restlessly under the table as I anxiously scan the entrance for her appearance. Looking at my watch, I remember that she still has plenty of time to arrive. In my opinion, if I'm not early, I'm late; I forget that not everyone abides by that axiom.

A man in a tuxedo plays soft music from the piano in the corner. Part of me worries this restaurant is too formal for a first date. The other part of me wants to show off and impress Elizabeth, so the fancier the better. I tug at the tie around my neck to loosen it a bit and let some air down my collar. At first, sitting near the lit fireplace was pleasant and romantic. Now that sweat is rolling down my back and gathering under my arms, I'm full of regrets.

Just as I'm about to wave down a waiter to change location, Elizabeth begins walking towards my table. Her sandy blonde hair is pulled back in a bouncing ponytail with two wisps on either side to frame her pretty face. I focus all my attention on her smile and try to ignore the way her blue dress clings to her curves. I'm not celibate by any means, but it has been awhile.

"Evening, Reverend Collins," she says, sitting down gracefully in the chair the waiter pulled out for her.

"Evening, Elizabeth. Please, call me William," I gently correct her. I don't need to be reminded that I'm her preacher. This situation is weird enough as it is. "How was your day?"

"You know you can just call me Lizzy," she reminds me. "The kids are always crazy on Fridays. Other than that, it was okay." She picks up her menu and begins perusing the options. What kids is she talking about? It takes my brain a second to realize she's talking about her students.

"I suppose they are excited about the weekend," I reply, also perusing my menu.

"I am, too, but I don't spend the day screaming and throwing paper airplanes." Elizabeth groans and closes her eyes for a moment.

"True." I'm at a loss as to how to proceed. She's clearly annoyed now and I'm unsure how to fix that. Fortunately, the waiter returns to take our order and I can change the subject once he leaves. "How are your parents?"

"They're good." She doesn't elaborate.

"Good." We stare awkwardly at the vase of red roses in the middle of the table and avoid eye contact. The sweat from my back has made its way to my waistband and my discomfort grows. I rest a hand on my glass of ice water to cool down. "What do you like to do for fun?" I really should have Googled conversation starters for first dates.

"I like to read and spend time with my sisters." She sips her water and eyes me coolly.

"What do you like to read?"

"Romance books." She stares at me, daring me to say something snarky about her favorite genre.

"Ah," I reply, clearly failing to demonstrate my wit and enormous vocabulary. There's nothing wrong with reading romance books per se, I just think there are better genres for expanding your mind and challenging your intellect. The waiter returns and fills our wine glasses. I'm not much for drinking; however, I'll take all the help I can get with this date. Both Elizabeth and I sip our wine as if we're relieved to have something else to do.

If not for the piano music, the silence of our conversation would be deafening. Elizabeth keeps looking around the room, seemingly admiring the paintings on the walls, though it's clear she's just as uncomfortable as I am. Finally, our dinner arrives and we can use eating as an excuse to avoid talking.

This is not at all how I thought tonight would go. I imagined easy conversation, laughter, kissing her good night outside of her apartment. Instead, I get the feeling she would literally rather be anywhere else than here with me. The steak in my mouth tastes like rubber and, with each chew, I resist the urge to spit it out and just leave the restaurant in utter embarrassment.

Since this night can't possibly get any worse, I may as well tell her why we're in this situation.

"You may be wondering why I asked you to dinner," I begin. She finally makes eye contact with me and gives me her undivided attention. "I'm in search of a wife and I thought, maybe, that could be you." They say ripping off a bandage is less painful than tugging it off a little at a time. Judging by Elizabeth's expression, I doubt that very much.

"Wait, are you asking me to marry you?" Her eyes widen and her lips part as she waits for my answer.

"In a manner of speaking, yes." I lean forward and gently grab her hand from the table. "It's crazy and we don't really know each other, but I have to get married soon so I can keep my job. You're a good person and you come from a good family. Once we're married, we can get to know each other better. What do you say?"

Elizabeth pulls her hand away from mine and covers her mouth as she starts laughing. Her raucous laughter is drawing attention to our table. Austere older couples glance our way with disdain as Elizabeth's laughing fit, snorts and all, continues.

"I don't see what's so hilarious," I snap. "I don't appreciate your laughter at my question."

"I'm sorry," she says, finally calming down and controlling her amusement. "I've just never heard something so ridiculous in my life." She dabs at her eyes with her napkin. "You can't be serious."

"Why not?"

"People don't propose marriage to strangers." She shakes her head and drinks the rest of her wine.

"We're not strangers. You go to my church," I point out. Her eyes narrow and it's clear she's going to say no. "Will you please just think about it?" I plead.

"Fine," she sighs, rolling her eyes. "I'll think about it." Thinking about it isn't going to change her answer, but I could use a little false hope right about now.

"Well," Elizabeth says, standing up from her chair. "This has been super weird so I'm going to go now." Looking down at me with a sad smile, she says, "I'll give you my answer soon." She walks out just as gracefully as she had walked in.

I rest my head in my hands and exhale so loudly I'm sure the kitchen staff can hear me. I've never been so embarrassed and flustered in my life. If this is how all the dates are going to go, I may as well start searching for a new job right now.

Chapter 3
Charlotte

Nick, Eddie, Rob, and Dad are bunched up on the sofa screaming at the basketball players on the giant plasma TV in the living room. They left the dinner table without even bothering to clear their plates. Mom says nothing as she scrapes their dishes and empties their glasses before placing them carefully in the dishwasher.

"You really should make them do that. You cooked everything." It kills me how she still spoils them and treats them like children even though they are all in their twenties.

"I've got it. Let them enjoy their game," Mom says. I sigh loudly and refuse to surrender.

"That's not the point. You think that because they are men, they are excused from so-called womanly tasks and that's not fair. They can pick up a plate and carry it into the kitchen. It's not hard," I point out.

"Charlotte," she cautions, "one day, if you have sons, you'll understand. Of course, you'd need to be married first and we both know that's not happening any time soon." She slams the dishwasher closed with a thud. "Although, there is something your father and I need to talk to you about in regard to that topic." She wipes off the counter and calls Dad into the kitchen.

"What is it?" Dad bumbles into the kitchen with his readers on and a newspaper in his hand.

"Tell Charlotte what we talked about earlier," Mom prompts Dad who, placing down the paper and his glasses, gives me a sad look. He clearly doesn't want anything to do with this situation.

"It's time you got married," he says bluntly and with more awkwardness than I thought could exist in one moment. I physically have to close my mouth with my hand or my jaw will fall off my face. What did he just say? I must have misheard him. This is so weird. What is even happening right now?

Eventually, I regain my composure and my ability to speak. "You two act like I haven't been trying to achieve that goal for the past few years. You really should just give it up. I have." After years of bad dates and crappy boyfriends, I'm convinced love either doesn't exist or it's just really good at hide and seek.

"Charlotte," Mom begins. "Maybe you're not..."

"What? Not trying hard enough? I was out with Lizzy and Jane last weekend and, despite one guy seeming interested at first, he picked Jane instead! I'm so tired of these superficial men and their one-track minds." I roll my eyes and notice Dad cringing at my words. "Sorry, Dad."

"Your father and I have been talking and we think you should go on a date with Jay Dunham. He's just finished graduate school and his parents were thinking you'd be a good match." She looks so pleased with her suggestion.

"Jay? Jay Dunham?" I start laughing in spite of myself. "Jay is gay, Mom, so I don't think he and I are a good match." I turn to gauge Dad's response to all of this, yet he avoids eye contact. He knows this is ridiculous.

Mom sighs and starts rubbing her chest with her right hand. She had an "episode" a few months ago that put us all on edge, so now Dad is on high alert.

"Nori, you're stressing yourself out. Remember your heart." Dad walks over to Mom and takes her hand.

"Stop coddling me." She reprimands him and resumes rubbing her chest. "I'm fine. I take my heart pills every day like the doctor said."

"Mom, this is nothing to stress over. The boys will have fiancés before you know it and you can stop worrying about the burden of your only daughter." My tone is tight and my voice is clipped, far more antagonistic than I should be with my own mother. Both she and Dad stare at me in surprise.

Changing my tone, I take a deep breath and say, "Look, I'm sorry. I appreciate your help and I recognize that you have good intentions. However, you're just going to have to accept that fact that I'm a crazy cat lady and no man will ever want me to be his wife." As I speak, my eyes begin to water so I blink quickly to make the tears dissipate. "Thanks for dinner. I'll see you next weekend." I quickly hug them both, yell bye to my brothers, and head outside.

Once I get in my car, I sigh and lean back against the seat. Charlie's rejection last night and Mom's suggestion tonight has me feeling more than disheartened. Is this what rock bottom is like? The bottom of the barrel? Being between Scylla and Charybdis? My mind floats back to what Mom said a few months ago when we were watching "Say Yes to the Dress" together.

A very happy blonde woman was introducing herself on the screen and talking about how she met her fiance. Her name and age appeared below her: Lyndsey, 27.

"She seems a bit old to just now be getting married," Mom muttered to herself, her eyes glued to the screen. At first, I don't think she realized she said that out loud. As realization dawned on her face, she turned towards me and opened her mouth, but I cut her off.

"Actually, Mom, 28 is the average age women are getting married these days. People don't get married at 20 that often anymore." I crossed my arms and dared her to respond. We watched the rest of the episode in silence.

At this point in my life, I'm sorely tempted to hire someone to pretend to be my boyfriend at my next family get together just so they'll leave me alone about it. It would make Mom so happy knowing I have a man in my life, a man I might marry and have a family with. Marriage shouldn't be a requirement for a woman's happiness, and I know I shouldn't live my life according to my mother's expectations, so why does her disappointment hurt so much? I wipe my eyes with my sleeve and start my car. These are all questions for my stress journal when I get home.

Once I arrive home, I'm so glad I have the place to myself; Lizzy is out on a date tonight. Settling on the couch with a cup of tea and a book, I eagerly enter a fictional world far different from the real one. After two chapters, I'm disturbed by the buzzing of my phone with a text message.

Dad: "Sorry about your mom, kiddo. She just wants you to be happy and to her, that means being married."

I want to shove the phone into the couch cushions and pretend I didn't get the message. I had finally put that conversation in the past and now I'm right back in it. Every time Mom brings up the fact that I'm single, she acts like I'm single on purpose, like I have hundreds of guys begging me to marry them and I'm turning them all down with glee. Every guy I date turns out the same way and I'm tired of it. I'm tired of putting myself out there and getting rejected. Guys my age want someone younger or prettier and I can't change either of those things about myself.

Me: "I know. Love you."

He tries his best to balance out Mom's crazy, so I don't blame Dad for the weird Jay-centered ambush. Cleo climbs into my lap and rubs her face against my book begging for attention. "Okay, needy girl." I set the book down and run my hand down her soft, fluffy body. "We are independent women. We don't need men. Right, Cleo?" She *mrows* in response and starts kneading my lap.

Tony, not to be outdone, also climbs in my lap and demands pets. "We'll make an exception for you, Mr. Man," I say, laughing to myself. At least I have my cats to keep me company. Oh, God. I really am an old maid, cats and all.

Before I can start having my weekly existential crisis, the front door opens and Lizzy enters. She takes off her coat and walks over to the couch with a weird expression on her face.

"What happened?" I ask.

"I just had the weirdest date ever!" Lizzy squeals in between bouts of laughter.

"Did he bring his mother with him?" I ask, remembering my very uncomfortable date with Howard three months ago.

"No, though it was just as awkward," Lizzy promises me. "He asked me to marry him!" Her eyes are bright with astonishment. "How crazy is that?"

"That is very crazy," I respond coolly. Given Lizzy's beauty and outgoing personality, I'm honestly surprised this is the first time a man has proposed to her on a date. If she wasn't so picky, she'd be married by now. She keeps waiting around for Mr. Right. I'd be happy with Mr. Right Now.

"I thought he was joking at first, so I laughed." Lizzy plops down on the sofa next to me, causing the cats to leap from my lap to the nearby cat tree for safety. "Turns out, he was serious and did not appreciate my laughter."

"He sounds delightful," I respond sarcastically.

"I think you should go on a date with him," Lizzy suggests, a mischievous glint in her eyes.

"What? Why? I don't even know him." This is insane, even for Lizzy, the queen of insane ideas.

"I just have a feeling that you two would hit it off." She shrugs and leans back against a throw pillow.

"Should I be flattered or offended considering you only have negative things to say about him?" I cross my arms and give her my best side eye.

"He's a good guy," she assures me. "Nothing is wrong with him. He's just not right for me. He's more your type."

"My type? What do you mean?" I ask, prepared to be completely insulted.

"Serious, nerdy, well put together; the complete opposite of what I go for." She laughs lightly at her self-deprecating comment. "You should meet him," she suggests.

"You think I'm that desperate to get married?" I throw my hands up in the air in frustration.

"I think your family is," Lizzy points out.

"You have no idea. They just tried to set me up with a family friend's son who has zero interest in dating women. It was humiliating!"

"So, what have you got to lose? He could be the secret love of your life." She clasps her hands to her chest dramatically. She's been reading too many romance novels.

"Answer me this. If he hadn't proposed to you, would you have seen him again?" I don't want Lizzy's sloppy seconds, regardless of how much her ridiculous idea is beginning to appeal to me.

"Ugh, no. Like I said, he is not my type. Besides, I have my eye on someone else." She smiles to herself and blushes a little.

"That Darcy guy? He was a jerk." I roll my eyes. Lizzy likes a challenge when it comes to love, and I imagine he'll give her one.

"A hot jerk!" She giggles and winks at me. I roll my eyes as she hands me her phone. "That's him, your future husband, William Collins."

"Ha ha, you're so funny." I glance down at Lizzy's phone, fully expecting to be disappointed. He's 5'11", thirty years old, wears black rectangular glasses, has a full head of hair (I cannot abide bald guys), and appears neither overweight nor overly muscley. I suppose he has what some people refer to as a swimmer's build: lean, but strong.

He has a stiff smile, one I would call a "customer service" smile, forced and painful, waiting to disappear into an unhappy frown the moment the "customer" disappears from view. I wonder who asked him to smile like that, what person poised him against the brick wall, stepped back and shouted, "CHEESE!"

"As you said, on the plus side, he's not ugly," I admit. He's got a sort of nerdy hotness about him, like he plays video games late into the night and would enjoy a Dungeons and Dragons campaign with his friends. I scroll though his social media profile looking for red flags, stopping to read over his employment and education, the things that really matter to me. "Oh, he has a doctorate...in divination? He's a *pastor*?" My voice goes up at least two octaves causing both cats to jump from the cat tree in surprise.

"Oh, yeah, I forgot to mention that." Lizzy giggles. "He's actually the head pastor of my church." She looks a little embarrassed by this fact.

"You went on a date with your *pastor*?" I stare at her, my mouth agape. This is the second time tonight I've had to force my jaw back into its rightful place. That is...super weird. I can't imagine going on a date with the pastor of my church. That's probably because he's fifty years old, has a pot belly, and is very bald.

"Not because I wanted to!" She clarifies. "Mom said it was an honor that he asked me and if I didn't go the family's reputation would be ruined and her nerves would be shot, blah blah blah." She waves her hand around, erasing her mom's invisible nerves.

"That's still weird." I hand the phone back to her. "And you think I should go out with him? Your pastor? The guy who asked you to marry him on the first date?"

"It could work!" She insists. "Besides, you were just saying last week how you wanted to already be in a relationship and skip the dating part. This sounds like the way to make that happen."

"You have a point, though that's not entirely what I meant." The more she reasons with me, the more appealing this crazy idea is becoming. "Is this guy just proposing to every woman he dates?"

"That's what it seems like. He said he needs a wife to keep his job."

"So," I pause to register this new information. "If I go on a date with him, he'll marry me, even though we don't know each other, because he needs a wife?"

"That's the deal." She stands up and walks toward her bedroom. "Your parents would definitely approve and, who knows, maybe you'll fall in love." She flutters her eyelashes and blows me a kiss.

This is a lot to process. I bend down to pet Cleo and Tony and they follow me to my bed. They roll themselves into a black and white yin yang sign on my pillow. I let my curiosity get the better of me and start Googling this mysterious William Collins. A Wikipedia page comes up for Hilltop Church and, despite knowing that Wikipedia isn't the most credible of sources, I read every line.

There's not much about William himself here, other than the fact that he's the head pastor of this church. I had no idea Lizzy's church was so huge! If this article is to be believed, there are over two thousand members of William's congregation, which means that, technically, Hilltop is classified as a "megachurch." It puts my parents' church to shame. They get fifty people there for the holidays and less than twenty on a typical Sunday. If William's church has that many members, the offering each week must be insane! How much money does this man make? He's no humble country preacher, that's for sure.

Cleo leaves the pillow and starts purring around my waist, which is her reminder that it's time to go to sleep. That's just the thing I need to bring me back to reality and climb out of my rabbit hole. I can't actually be considering marrying a guy I don't know, can I? This is crazy, absolute lunacy, and yet...

I set my phone on the dresser to get ready for bed. If Mom hadn't tried to set me up with Jay, I probably wouldn't have given Lizzy's idea a second thought. After years of being ghosted, cheated on, and overlooked, that suggestion (that and being so freshly rejected by Charlie) is the straw that broke the camel's back. So here I am, still thinking about it, my brain going a mile a minute preventing me from drifting off into blissful slumber.

Since I've always been a logical person, I pick up the pen and notepad I keep by my bed and start making a list of the pros and cons of this absurd situation. Maybe this will calm my mind.

PRO:

I would be married, therefore no longer single and an object of ridicule to society.

He doesn't seem like a terrible person, though it is weird he's okay with marrying some random woman to keep his job. (That could also go on the CON list.)

He's desperate, so this might be my only chance.

Mom and Dad would be happy. I wouldn't be their old maid daughter anymore.

I might be happy. He might be right for me. (Do "mights" count as pros if they are possible though not probable?)

CON:

This is crazy! People don't do this!

He's a complete stranger.

He ends up being super weird and I'll be sacrificed during some elaborate wedding ritual. (Okay, that one is pretty far-fetched, but I'm not ruling anything out.)

I send up a quick prayer for guidance before one last look at my list of pros and cons. Cleo and Tony rub their faces against me and gaze at me, waiting for me to turn off the light.

Sighing, I turn to them and say, "Until God says otherwise, I'm left with the only sensible conclusion: when life gives you lemons, you marry the lemons."

Chapter 4
William

Considering how disastrous and awkward our first date was, I really don't think Elizabeth will show up for our second date. The whole thing has been so awkward and stilted from the get go. She was clearly uncomfortable and, while she's nice to look at, her intellect is lacking, which is an immediate turn off. She reads romance books, for goodness sakes.

However, I told her my situation and made my proposal. I decided honesty is the best policy; I am a pastor, after all. Understandably, she was surprised. She even laughed at me first thinking it was a joke. I wish it had been. Ever since last week when Cat gave me the list, my life has felt like some sort of comedy of errors. I gave Elizabeth time to think it over (whether she wanted it or not) and she said she would get back to me soon, which is what I'm currently waiting on.

The coffee shop is loud with the sounds of chatter and whirring coffee machines. The aroma of vanilla and espresso fills my nose and makes me slightly nauseous. I despise coffee; meeting here was Elizabeth's idea. I tap my foot impatiently as I check my watch for the third time in five minutes.

When I glance back up, a striking brunette woman is quickly approaching my table. The afternoon sun streaming in through the windows casts a halo around her head and my heart jumps into my throat. Without a word, she pulls out the opposite chair and takes a seat.

"You're not Elizabeth," I remark, swallowing hard, completely caught off guard by this presumptuous stranger and forgetting all my manners.

"And you're not Chris Evans," she replies, a nervous smile playing on her lips. "Any other astute observations, Captain Obvious?"

"Um, uh, no," I stammer out. Who is this woman and why am I suddenly a little nervous?

"I'm Charlotte Lucas. Lizzy is my best friend. She thinks I'm a better match for you, so she sent me in her place." Her dark green eyes rake over me; its unnerving and sensual at the same time.

"How thoughtful of her," I say sarcastically, quickly forcing myself to break eye contact with her. There's something about her that intrigues me, though I can't put my finger on exactly what it is. She's attractive in an unexpected way, a non-stereotypical way, though that's not the only reason she has my attention. There's a powerful aura about her, like she's entirely herself and no one can tell her who to be or how to live her life. It's intriguing.

"She wanted to surprise you," Charlotte explains, placing her large coffee in front of her on the table.

"Ah. I am certainly surprised. I assume this means her answer is, no?" I raise an eyebrow. Of course, I knew she would say no; I'm not an idiot. It still stings a little, though.

"Sorry to be the bearer of bad news." Charlotte's eyes soften with sympathy for my predicament. No man likes being stood up, much less having his marriage proposal rejected by a surrogate. "If it makes you feel better, I'm not entirely here because I want to be."

"What do you mean?" I lean forward, intrigued by her admission.

"Lizzy told me you're in need of a wife." She gives me a knowing, though not judgmental look. "If you'll have me, I accept." Her tone is so nonchalant it takes me a moment to realize what she said.

"Excuse me?" I tilt my head to the side like a confused dog. I can't be hearing her correctly. We just met. We know nothing about each other.

"You need a wife to keep your job and I need a husband to keep my family off my back." She lifts the lid of her coffee, stirring it slowly. Her pink lips form a perfect "O" as she gently blows off the steam. "I've been unlucky in love all my life to the point where I no longer believe it exists. This could be a very practical arrangement for both of us."

She brushes a loose strand of chestnut brown hair behind her ear and I can't help noticing how delicate her hands are. It strikes me that, unlike most women I know, her nails are bare and fairly short. Come to think of it, her whole look is effortless and natural: no caked-on foundation, no dark lines traced around her eye lids, no thick mascara clumped in her eye lashes. There's the slightest hint of a shine to her lips, the kind that comes from applying lip balm, but that's it. Interesting.

I drum my fingertips on the table and "hmmmm" as I consider her offer. Her eyes dart around the coffee shop, taking in everyone around us as she nervously avoids my stare. If Charlotte is offering, and she claims this is a mutually beneficial arrangement, perhaps it is worth considering. This would save me a lot of time dating women who will, undoubtedly, laugh at my proposal just like Elizabeth did. Charlotte's logic and practicality are impressive. The only problem is, she doesn't go to Hilltop, therefore she's not on Cat's list.

"Well, what do you think?" Charlotte picks up her cup and takes a long, languid sip, her green eyes assessing my expression.

"I'll have to talk to my boss first. She gave me a list of approved women who already attend my church. If she consents, I will consider it." I smile ruefully at the weirdest sentences I've ever uttered.

"She gave you a list? A list of approved women?" She practically chokes on her coffee in surprise. "Wow. That's intense, but it makes sense considering your position."

"I see Elizabeth told you a little about me." I raise an eyebrow in curiosity. "What did she say, exactly?"

"She said you're the head pastor at her church and you're a bit too serious for her taste." She finishes her coffee and glances at my wrist. "Nice watch, by the way. A bit pricey for a pastor I would think."

"This old thing?" I push back my sleeve and admire my Rolex. True, it had cost me a pretty penny, but I can afford it. "Let's just say I make more than the average pastor."

"Clearly." Her eyes take in my suit, noticing the fine tailoring, I'm sure. Emiliano is the best in the business and he charges accordingly.

"And what is your chosen profession?" I ask, relaxing my shoulders against the back of the chair. I find myself wanting to find out more about her, this woman who just might be my future wife.

"I teach history to teenagers. It's a great exercise in restraint and patience. Plus, it's a great way to learn improv." She smiles wryly. "I actually teach at the same school as Lizzy. That's how we met."

"Do you enjoy it?" The idea of spending hours upon hours managing teenagers while trying to teach them anything sounds absolutely terrible. At least she has a sense of humor about her job, unlike Elizabeth.

"Some days, yes, some days, no." We chat for a bit about the pitfalls of both of our occupations, each of us glad not to have the other's job. Our conversation is easy, almost effortless, both of us participating equally in a pleasant dialogue.

"If my boss approves of you and we get married, you won't have to work anymore. I won't stop you from working. However, financially, you wouldn't need to anymore." As my wife, she would be expected to take on tasks at the church and in the community, thereby making her full-time job more of a burden than a blessing. I won't bother her with that fact quite yet.

"Huh." She pauses. "I hadn't considered that." She thinks deeply for a moment. I can almost see the edge of doubt creeping into her mind.

"There's a lot of things to deliberate over, little details, really. Let me talk to my boss and we can work out all of that later." I reach into my wallet and pull out one of my business cards. "Here's my number. Text me so I have yours and I'll let you know our next steps." This whole thing is so formal, almost businesslike. This was, however, a much less awkward time than my date with Elizabeth, so there's that.

"Sounds like a plan." She immediately sends me a text. "I appreciate your willingness to consider me for your future wife." Her smile disappears as she shakes her head. "I feel like I just had a job interview."

"In a way, you did." I smirk as I stand up from the table. "I'll be in touch." Leaving the coffee shop, I resist the urge to look back at Charlotte to see if she's watching my exit.

She intrigues me, I can't lie. And while she's not a traditional 10/10 in the appearance department, she's attractive in a different way. I appreciate her wit, logic, and overall pleasant demeanor. Those things matter far more than appearance if our potential marriage is going to work. Elizabeth would have been nice to look at, but a life with a partner who doesn't challenge me intellectually almost sounds worse than a life of vanilla sex.

After arriving home, I email Cat's assistant to schedule a meeting. She wants a woman who already attends our church, so this could be complicated. However, Charlotte may very well be the solution to my marriage problem, especially if she is willing to get married fairly quickly.

From what I've seen in movies, women typically want a lot of time to plan their wedding and get things in order. In this weird situation, I imagine Cat will handle all of that, most likely arranging for the wedding to be at Hilltop with far too much pomp and circumstance. I'll probably have to talk her down from televising the affair, although it would be good press for the church.

Chapter 5
Charlotte

"Ms. Lucas?" Haley raises her hand to get my attention.

I walk over and ask, "Yes, Haley?"

"Why aren't there any pictures of Thomas Jefferson?" She asks, her young eyes wide and innocent.

"That's a dumb question, Haley," Brayden, her alleged best friend, says next to her.

"Brayden, that's not nice," I scold him. "There are paintings of him. Is that what you mean?"

"No, like pictures with a camera." Sweet, sweet Haley. She's very intelligent; she just lacks a little common sense sometimes.

"Um, well," I pause trying to come up with a way to explain the reason in a way that doesn't make her feel embarrassed. "That's because cameras hadn't been invented yet, dear."

"Told you it was a dumb question," Brayden says, a smirk on his smug face.

"Brayden, I will move you across the room if you can't be nice to Haley," I threaten. He rolls his eyes and gets back to his project on the presidents.

"So, paintings are okay for our project?" Haley resumes, pretending she never asked about photographs. I nod and resume roving around the classroom keeping the students on task.

It's been a few days since my meeting with William Collins and I have yet to hear back from him regarding my absurd proposition. Each day that passes makes me feel more and more ridiculous. It seems my pattern of being rejected by men is continuing. Not even a man desperate for a wife wants me. Maybe that's for the best. Maybe I'm meant to be single forever. Maybe I don't deserve love...

"Ms. Lucas!" Another student calls for my attention. I'm grateful for the distraction from my thoughts. Helping my students complete their projects takes up all my brain power for the rest of the day.

***

By the time I get home, I collapse on the couch and sigh. Another week of shoving historical facts into the minds of the next generation is complete. I finally have time to check my phone for the day. When I do, I'm alarmed to find a voicemail from Dad.

"Hey, Charlotte." His voice is tired and tight. "Don't freak out. Your mom and I are at the hospital right now. The doctors say she had a heart attack. Even though it was mild, they are going to keep her overnight for observation. She's in room 48 if you want to come by and visit her. Love you." Dad's voice stops abruptly as the message ends.

Oh, God! I leap up from the couch and head straight to the hospital. My anxiety rockets through my veins when I arrive and start searching for Mom's room. A nurse directs me down the right hall as the strong scent of disinfectant and fresh latex makes my eyes water.

"Mom!" I run through the door to her bed. She looks so helpless in the white bed, a giant pillow shoved behind her head and back, hooked up to machines that beep and whirr in rhythm with her breathing. I take her hand and she smiles at me.

"Hi, honey," Mom says, her face a little pale under the harsh fluorescent lights.

"What happened?" I ask her and then turn to Dad in case she doesn't feel like talking.

"I was feeling some pain in my chest and my arm. Your dad dragged me here against my will, though I guess it was a good idea." She looks over at him and rolls her eyes.

"It was much more dramatic than that, Sweetie." He sighs and turns toward me. "I hadn't been home from work maybe ten minutes before I heard her screaming in the kitchen. When I walked in, she had a bowl of batter at her feet and she was staring at her left arm. Her right hand was pressed to her chest. I called 911 and they brought us here about two hours ago." He runs his hand through his hair and stares lovingly at Mom. "She's stable. Staying here is just a precaution."

"I'm fine," Mom insists. The machine next to her beeps in disagreement. "No need to make a fuss about me."

"Did they say it was worse this time?" I ask Dad, still holding onto Mom's small, cold hand, both to support her and to stop my own hand from shaking. I might still be in shock that Mom had a heart attack. I'm only halfway processing the words falling from everyone's lips.

"They didn't say." Dad shrugs his shoulders.

"How are you feeling, Mom?" I ask, gently sitting on the side of the bed next to her.

"Good, I suppose. I'd like to go home, but that's not happening." She glares at Dad and then at the doorway as a doctor enters the room.

"Hello, I'm Dr. Jones," he says, greeting me with a practiced smile. "Your mother is in good hands, I assure you. She had a mild cardiac event and, though it is unlikely to repeat itself soon, an overnight stay is recommended purely out of an abundance of caution."

"Thank you, doctor," I respond. Everything he's saying sounds both correct and wrong at the same time. At that moment, all three of my brothers burst through the door causing immediate chaos.

"My boys!" Mom's face lights up as they surround her bed. Both the doctor and I are unceremoniously jostled towards the door and have no choice except to enter the hallway. As he awkwardly walks away, I lean back against the wall, close my eyes, and try to ground myself as best I can.

"Elephant, zebra, rhino, cheetah..." Naming off animals is my typical go to grounding exercise when I'm overwhelmed. Between my crazy students and Mom's heart attack, I haven't had a moment to relax and cool my anxiety all day. Overstimulation plus extreme stress equals utter panic. "...ostrich, hippo, warthog, panther, lion, gazelle."

"Charlotte?" A man's voice startles me. My eyes fly open and to my absolute surprise, William Collins is standing right in front of me. He's wearing another expensive looking suit, this time in charcoal gray with matching Oxfords. His blue eyes scan my face intently. "Are you okay? Why are you naming animals in the hallway?"

"William, hi, um, well," I'm stumbling hopelessly over my words as my brain struggles to process more new information. "The animals are because of anxiety and the anxiety is because my mom just had a heart attack."

"Oh! Is she alright?" The concern in his voice is touching, though, as a pastor, I'm sure this is just how he talks to everyone he sees in a hospital.

"They said it was mild and she'll be here overnight for observation." As I speak, the tears I've been holding back start to fall. I couldn't cry in front of Mom and Dad; that would just upset them more. "I could have lost her," I murmur, more to myself than William. I press my face into my hands and wipe off my tears with a shirt sleeve. I don't care that I'm not being graceful or stoic in front of this borderline stranger. He's here, he gets to see me cry.

"She's okay," he assures me. "She's right where she needs to be." His voice is very soothing and calm. He peeks around me and gets a view of Mom gushing over my brothers as they take turns hugging her. "Do you want to come with me to the cafeteria? I've been here all day and I could use some food."

"Yes, that would be a nice distraction." We walk together down the hall in a comfortable silence. Only after we get food and sit down does he resume speaking.

"My father died a few years ago," he begins, looking down at his sad bowl of soup. "A brain aneurysm. It was very sudden and unexpected. He was the picture of health."

"Oh, I'm so sorry. I can't imagine what that was like." I look at this well put together man in his expensive suit and ache for him. The very idea of losing either Mom or Dad makes fear rise in my chest and squeeze around my lungs. The doctor didn't seem to think Mom's heart attack was something to worry about. What if that is just something he said to keep us from panicking? How close to death was she?

"Time heals all wounds," he gazes at me and smiles wistfully, "or so they say. I'm not telling you this to gain your sympathy or your pity. I just wanted you to know that I'm here for you." He reaches across the table and takes my hand. His touch is soft, yet there's a reassuring strength in his fingers I find comforting. Despite the urge to withdraw my hand, I don't. My heart wants this overly familiar gesture to mean something, though my brain tells me this is probably just something he does to comfort his parishioners. We are just acquaintances, nothing more.

"I'm sure you say that to all the ladies," I tease, trying to lighten the mood. The corner of his mouth lifts up in a half smile as if he might laugh. I'd like to see him laugh, really let loose and shake his stoic persona.

"Only the ones I might marry." His half smile evolves into a playful grin and my breath catches in my throat. He's so handsome when he's being genuine and not just putting on a persona. I'd be lying if I said I hadn't been thinking about him on and off since I first met him. Like Lizzy stalking Darcy, I've been all over William's social media pages. Each profile is a carefully crafted image of a precise, professional, perfect man who takes his job very seriously. He came off as a little cold and stern at first, so I'm delighted to find that he's human underneath the preacher persona.

Just as quickly as it arrived, his grin is gone and replaced by his standard professional expression. "Speaking of marriage," he clears his throat and releases my hand. "I met with Cat to discuss your proposal." And just like that, we're back to formal business matters.

"And what did she say?" My hand is exposed and cold, like my security blanket was tugged away without warning.

"She said she needs to do a background check on you before we can proceed." He dips a cracker into his soup and takes a bite.

"I'm not a secret criminal if that's what's she's worried about. I wouldn't have been hired to be a teacher if I was." Background checks are fairly common procedures and I have nothing to hide, so I should pass with flying colors.

"It's more so about your social and personal background, who you're related to, where you live, any inappropriate things you've posted online, stuff like that." He moves his soup aside and rests his elbows on the table. His fingers interlock as he rests his chin on his hands and his blue eyes rove over me as if he's studying my soul.

"As a teacher, I'm familiar with keeping my image squeaky clean." I cross my arms and look him square in the face. "I resent what you're implying."

"It's merely a precaution, I assure you. Cat just wants to be thorough." He glances at his watch. He does that a lot.

"I should probably get back to my mom," I say, standing up and pushing in my chair.

"I didn't mean to offend you," he explains, also standing up.

"I understand," my tone is tight and unforgiving. "I guess I'll keep waiting to find out if I'm good enough." I turn and start to walk away.

"Charlotte," William reaches out and grabs my arm with the politest little tug. "This has nothing to do with who you are or your personal worth. It's all about the church's image. There are things even I..." He clenches his jaw and stops speaking.

"Even you...?" I raise my eyebrows and prompt him delicately. What secrets is he hiding behind his polished image?

"Never mind. I'll tell you what Cat says soon." His frown deepens and his eyes briefly betray his inner turmoil. He lets go of my arm and walks quickly down the hall. As I watch him walk away, my curiosity about Reverend William Collins grows. Who is he underneath all that polished pride and pompous persona? And will I get to discover his dark secrets, or will Cat find me unworthy?

"Wait," I call out, an idea suddenly occurring to me. "Would you mind coming to my mom's room and praying over her?"

"Of course," he turns back to me, raising an eyebrow at my change of attitude, agreeing to my request more so out of professional obligation than choice, I'm sure.

Once we reach the room, I enter with William close behind me.

"Mom?" I get her attention away from my loud brothers for a moment. At first, she narrows her eyes at my interruption. Then a charming smile replaces her annoyed expression when she sees William.

"Well, hello! And who do we have here?" She puts on her best customer service voice and gives William all her attention.

"Mom, this is Reverend William Collins. William, this is Eleanor Lucas." With my formal introduction done, William extends his hand towards Mom and she shakes it firmly.

"I'm a friend of Charlotte's," William explains.

"A *friend* of Charlotte's?" She looks past him and at me with surprise.

"Yes, Mom, I have friends," I reply, rolling my eyes. Granted, my friends are typically women, so her surprise is well warranted. I've brought William here for two reasons. The first being to pray over Mom's health. The second is to meet Mom so that, assuming Cat approves of me, William's existence in my life isn't entirely a shock to her later on. I refuse to be the cause of a second heart attack.

"I see," Mom's eyes flick up and down William's body assessing him for imperfections. Finding none, she releases his hand. He turns to Dad and shakes his hand as well. Dad appears just as surprised as Mom that I have any connection to a man, friend or otherwise. He nods at William politely before introducing my brothers. After more handshakes, William moves to the head of the bed and places his hand on Mom's shoulder.

"Charlotte asked that I pray over you. Is this something you're comfortable with?" His voice echoes with authority in the small room. Mom nods and we all bow our heads.

"Dear Lord, we come to you today to humbly ask that you help Eleanor with her healing and recovery. Please surround her with your love and grace as she regains her strength and gets back to her regular routine. Please support her family as they aid her in this time of renewal, giving them patience and energy to care for her and her needs. We ask all of these things in Your Son's name, Amen."

As William finishes his prayer, a sense of peace pervades the room. My shoulders are lighter and I can breathe easier. I always forget how powerful a prayer can be, especially a prayer by someone who is truly connected to God. Looking up from the floor, William and I lock eyes and a shiver runs through my body. His gaze is intense and inviting at the same time. I'm both afraid and aroused.

"It was nice to meet you all," William says, waving good bye to my family as he walks out of the room. Before he completely exits, he turns around and glances back at me one more time, a fleeting smile on his lips. Warmth floods my veins, making my chest constrict and my fingers tingle.

Mom's voice brings me back to the situation at hand. "Charlotte! You didn't tell us you were seeing someone!"

"Well, it's complicated," I explain terribly.

"That's no excuse," Mom says, her tone irritated. The machine wired to her chest starts beeping aggressively.

"Nori, you need to relax," Dad cautions, pointing to the heart monitor. "We can interrogate Charlotte tomorrow."

Mom *hmphs* and crosses her arms. Nick, Eddie, and Rob take turns hugging Mom before leaving. Rob, my youngest brother, stays behind for a moment after Nick and Eddie have left.

"You're dating a preacher?" He asks incredulously.

"Um, sort of," I hedge. Rob and I have always had the closest relationship out of all of my brothers. I want to tell him the weird truth of the situation, just not in front of our parents. "I'll explain later," I promise. He nods and heads out.

After my brothers leave, Dad and I take turns at Mom's bedside all night despite her insistence that she's fine and we should go home. I can't get over how fragile she looks in the white bed. She's always been the strong one in the family, the one in charge of everything, the one we all turn to with our problems and stresses. She could have died today if Dad hadn't gotten home when he did.

While she sleeps, I bow my head and send a quick prayer to God thanking Him for giving us more time together. Mom can't die before I get married. Even if the marriage is more one of convenience than love, I'll do whatever it takes to make her happy.

Chapter 6
William

"I approve of her," Cat's words reverberate across the room and straight into my brain. We just finished discussing the budget for next month's mission trip and it takes a moment for me to realize what she's referring to.

"You approve of Charlotte?" I ask. "To be my wife?" I really didn't think she'd accept any woman who wasn't on her list. Despite my hesitations over this whole situation, I had a slight hope that Cat would find Charlotte to be acceptable. I've only spoken with her twice in person, yet she's starting to grow on me.

"Reynolds and Dillard couldn't find anything damaging or even remotely concerning about her, and they're the best in the business." Leave it to Cat to have two private investigators on her payroll. "Her image is squeaky clean, her social media presence is minimal, and her job is one people typically hold in high regard. The only negative thing about her is her age." Cat frowns and shakes her head. "I would have preferred her a bit younger for childbearing reasons. I would have also preferred you married sooner, so I can't complain about that too much."

"She will be so pleased to hear of your approval," I respond politely, resisting the urge to roll my eyes at her last comment.

"And since you've found someone in record time, there's no reason why we can't have the wedding within the next few months," Cat states, staring on the numbers on her computer screen instead of my shocked face.

"The next few months?!" I stammer. "You said I had a year." My heart is pounding so fast I wonder if it will burst from my chest.

"A year to find someone," she points out. "Now you have someone, so the sooner you wed, the better." She quickly glances up at me over her screen. "And I'd like to meet Charlotte to get her opinion on a few matters before I begin planning."

"Um, yeah, sure," I reply, only partially comprehending her request. "I'll contact her immediately and have the meeting set up ASAP." My responses are automatic at this point. My mind is too busy pre-panicking about actually being married to Charlotte and what all that entails.

"I'll have Davis draw up a standard pre-nuptial agreement as well. She can sign that when I meet with her." It baffles me how matter of fact Cat is being about all of this, about my life, my future, my happiness. Is this job really worth surrendering this much control over my own choices and actions? Any other church would gladly take me; I'm excellent at my job.

Behind Cat, the large portrait of my dad glares down at me, his stern eyes reminding me that I can't leave. Doing so would tarnish his reputation and bring shame to our family name. He made our family's commitment to the church very clear when Mom decided she'd had enough and just walked out one day. He chose the church over her and I haven't seen or heard from her in over ten years. Like him, I was called to be a minister, and his people became my people when he passed away. I can never leave them; I need them just as much as they need me.

"Sounds like a plan," I respond, pulling out my phone to text Charlotte about this very important update.

"William," Cat commands my attention. When I make eye contact, I'm surprised to see her typically harsh expression has mellowed. "Being married will be good for you, I promise." Her care and concern about my personal well-being were never in doubt, though it is still nice to hear her admit to it.

"Now," she says, pointing back at her spreadsheets. "Before I take these records to the committee, let's talk about last month's expenditures. It looks like we still owe $3,500 for the plumbing repairs in the basement kitchen."

"Really? I thought for sure we paid for that already."

"Clearly not. This is why I have to oversee the finances when things like this slip your mind." Cat reproves me, though I don't think I deserve it. I know for a fact that check went out because it was the last thing my assistant, Sierra, mailed before she left for maternity leave. Not wanting to cause further tension, I simply nod and make a note to pay that bill. Again.

After discussing every last penny spent on travel, church renovations, and the new playground, I'm finally free to check my phone for Charlotte's response.

"Now what?" Her response is short and right to the point. Now what, indeed? Do we date? Do I get her a ring? Do I ask her dad for his blessing?

"Yes, hi, Mr. Lucas? You only just met me and I barely know Charlotte, but I was wondering if I could marry her? Thanks!" What father wouldn't find that odd and immediately refuse? I then remember Cat's request to meet with Charlotte.

"You need to meet with Cat to iron out some details about the wedding and other stuff." Now really isn't the time to bring up signing a pre-nup or discussing the more private aspects of our upcoming marriage.

"Could I do that on Sunday after church? Lizzy invited me to come this Sunday. I want to see how good you are at your job."

"That should be fine. See you on Sunday." I'm suddenly very nervous about my next sermon.

In the blink of an eye, its Sunday morning and I'm putting the final touches on my sermon when Josiah enters my office.

"Morning, William," Josiah greets me, a broad smile on his face.

"Morning, Josiah," I respond in kind.

"And what exciting topic is today's sermon on?" He sits down on the corner of my desk and turns my laptop screen around. "Ah. A message on compassion, how unproblematic."

"You're more than welcome to give a message any Sunday you like," I point out, annoyed at his comment.

"Not sure Cat would approve of the Youth Minister giving a sermon, especially not the one I have in mind."

"Always trying to stir the pot," I shake my head and turn my laptop back towards me.

"And what's wrong with that?" he argues. "A message that relates to modern issues or points out the flaws in our system might actually wake up some of the hypocrites in the pews. Our church needs a change." Josiah stands up from my desk and puts his hands in his pockets. "You have to admit, things have gotten pretty stale here lately."

"That's purely your opinion," I retort, getting a little heated. "This is the message Cat approved, so this is the message I'm giving." I jab my finger on the mousepad and send the document to the printer. Grabbing it quickly from the tray, I staple it forcefully.

"We'll have to agree to disagree, as usual." Josiah gives me a wry smile. "You seem more tense than usual today. What gives?"

"My future wife is going to be here," I blurt out without any ceremony or pretense.

"Your what?" Josiah's eyes widen and his jaw drops. He grabs my shoulders with both hands and shakes me a little. "What are you talking about? You're not even dating someone!"

"Long story short, Cat demanded I get married for the church's image. I found a woman who is willing to marry me and so, technically, I'm engaged." I gently remove his hands from my shoulders and place my sermon in a blue folder on my desk.

"Wow." He puts his hand to his head as if he's dizzy. "What would have happened if you told Cat no?"

"She would've fired me."

"Wow," Josiah repeats, now rubbing the back of his neck with his hand. "I would have quit on the spot."

"Well, you don't have your father's legacy literally hanging over your head." I nod towards the large portrait of Dad on the wall behind my desk.

"True." He buttons his suit jacket and shuffles his feet. "Do you like her?"

"That's immaterial," I grab the folder and start walking toward the door. The fact is, I don't know how I feel about Charlotte in terms of romantic feelings. Physically, I am attracted to her and the idea of having sex with her appeals to me greatly. Emotionally, it's difficult to determine whether or not I can love her. So far, although we've only had a handful of interactions, we seem compatible and I enjoy talking with her; that's a good place to start. As long as I keep viewing our situation logically, I won't risk any sort of hurt feelings or a broken heart.

"If you say so." Josiah says, following me out the door toward the sanctuary. "Keep me updated, would you?" He holds out his fist and I bump it reluctantly. We part ways as he heads to the pews and I walk up the steps to the pulpit. As I take my seat high above the congregation, I can't help searching the pews for Charlotte.

She's sitting with Lizzy and her family in the third row, the Bennett family's usual pew. Knowing she's out there, so close to the front, has me tapping my foot and pinching my sermon between my fingers. It's a wrinkled, crumpled mess by the time I stand to read from it. Looking out at my parishioners, pride overpowers the nagging sense of apprehension every time my eyes glance in Charlotte's direction. I can do this.

Chapter 7
Charlotte

I've always thought of churches as peaceful places, even when I was young. When other children giggled and colored during the sermon, I relished the beauty of the sanctuary. It was my safe space from the world, and though I'm not as adamant a church goer as I was in my youth, I still find it to be a place of solace.

Unlike the church I grew up in, this church is massive. I get the feeling it started as a normal sized church and then expanded through renovations over time. It has two floors, several TV screens on the front wall, a banquet hall, a massive stage for the choir and band, gorgeous giant stained-glass windows along the sides with one directly behind the pulpit, and more rows of pews than I can count.

I tried to calm my nerves by counting everyone here, but I keep losing track once I hit over two hundred. If anything, counting the people has only worsened my anxiety as I realized each one of these hundreds of people will soon be my congregants just as they are William's.

All throughout the service, I avoid staring at William, or should I say, my future husband. My mind keeps wondering what his boss could possibly want to meet with me about and I can't focus on anything happening in front of me. Lizzy has to keep nudging me when it's time to stand and sing. She knows that William has tentatively agreed to marry me. I just haven't told her that I've been approved to marry him. I'll wait until after my meeting with the mysterious and terrifying Cat De Bourgh to reveal that information.

After the overflowing offering plates finally make their way back to the front of the massive church, William stands and approaches the podium. There are screens on either side of the stage that project his image so the people way in the back and up top can see him clearly. His hair is perfectly coifed, his light gray suit tailored, his tie a stark deep red against his white button-down shirt, and his bright blue eyes shine brightly behind his black frames. A broad smile lights up his face as he surveys his kingdom; he is clearly in his element. Placing a stack of papers on the stand and flattening them out, he begins speaking.

"Put on then, as God's chosen ones, holy and beloved, compassionate hearts, kindness, humility, meekness, and patience, bearing with one another and, if one has a complaint against another, forgiving each other; as the Lord has forgiven you, so you also must forgive. The word of God for the people of God..."

"Thanks be to God!" The crowded pews chant as one.

"These words come to us from Colossians 3:12-13." He pauses as one screen replaces his image with the Bible verses he just read. "Forgiveness and compassion are two key traits we as Christians must learn to cultivate in the garden of our heart." He places his hand over his actual heart as he speaks.

His metaphor is quite nice, though I hope there's actual substance to it. He continues his sermon and my attention fades away as I contemplate what our future life together will look like. I never thought I would be a preacher's wife. I'm not entirely opposed to the idea, obviously, it's just unexpected. I picture myself sitting in the front pew, dressed in a matching blue skirt and jacket, a string of pearls around my neck. That's one thing I've noticed about this church that I'm not a fan of: everyone is so painfully formal, both in dress and in action. Even when greeting each other, they shake hands and smile politely; there are no hugs, no hearty laughs at familiar teasing, no genuine happiness to see the other person.

This is quite different from the church I grew up in. A typical Sunday service is given to, at most, fifty people all dressed in their Sunday best, whatever that means to them. I had originally planned on wearing jeans and a nice blouse today, until Lizzy's horrified expression told me that was the incorrect thing to wear. We compromised when I chose one of the dresses I wear to teach in. I wonder if William ever gets tired of wearing a suit. Each time I've met him, he's worn a suit. Does he wear them around the house? I guess I'll find out soon enough.

"...and so, by being compassionate to others, we, too open ourselves to greater joy and salvation. Let us pray." William raises his hands up to the heavens and bows his head. I can't believe I zoned out for the entire sermon. I don't think he'll interrogate me on what he said, or would he? I'm nervous enough about meeting Cat; I can't handle a pop quiz, too.

Soft piano music plays as everyone stands up and exits the sanctuary. I stand in the pew with Lizzy's family and watch as William descends onto the main floor and makes his way to the back of the church. The people part for him like he's Moses and they're the Red Sea. The power he has here is quite impressive, I can't lie. I tell Lizzy to go on and I'll catch her up later. I don't know where to go next, so I'll sit and wait for William to find me once everyone is gone.

As people leave, the church starts to feel overwhelmingly large, almost oppressive in size. I lean back against the pew and admire the stained-glass windows that decorate the side walls. I've always had a fondness for churches. There's just something about their structure, purpose, and over-all feeling that speaks to me.

"Charlotte Lucas?" A woman's voice jerks my face to the right and away from the beautiful windows. She's an older woman, probably in her late fifties with black, tightly curled hair, and wearing a floral print pantsuit (I didn't even know such things existed). Aside from her garish outfit, she's very put together and professional. Her eyes narrow at me from behind large, round glasses as she waits for my response.

"Yes, that's me," I practically stammer, completely caught off guard.

"I'm Cat De Bourgh," she says, looking down her nose at me. "Come with me." I quickly stand and follow her through the back doors of the church. She's just as intimidating as I thought she would be. My anxiety is rising, making my palms sweaty and my knees weak. "Take a seat," Cat commands, pointing to a chair in front of her desk. I collapse into the seat, my legs giving out entirely.

Sitting down in her swivel chair, she places her elbows on the desk and steeples her fingers. Even while sitting down, she exudes power and authority. Glancing at me as if assessing my worth, Cat sighs. "William probably told you that I did some investigating into your background and your life, essentially."

"Yes, he did." I nod and grip the sides of the chair to keep myself steady. I do not like confrontation, especially when it involves someone giving their opinion of me or what I've done. It's why getting classroom observation feedback is the worst part of my job.

"I will tell you I was impressed by your squeaky-clean image and reputation. There isn't even a single picture of you in a bikini online. It was refreshing." She slides a packet of papers from the side of her desk to the center. "While I would have preferred someone who is already a member of Hilltop, you are perfect otherwise." She allows a small smile to crack through her severe expression. It's more unnerving than reassuring. "Let's talk business, shall we?" She hands the packet of papers to me. As I take them, their weight surprises me and I almost drop them.

"What's all this?" I thumb through the papers, catching glimpses of legal terms between lettered and numbered sections of text.

"That is your pre-nuptial agreement. I assumed William told you there would be one." She raises an eyebrow at my confusion. "Either way, before you walk down the aisle, you will need to sign this contract. It's a standard agreement, mainly focusing on ensuring William keeps all of his assets should you do something foolish like try and divorce him. Not that I particularly think you are the gold-digging type, but I prefer to cover all my bases."

"Okay…" I reply hesitantly, still processing the document in my hands.

"Now, as for the wedding, I'll be handling the planning, though your opinion will be asked for certain things along the way, such as flower choice and color scheme. I'll select a dozen dresses for you to choose from." She starts jotting down notes on a notepad. "It will be a large-scale affair, possibly televised on the local news channel. I'm thinking late May, early June so you can wrap up your school year without issue."

"That's only three months from now," I protest. "William told me he had a year." I'm pinching the stack of paper tightly between my fingers. My chest constricts and my neck stiffens as her words sink in. I want to get married in case anything else happens to Mom, but…

"The sooner the better," she replies, not even looking up from her notes. "Now, you'll need to start attending services regularly so you can get familiar with the members. We'll announce your engagement next Sunday, so dress accordingly."

"Okay…" I glance down at my buttercup yellow, knee length dress. My chest, what little of it there is, is completely covered; even my shoulders are hidden from sight. It's one of my favorites and I specifically wore it to boost my confidence today. "May I ask what's wrong with my outfit?" What is with these people and what I wear? I look pretty damn nice today!

"It's fine for a regular congregant," she waves away my question with a sweeping hand gesture. "But as the head pastor's wife, there are higher standards. You are part of the face of Hilltop. You will be who people envision when they think of the church. You'll be part of our marketing, fundraising, and member retention programs, or at least your image will be. How you look matters, not only with your clothes, but with your attitude and with how you interact with everyone here. The sooner you realize and accept that, the better off you'll be." Her expression is cold, calculated. I keep looking for some type of compassion in her eyes, something that says she understands and has sympathy for my situation; it's not there.

"Whatever, bitch," is what I want to say. Fortunately, my anxiety keeps that inside and I say, "Okay" instead.

"Your job between now and next Sunday is to read over and sign the pre-nup. Any questions?"

"Not right now." That's not entirely a lie. I have one million questions. I just can't think of them right now with her staring at me and this huge stack of papers in my lap. My heart beats so loudly in my chest; she has to hear it, too. A subtle buzzing whispers through my body, a warning sign that I'm seconds away from an anxiety attack. I have to get out of this room before I start hyperventilating.

"You may go," she says, dismissing me both verbally and with a wave of her hand.

"Thank you," I murmur before power walking out of her office and into the hallway beyond. In my haste, I immediately crash into William. He must have either been passing by or eavesdropping on my conversation with Cat. He and I both fall to the floor in a tumble of flailing limbs and mumbled "oofs!"

With William right underneath me and my body lying on top of his, I'm hyper aware of how lean and powerful his body is. From his tailored suits, it was already clear he's in good shape; this just confirms my suspicions. Lying on top of him like this, forces me to think about what it would be like to have sex with him, so now that's all I can think about.

I was already having a difficult time breathing, and this certainly does not help. I press my hands on the floor above his shoulders in a pathetic attempt to raise myself up. In the process of doing so, I somehow manage to slide my hips up and down his crotch, thus making this awkward situation so much worse.

Despite being completely flustered, I can't help noticing a hardening underneath my hips. Is he...hard right now? In response, my pussy begins to throb. Down, girl! My dry spell is not helping this situation at all.

In one fluid motion, William slides his hands under my armpits and gently rolls me to the side. The hem of my dress slides up and I catch him glancing at my thighs. Blushing deeply, he huffs to himself and stands up. Straightening his suit, William reaches a hand down to help me up. I accept his help and finally pull myself off the ground.

"Sorry about that," I apologize, my face warm with embarrassment. I start wiping imaginary dirt off my dress to avoid William's intense gaze.

"No, that's my fault, I wasn't looking where I was going," he apologizes as well and firmly tugs his jacket down to cover his groin. My suspicions are confirmed. "How did your meeting with Cat go?"

"Um, it was a lot." My mind is going a hundred miles an hour. Between meeting with Cat and unexpectedly seeing William right after, I can't catch a break. At least bumping into William and accidentally humping him momentarily distracted me from the crawling anxiety inside of me that Cat created.

"What's this?" William bends to the ground and picks up the pre-nup. Flipping through it, he presses his lips together and frowns. "She got this together a lot faster than I thought she would. Sorry I didn't warn you." He rubs the back of his neck and checks the time on his watch. "Do you want to go through this together so I can answer any questions you have? I have time between now and my next meeting." He looks at me so earnestly and hopefully, the complete opposite of how Cat looked at me. My heart melts a little at his offer; I want to take him up on it, just not now.

"I'm a little overwhelmed right now, to be honest. Maybe another time?" I would really like to get off this roller coaster ride of emotions ASAP.

"Understandable. Once you've processed everything, let me know and we can catch up." His expression softens and he smiles reassuringly at me.

"Okay. See you later, Will." I shove the contract deep into my purse and turn to go.

"I prefer William," he corrects me, his voice assertive and commanding. A small shiver runs through my body at his bold tone.

"William sounds so fancy, like you should be a duke or something," I tease, deciding to push his buttons a little bit. "I'm going to call you Sir William from now on." After having his hard body underneath mine, I can't help being a little flirty.

"In that case, I'll start calling you Lady Charlotte." A mischievous smile plays on his lips and his eyes darken as he completely drops his preacher persona. Is he flirting back? No, that can't be right. He's just playing along with my joke. Or is he?

"That's only fair," I respond with a wink that's more spastic than sexy, I'm sure. "Bye, Sir William." Before I can embarrass myself further, I start following the exit arrows until I'm out of the building and back in the parking lot. Once I'm in my car, the weight of the past hour hits me like a linebacker and I slump against the steering wheel. Between Cat's haughty condescension and William's unexpected flirting, my brain and body are running on overdrive.

Can I do this? Should I do this? It all seemed so simple before today, before I was handed a hefty pre-nuptial agreement and informed of Cat's expectations of me.

Arriving home, I lay the packet on the coffee table and flop on the sofa next to Lizzy. She pauses her movie and leans forward to examine the contract.

"What is this?" She flips through the first few pages and squeals excitedly. "Oh my God! Is this a pre-nup? Are you actually marrying William?"

"It seems that way," I mutter under my breath as I hug a throw pillow.

"How exciting!" She smiles broadly and grabs a highlighter from the pen cup on the table.

"What are you doing?" I raise an eyebrow at her.

"Annotating." She uncaps the highlighter and begins reading the contract. English teachers. I roll my eyes.

"You have fun with that." I gesture at the document and stand up. I'll let Lizzy read through that monster and tell me what I need to know going forward. "I'm going to take a nap."

"Want me to wake you when I'm done?" She glances up at me briefly. Assuming it will take her at least an hour to get through the pre-nup, I nod and she resumes her highlighting.

Before I'm ready, Lizzy is jostling my bed and whispering, "Charlotte. Wake up. Charlotte."

"Did you speed read the thing?" I ask grumpily, my eyes still closed, hands clutching the sheet close to my body.

"Skimming and speed reading are not the same thing," she retorts. "Now," she lays down next to me and makes herself comfortable. I open my eyes to glare at her. She ignores me and continues speaking. "From what

I can tell, there's nothing really scary or concerning in here. It's mostly just to protect the church and his assets should you two ever divorce. Nothing in here about how many times a week you should have sex or how many kids you're expected to pop out."

"That's good," I groan.

"Have you thought about that part of the marriage any?"

"Kids?" I ask confused.

"No, sex." She waggles her eyebrows at me and smiles cheekily.

"Not really," I say, blushing. I'm full of lies today.

"I don't believe you," Lizzy says, gently swatting at me with the contract. "What if he's really bad at sex? What if he's a virgin?"

"I don't know, Lizzy!" I sit up frustrated. "I'm having a lot of doubts right now and you're not helping."

"Did Cat make you nervous?" She asks tenderly. "She has that effect on people."

"She was so intimidating," I admit. "And she has a lot of expectations of me once I'm William's fiancé. I never thought there would be so much involved with marrying him."

"Well, you're not just marrying him, Charlotte. You're also marrying Hilltop." She gives me a sympathetic look. "But, hey." She leans her shoulder against me. "You don't have to do this. You can change your mind. You haven't signed anything yet."

"Even with all these new expectations, the pros still outweigh the cons," I say, pointing to my list by the bed. I rest my head in my hands in defeat. She moves my hands away and turns my face towards her.

"If this is what you want to do, you can do it." Her eyes are full of conviction. "It can't be as hard as corralling a bunch of boisterous teenagers, and you do that every day!"

"You're right." I smile at her joke. "It will be an adjustment, but I can handle it. I'm just going to focus on the pros of the situation and get to know William better every chance I get."

"So, will you be coming to Hilltop every Sunday now?" She smiles eagerly.

"Yep." I pop the "p" for emphasis.

"In that case, we need to go shopping!" She claps her hands together like a child who just got a new toy.

"Lord, give me strength!" I joke as she drags me from the bed.

I got this.

I can do this.

I'm doing this.

Chapter 8
William

I set the open ring box on the corner of my desk as I work on this week's sermon. The diamond gleams brightly under my desk lamp like a fallen star. I've invited Charlotte to my house for dinner tonight to officially propose and it's all I can think about. It's foolish to be nervous about a proposal that she accepted/suggested two weeks ago, and yet, a slight panic lingers in my chest when I imagine the moment.

Saving my progress and closing my laptop, I turn my chair around so that I'm face to face with the almost life-size portrait of Dad behind my desk. He's dressed in his usual suit and tie, wire frame glasses, and polished black Oxfords. His expression in the picture is happy and relaxed, small wrinkles sit at the corners of his eyes, and his cheeks have a slight pink to them, as if he had just come in from the cold. This picture was painted before Mom left, before Dad forgot how to smile, and before he decided that if he wasn't happy, no one else would be either.

For too many years, I hoped Mom would return and Dad would apologize for choosing his job over her. Each time there was a big church event, like a homecoming or a famous guest pastor giving a sermon, the optimist in me would rise and expect her to return. After years of disappointment, I finally gave up. Dad made his choice and Mom made hers. She didn't even show up to his funeral.

Leaning back in my chair, I give the portrait a hard glare. Holding on to Dad's legacy was a challenge at first since my way of preaching and interacting with the church members was more generous and compassionate than his. Some factions in the church were resistant to my methods at first, but with Cat's help I eventually won them over. There are still days when I can feel Dad's disapproval and disappointment fall on me in waves no matter how much I try to ignore it. He was never one to give pep talks or life advice, and that's what I really need right now.

"Well, Dad, looks like I'm getting married," I tell the portrait. Most people would talk to their deceased dad in a cemetery; I talk to his portrait. It's more convenient than trapsing through a graveyard and, honestly, I'd rather talk to their face than their gravestone.

"I'm marrying a woman I don't even know in order to keep my job, technically your job." I sigh heavily and grab the ring from my desk. "How am I supposed to make this marriage work? What if we hate each other? What if we're just roommates at the end of the day?" I stand up abruptly and run my hand through my hair. "Or what if..."

My sentence hangs unfinished as I glance up to the simple wooden cross delicately perched above the portrait. A sense of calm floods my soul as the image of Charlotte from the coffee shop, her hair and face glowing in the sunlight, enters my mind. Her easy smile and confident aura pulled me in immediately. In that moment, God was there.

"I just have to trust, don't I? Trust that this will all work out, trust that this is God's plan for me, trust that I'm doing the right thing for me and for Hilltop." I slip the ring box into my pocket and grab my car keys. "Thanks for the chat, *Father*."

When Charlotte arrived, I was surprised that she's dressed so formally and so...old. She's dressed like an old church lady, pearls and all. Her dark hair is pulled back in a tight bun and she looks super uncomfortable.

"Your house is quite large," she notes, looking around the foyer and into the rooms beyond.

"Yes, it's my family home. My great grandfather built it decades ago." This sturdy house has made it through fifty years with only minor need for renovation and repair. It wasn't always this large. With each generation, more rooms and floors were added. My grandparents had six kids, so a big house was a necessity. As an only child, the house always felt too large, too spacious. I can't help wondering if future children, my children, will fill these empty rooms. Does Charlotte even want kids? That's not something I should assume about her. What if she doesn't?

Forcing the jarring thought aside, I guide Charlotte to the dining room and pull out her chair. She smiles up at me appreciatively. Children are a conversation for another day.

Dinner revolves around small talk since neither of us seems willing to bring up the pre-nup agreement. Halfway through dinner, I realize she hasn't touched her steak.

"Are you a vegetarian?" I ask, resting my utensils on the side of my plate.

"Sort of. I don't eat red meat. Chicken, fish, and pork are fine, I just can't stand the idea of eating a cow." She smiles sheepishly at me and pushes her plate to the center of the table. "Sorry, I should have told you."

"No, I'm sorry, I should have asked." I fume silently to myself, clenching my fist into a ball on the table. I feel like an inconsiderate jerk. "Do you want something else to eat? I can order something or find something else in the kitchen."

"That's alright," she assures me. "I'm too nervous to really eat much anyway." She's nervous? What is she nervous about? She's not the one proposing later.

"I'll remember that you don't eat red meat from now on. I guess this is going to be a learning process for both of us."

"About that," she gets up and disappears for a moment. Returning, she lays a stack of paper on the table and a small notebook. "I thought it would make things easier if I wrote down a couple of things about me." She slides the notebook down the table. I pick it up eagerly.

"That's an excellent idea!" I open the notebook and notice that there is a table of contents in the front with everything neatly labeled in flowery cursive. I'm impressed by her organization and forethought.

"If you wanted to do something similar, I would appreciate it." She smiles encouragingly at me. "I would have gotten you a notebook, but you strike me as someone who would rather type than handwrite something."

"What makes you think that?" I raise an eyebrow at her remark. She's very observant and I'm very intrigued.

"Your sermon was typed up. Plus, you're very put together and tidy. Handwriting can be messy." She quickly swipes a loose hair behind her ear, as if afraid I'll notice such a small imperfection.

"You don't strike me as a messy person," I counter.

"You should see my apartment," she laughs lightly and fidgets with the buttons on her jacket. "It's organized chaos, but chaos nonetheless."

"Be that as it may, you're certainly very well put together tonight," I say, my eyes raking over her formal attire. I want to mention that fact that she looks uncomfortable; however, that would be rude. It's hard to know if her physical discomfort is because of her outfit or because of the situation we're in. Awkward tension floats over us like an overinflated balloon.

Before she sat down, I couldn't help but notice her rather sizable ass. She's definitely not a small woman and I'm not mad about it. Based on the way her suit jacket is looser up top than at the bottom, she's not packing double D's and I can't help wondering what her smaller, perky breasts would feel like in my hands. I've never been with a woman with small tits before. The thought has my cock hardening.

"Well, Cat told me I needed to dress better at church, so I thought I would go ahead and start dressing this way all the time to get used to it. I'm going to be part of the Hilltop image, after all."

"I see." Of course, Cat would want her to "look the part" early on, though it seems be bit unfair to expect her to adhere to that expectation 24/7. "I want you to be comfortable around me, so don't worry about all that when it's just us." The word "us" lingers between us like a brand-new fragrance which we both inhale slowly. It's not an unpleasant odor, not heavy or over powering, more like a like body spray that lightly mists the skin, a flowery scent lingering just along the edges of personal space.

"Oh, okay." She unbuttons her jacket and places it over the back of the chair. Pale shoulders dotted with freckles catch my eye and I feel like a middle school boy eager for the slightest bit of exposed skin. I've been so busy with work I haven't had time or energy to have sex with anyone for about six months now.

With Charlotte, my future wife and lover, here in front of me, this is like the world's slowest striptease. The way the pearls run around her smooth neck have me itching to give her a different type of necklace. The urge to grab her by the throat and watch her lips part in pleasure has me on the edge of my seat.

"Doesn't that feel better?" My tone has unintentionally moved from polite to suggestive. I need to reel in the primal part of me, even though I'm dying to let it loose.

"Yes, much better." She blushes briefly and glances down at the papers in front of her. "Oh, here's the pre-nup. I went ahead and signed it. I didn't see anything concerning." She pats her hand on the stack of paper and flashes a friendly smile.

"Should I assume that signing this means you are 100% on board with marrying me?" I ask tentatively, standing up and moving to her end of the table. I pick up the contract and flip through the pages, noting her signature in all the right spots. Cat will be pleased.

"More like 90%," she admits, staring up at me with her deep green eyes.

"What can I do about that remaining ten percent?" I'm like a used car salesman trying to make the last sale of the day to get my commission. I set the contract down and stand beside her, placing one hand on the table and the other on the back of her chair so that we're face to face. The scent of black cherries fills my senses as I breathe her in. Her eyes widen in surprise at my daring closeness.

"A strong marriage, even one for convenience, relies on two things," she pauses and licks her lips. Watching her tongue dart out to quickly moisten her lips has me practically panting. "One, communication between both people to ensure both are getting what they need from the relationship. And two," Charlotte takes a deep breath. "Chemistry."

"Chemistry," I repeat back, my voice dropping an octave and becoming a deep whisper. A crimson flush comes over her pretty face as I put my hand to her cheek. "Should we take a chemistry test, then?" I suggest, my cock straining at my pants, begging to bury itself inside of her pussy.

"That would be wise," she admits, her breathing becoming shallow, the quick rise and fall of her chest betraying her futile attempt at controlling her nervous desire.

"Before we begin," I pause, remembering she has no idea what she's about to get into. "You should know that I have certain expectations and desires when it comes to sex. Despite being a preacher, I need more than just the missionary position."

She smiles nervously at my sad little joke before saying, "Okay..."

"I'm someone who needs control, someone who needs a willing submissive to pleasure and dominate." At my words, her eyebrows raise up and her eyes alight with surprise and a hint of intrigue. "That being said, if my particular sexual proclivities are not what you signed up for, tell me now and I'll rip the prenup in half. You can walk away without any repercussions whatsoever. I won't even make you sign an NDA." Cat would be furious if she knew what I was saying. No NDA? I barely know this woman; I must be crazy!

"I..." Charlotte glances from me to the signed prenup sitting at my end of the table. "I think I'm okay with this."

"Excellent." Tamping down my excitement at her consent, I keep my voice calm and low. "Now, when I give you an order, you follow it or there will be consequences, Lady Charlotte." I lick my lips and give her a roguish grin.

"Oh!" Her cheeks pinken and her breath catches in her throat as she realizes what I'm saying.

"Stand up." I add some bite to my words and she immediately rises. Women assume that because I'm a pastor, I'm a submissive man, one who follows a woman's lead in bed, one who lies back and makes her do all the work. It's time to teach Charlotte I'm not the man I appear to be. Our first lesson is tonight.

"Follow me." I lead her down the hall to my bedroom, soon to be our bedroom.

"In here," I gesture for her to enter the room first. I grope through the darkness until I find the floor lamp and turn it on. A halo of light hangs over us filling the room with a soft white glow. She reaches the bed, then turns to face me, waiting for my next order. I'm in charge here; we both know it.

"If at any point you feel uncomfortable and want to stop, you will tell me so immediately. If I do something that causes you pain or discomfort, you will tell me to stop by using a safe word. Now, choose your safe word."

"Safe word?" She thinks for a moment. "Waffles?" That might be the weirdest safe word I've ever heard, but no matter.

"No means no here, always. Don't do anything you're not okay with, got it?" I walk towards her and stop once I'm only one step away. She nods her consent and I reach for her neck, the neck I've been wanting to wrap my hand around all evening. Inhaling her delicious cherry scent, I clench my hand around the sides and give her a gentle squeeze. "Good girl," I moan.

Her pink lips part just like I imagined they would. What I hadn't imagined earlier is the eager smile that's lighting up her face, as if this is exactly how she likes to be handled. Every nerve in my body is on fire with need, need for her, need for this woman God placed in my life. Once I kiss her, there's no going back, no stopping, no reversing of the moment. My life before Charlotte is over; there is only life with her going forward.

I pull her close and press my lips to hers, relishing her sweet, soft kiss. It's just an appetizer and I want the whole entrée. Pulling back, I reach into her hair and release it from the tight bun it's been in for far too long. Her chestnut locks fall around her face as she sighs with relief like I knew she would. "I told you to be comfortable," I growl in her ear.

"Yes, Sir William," she responds, locking eyes with me, watching me closely for my reaction to her words. Her submissiveness has me craving her in the worst way.

"Lady Charlotte," I murmur into her smooth neck before giving her a slight nibble. "Take off your clothes."

"Yes, sir." She unzips her skirt and lets it slide down to the floor. Next to go is her top which she rolls up and over her head before dropping it next to her feet. Standing here in front of me in her very lacey black panties and bra, she exudes confidence and raw sexuality. As I take in her mostly naked body, I admire her small, perky breasts and her deliciously large ass. She's a contradiction in curves. I walk behind her and give it a hard squeeze as if testing a new mattress for firmness. She giggles nervously before regaining her composure.

"Perfect." I reach around her and run my hands over the curves of her breasts, letting my fingers linger on her hardening nipples a moment too long causing her to release a small whimper. "You look amazing, Lady Charlotte, good enough to eat." I move her hair aside and languidly kiss her neck from ear to collarbone, my teeth lightly grazing her skin. "Would you like that, Lady Charlotte? Would you like me to eat you?"

"Yes, Sir William," she says, her breathing hard and fast. I wrap my hands around her waist and let a few fingers slide beneath her panties, searching for her clit. "Oh!" She cries out as I make contact with her soft folds, already wet with anticipation. I slowly let my middle finger sink into her dripping entrance. She lays her head back on my shoulder and moans loudly.

"That's right, tell me how good it feels when I touch you. Tell me what a good job I'm doing." Between her moans and her round ass right against my cock, I'm harder than steel right now and it is borderline painful. I want, no, I need to fuck her.

The more I move my finger in and out, relishing in her glorious wetness, the more she relaxes against me, trusting me with her pleasure and her weight. Her legs are starting to buckle and, even with my firm grasp on her hips, I need to lay her down before we both fall. I'm more of a cardio guy than a weight lifter; I have the endurance to go all night, just not the ability to hold her up the whole time.

Removing my hand from her warm center, I move in front of her and unbutton my shirt. She watches me undress, her eyes hazy with lust, her cheeks flushed with pleasure. Pride washes over me as her eyes rove over my naked upper body. I may not have muscular tree trunks for legs, but swimming does keep my upper body in great shape.

"Not what you expected?" I tease, taking a step toward her.

"No," she whispers to herself, reaching her hand out to touch my chest. I allow her fingers to briefly trace over my tattoo before I pull her face to mine and crush her lips with my own. The force of my kiss pushes her down onto the bed so she can fully relax her body and I can better focus on her needs.

I straddle her hips and kiss her neck, collarbones, and the exposed parts of her breasts. Her soft moans are driving me wild. I reach behind her and unclasp her bra, freeing and pulling each breast into my mouth and alternately sucking and licking her nipples until her body is completely arched into mine and off the mattress.

"William!" She cries out, pressing her hips up into mine, desperately seeking release. "Please!"

"My good girl has such nice manners," I remark, kissing down her stomach to her soaking panties. "Please what? Use your words."

"Please fuck me," she says, biting her bottom lip to fight against the delightful agony of her impending pleasure.

"Since you asked so nicely," I respond. With a hand on either side of hips, I rip off her panties and throw them on the floor. With her delightfully hairy pussy exposed, I have to restrain myself from immediately going in for a taste. The scent of her arousal has my mouth watering.

I kiss her inner thighs slowly as I make my way from her knees to her broad hips, enjoying her soft curves along the way. I'll never get over the perfection of the female body, each curve and swell made by God for human pleasure. In this case, Charlotte's body for my pleasure. Placing myself between her deliciously voluptuous legs, I spread them as far as they'll go. My fingers skim the surface of her inner thighs, causing them to slightly tremble.

"Stay still," I caution her, knowing full well she will clamp them together the moment I start tasting her. Reluctantly, I remove my glasses and set them on the night stand. As much I want to keep seeing her in 20/20 vision, those things really get in the way for what I'm about to do.

I slowly run my tongue up and down her folds, my eyes rolling back at how good she tastes. Her body shivers and her legs shake, but she keeps them spread for me, just like I asked her to. "Such a good girl," I murmur against her warm pussy. "You taste so good, so irresistible." She cries out in pleasure as I tongue her entrance, my lips wandering up and down her sensitive center. I don't need my glasses to know she's enjoying this, just my ears.

"Oh, William!" She reaches down and grabs my hair, pulling me snugly against her. I chuckle and slide my tongue up to her ready clit.

"That's right. Show me how much you want it!" My tongue swirls around her clit and her legs clamp firmly around my head. "Keep your legs open!" I command, prying her legs open with my hands and holding them in place, my hands pressed deep into her quivering thighs. Normally, I would punish her for making me repeat an order; however, our first time together is neither the time nor place. Each of her moans encourages me to keep going, despite the fact that my cock is demanding release and I'm unsure how much longer I can restrain myself.

"Right there!" Charlotte exclaims suddenly, urgently pushing her pussy against my lapping tongue and losing herself in the moment. I keep my momentum, letting her lead my motions by how forcefully she humps my mouth. I'll give her control for now; I'll regain it soon enough.

"Oh! My! God!" She practically screams as she comes, breathing hard and fast while her orgasm rocks through her body. I slow down and languidly lick her pussy as she comes down from her high. If not for my insistent cock, I could stay here all night savoring her heady flavor. Once her breathing slows to a more regular pace, I remove my face from between her legs to look at her.

Her face is flushed and she's grinning from ear to ear. "You passed the test," she says, her voice husky and low.

"But Lady Charlotte," I begin, releasing her legs so they fall down on either side of my waist. "That was just the short answer part. I have yet to tackle the essay portion."

"What?" She asks, her tone both incredulous and excited. "I don't know if I can take anymore." She smiles blissfully and gazes up at me, waiting for me to surrender.

"You can, and you will. You will take my cock like the good girl you are and you will come around it while I watch you fall apart from pleasure," I growl as stand up to take off my pants. I quickly grab my glasses and slide on a condom before placing myself between her legs once more. "I'm going to watch you shake and quiver as I enter you, stretching you to fit me like a perfect glove. With each thrust you'll realize your pussy was made for my cock." I place my hands on her hips and delight in how her body is already quaking in anticipation.

"You're so...big," she points out, reaching her hand out tentatively to stroke my cock. Her soft fingers trailing along my shaft cause me to grip onto her hips so hard I worry I'll bruise her. The beginnings of light bruises mark the inside of her thighs where I held her legs spread earlier.

"You can take it," I assure her, swatting her hand from my cock and rubbing the tip of it against her clit. She moans loudly in response so I move down to her entrance, dipping my cock into her fresh arousal. "So wet for me again, Lady Charlotte? Good girl." I slide a hand up her stomach and to her breast where I knead her nipple until her hips are bucking against my cock. "I knew you could do it. I knew you wanted more." At first, I ease into her, checking to make sure I won't hurt her upon entry.

"Oh!" She screams out and covers her mouth with her hand as if shocked by her volume. I pull her hand away and shake my head.

"If you aren't screaming, I'm not doing a good job." With a single, solid thrust, I'm inside of her. Immediately, I'm overwhelmed by how tight she is. "Damn, Lady Charlotte, you feel so fucking good." I lean down and bite her neck, trying so hard to just enjoy the initial feel of her pussy clenched around my cock. It's too good to resist for long.

I find myself losing control and fully pounding into her, lifting her hips off the mattress with each thrust. She matches my grunts with soft, echoing "ohs" that quickly escalate into louder "OHs," interspersed with "William! William!"

"That's right, good girl, taking my cock like I knew you could." I grab her neck and admire the way my hand molds to her delicate throat. Rather than looking away like most women would, Charlotte meets my eyes with her own and smiles mischievously at me. "You like that, Lady Charlotte? You like my hand on your neck and my cock in your pussy?"

"Yes!" She blurts out. "A thousand times, yes!" She reaches a hand down to her clit and starts rubbing herself vigorously.

"No!" I smack her hand away and replace it with my own. "You will come from my touch and my cock alone. Now, come for me!" I roar, my fingers moving deftly up, down, and around her swollen clit as I hump her in a wild, animalistic frenzy.

"I'm coming!" She screams as her walls tighten around me, pulsing and squeezing around my cock. The climax building inside of me erupts and I explode with every ounce of energy in my body. The world seems to vibrate for a moment and I worry I might pass out. Slowly pulling myself from her, I take a moment to recover. My breathing is raspy and ragged, but so is Charlotte's. I roll over to the side and sit up on the edge of the bed. I wonder what's going through her mind right now. She's clearly sated and spent; two things I take great pride in achieving.

"I didn't know preachers were allowed to curse," she says, more to herself than to me. I chuckle and lay down beside her.

"We're allowed to do a lot of things, just mostly in private," I respond, laying a hand on her stomach and watching it rise and fall with her breathing.

"I also didn't know preachers could have tattoos." She turns her head to face me, her eyes lingering on my chest and upper arms. "Doesn't the Bible say that's not allowed?"

"Actually, when read in its proper context, verses against tattoos are about getting tattoos as a way to worship other gods. As long as that's not what they are for, tattoos are fine. I wrote my master's thesis on the issue, so I would say I'm pretty well versed on the subject. Pun intended." I grin broadly and she smiles back at me.

"I like that about you."

"My tattoos?" I ask.

"I like that too," she laughs and continues. "What I mean is I like how you're unapologetic about how intelligent you are. I don't think I could be married to someone who wasn't intellectual." The word "married" lingers on her tongue for an extra beat, almost like she's fully tasting the word for first time, really contemplating its full flavor palette.

"I see we are of like mind in that regard." I'm relieved she finds my intellect attractive, most people don't. They think I'm showing off when I'm simply explaining or elaborating.

"Where is your bathroom?" Charlotte sits up and searches for her discarded clothes.

"Right through there." I point to the door on the right wall and she disappears into it. While she's gone, I clean myself up and dispose of the condom. My relief that we connect sexually is palpable. I had been so worried about having a wife who was either bad at sex or didn't enjoy sex, I hadn't even contemplated the possibility of a wife who would actually suit my physical needs. This just might work after all.

Charlotte emerges from the bathroom fully dressed just as I finish buttoning my pants. Her hair is back in a neat bun and all I want to do is release it and pull her to me once more. Even if we never develop more than friendly feelings for each other, at least the sex is good, and I can live with that.

"Well, that was fun," she says, smiling playfully at me.

"Did I eliminate the remaining ten percent of your doubt?" I ask, walking with her to the dining room where she grabs her jacket.

"Absolutely. I can definitely say I'm one hundred percent on board with marrying you now." She slips on her jacket and giggles as she blushes lightly.

"In that case," I reach into my pocket and grab the small black box. I'm relieved it's still in there after all the undressing and redressing I've done. I pull it out and get down on one knee. "Even though you basically propositioned me weeks ago, it's only far you get an actual marriage proposal." As I open the box, she covers her mouth with her hand and her eyes widen in surprise. "Charlotte Lucas, will you marry me?" Despite knowing she'll say yes, my hand shakes.

"Yes," she answers, tears coming to her eyes.

"Are you sure? Crying isn't usually a positive thing."

"Yes, well, I cry a lot so you might want to get used to it." She smiles faintly before continuing. "I know this isn't real, we're not in love, we barely know each other, but...I never thought anyone would ever propose to me. They're happy tears."

"That's a relief," I reply, sliding the ring onto her finger with ease.

"How did you know my ring size?" She lifts her hand to her face to examine the ring closely.

"Elizabeth gave me one of your rings to take to the jeweler's," I explain. "Do you like it?"

"It's lovely, thank you." She quickly wipes two small tears from her cheeks and kisses my cheek. "I suppose I'll see you on Sunday? Cat said that's when you'll announce our engagement."

"Yes, she's already written up a statement for me to read." I would have rather written my own betrothal announcement, but Cat is in charge of this whole situation whether I like it or not.

"How romantic," Charlotte says, rolling her eyes. "Oh, by the way, would you be able to come to my parents' for dinner tomorrow night? I want to tell them about it before you tell the church."

"Of course," I reply. I'm reminded of the sad fact that I don't have my own parents around to share the news with. I keep my expression neutral as I write down her parents' address. At least Charlotte won't have any meddlesome in-laws to worry about.

"See you tomorrow, William." She says cheerfully.

"Drive safe," I say as I open the door and watch her leave. Walking back to the dining room, I pick up the notebook Charlotte gave me and head to my office. I'm surprised to find that I'm eager to learn more about her after just having seen her.

There's something about her that I can't put my finger on, something that has me hungry for her body and her mind. Opening the notebook, I start at the first section: "Basic Details About Me You Can Probably Find on the Internet." I chuckle at her title. Intelligent, attractive, and funny? Thank you, Lord!

Chapter 9
Charlotte

"**I** never thought this day would come!" Mom clasps her hands together and smiles broadly at me.

"Thanks for your constant belief in me," I respond, sarcasm dripping from my voice.

"You know what I mean!" She clarifies, giving me a huge, unexpected hug. "Charlotte's boyfriend at a family dinner! I'm so excited I forgot about the potatoes on the stove earlier and they boiled over everywhere." Turning on the mixer and dropping in half a stick of butter, she begins mashing said potatoes.

"Not the potatoes!" I mock, smiling cheerfully at her. Despite how anxious I am about William at a family dinner, I'm in a pretty good mood, probably from having two orgasms last night. Knowing that we connect sexually has lifted a huge burden of doubt from my shoulders. At least if we're married, I'll be getting laid on the regular, and that's worth all the other ridiculous expectations as far as I'm concerned.

"Go set the table," Mom says, shooing me out of the kitchen. I grab a bunch of cutlery, plates, and napkins and do as I'm told. Just as I set down the last plate, there's a knock at the front door.

"I'll get it!" Eddie jumps from the sofa and reaches the door before I can make a move in that direction. Damn him and his former track star skills!

He opens the door and there's William, dressed in his usual suit and tie, carrying a bunch of flowers. "For me? You shouldn't have!" Eddie grabs the flowers and moves aside. "Come in! The gang's all here."

William enters the room looking a little shaken up. I don't think he was expecting such an exuberant welcome from my brother.

"You take these back and I'll take your coat." Eddie shoves the flowers back at William and practically yanks his coat off of him.

"Eddie! Chill! You're freaking him out!" I walk over to them and jokingly shove Eddie towards the living room. He smiles impishly and holds up his hands in surrender before leaving us alone. "Sorry about that. Everyone's excited you're here."

"Even you?" His eyes are telling me he wants to fuck me right here, right now, and I have to press my legs together to stop the building tension in my center. As I do so, I wince a little as my inner thighs touch each other. They're a little bruised from how hard he pressed my legs open last night; a small price to pay for so much pleasure.

"Yes," I admit, "Even me." I watch his eyes darken at my admission. I turn away from him before I lose control and use his tie to pull him closer. Sex with William was certainly memorable and very, very enjoyable. The moment he ordered me to stand, the feminist in me wanted to fight back and remain sitting. My body, however, had other thoughts. Each command he gave me had me pulsing with desire.

After a week of decision fatigue, it was both exciting and a relief to not have to think for once. God, it was so nice to have a man take control and know how to please a me in bed. And the way he praised me? Immediately wet, immediately, and that was before I even saw his sexy tattoos. Never in a million years would I have guessed he had any. One in particular stood out to me above the rest: the word "*Lazarus*" across his chest in bold black letters. I was a bit too preoccupied to ask about it last night, though I definitely want to know more about it soon.

"I'm glad to hear it. These are for you," he says, handing me a bouquet of irises and daffodils, my favorite flowers.

"I see you've been reading my notebook," I smile and take a deep inhale from the bouquet.

"Forewarned is forearmed, or so they say." With Eddie, William had used his customer service smile. With me, he relaxes and let's a genuine smile escape and spread across his handsome face. "This one is for your mom." He holds up a bouquet of yellow roses.

"How lovely! This way," I say, leading him past the living room and into the kitchen. He can say hi to Dad and my other brothers later. Mom is the priority.

"Mom?" I say quietly, trying not to spook her as she diligently scoops the potatoes into a giant bowl. The doctor had told her to take it easy after her heart attack. That hasn't stopped her from whipping up a massive dinner for tonight.

"Yeah?" She turns around and immediately smiles when she spies William. "Reverend! So nice to see you again!"

"The pleasure is all mine," he responds and hands the roses to her. "These are for you."

"Oh! Aren't you the sweetest!" She grabs a vase from the top of the fridge and places the roses in it with water. I also grab a vase and do the same for my flowers. I'm so touched that William not only brought me flowers, but he read my notebook and learned which flowers I like the best. "Dinner's ready so go get the rest of the men and have a seat." Mom carries the bowl of potatoes to the table and I collect "the men," as Mom called them.

"William! Glad to have you here," Dad says, soundly patting William on the back and shaking his hand firmly.

"Glad to be here," William replies, a polite smile plastered to his face. He shakes Nick's, Eddie's, and Rob's hands and they all take their seats.

"Reverend?" Mom turns to William. "Would you mind blessing our food?" I really wish she would just call him William. She seems to take a certain amount of pride in the fact that he's a pastor, like having him here is some kind of honor.

"I wouldn't mind at all. Let us bow our heads." William says a quick yet efficient blessing and we start passing the food around. Once everyone has filled their plates, Mom starts peppering William with questions as if I'm not there.

"How long have you two been together?" She asks, daintily slicing up her chicken breast.

"Not very long," William replies, not lying but also not telling the truth. Who gets engaged after a month? Me, I guess. I nervously touch my engagement ring hidden in my pocket. I'm hoping the right moment will present itself before I slip it on my finger and make my announcement. Even though I just put it on last night, my finger feels naked without it. I find its small weight comforting, a materialistic reminder of the commitment I've made to William.

"How did you meet?" She throws another question at him instead of me.

"Through Elizabeth Bennett. She attends my church." William flashes me a small smile. My heart flutters a little at his attention. Ever since he rocked my world twice last night, I've developed a bit of a crush on him. Yeah, I'm crushing on my fiancé. That's not weird, right? Right?

"I always liked Lizzy. She's a good girl." Mom passes the rolls around the table as I choke on my water. William fights back a chuckle at my reaction. "You all right, Charlotte?" She has a quizzical expression.

"Yeah, I'm fine," I sputter, coughing a little after the water finally goes down. My face is quickly turning red and getting very warm. Fortunately, everyone will assume it's from choking, everyone except William.

Dinner conversation quickly changes topics as my brothers start asking William about his favorite sports teams. Rob keeps giving me side eye glances and I remember I never did explain to him what's going on with me and William. I mouth, "Sorry" at him and he gives me an annoyed sneer.

William is interacting so calmly and naturally with my family; he is completely at ease and I'm impressed. My parents are enamored with him, and my brothers, aside from Rob, seem to like him so far. Thankfully, everyone's attention is on William so they don't notice my plate remains mostly full throughout dinner. I'm too anxious to eat much; each bite is a chore.

My right leg keeps bouncing out of my control and I wish I could magically increase my anxiety medication. A warm hand lands on my thigh and I freeze. I sneak a glance at William and marvel at his outwardly collected and pleasant demeaner as his hand moves soothingly up and down my thigh, calming my nerves. Just like with the flowers, I'm pleasantly surprised. He must have read the entire notebook because the section on my anxiety is towards the back.

I'm touched by both his literal touch and his effort in getting to know me. No guy I've dated has ever put this much effort into our relationship, and this relationship isn't even real or based on an already established emotional connection. William's hand reminds me to breathe slowly and count down from ten. When all this began, I was worried he would worsen my anxiety. However, it seems he might actually be good for it. I lay my hand on top of his to let him know I'm good now. I fully expect him to pull his hand away. To my surprise, it remains.

"Charlotte!" Mom gets my attention with a sharp tone. "You hardly ate anything. Are you alright?"

"Um, actually," I pause and everyone's eyes turn to me as the conversation comes to a stop. I slip my hand in my pocket and slide the ring on my finger. "I was too nervous to eat because I have an announcement to make." I glance around the table, my eyes starting at Mom and making their way from her to Dad, from Dad to Nick, from Nick to Eddie, from Eddie to Rob, and lastly from Rob to William. His clear blue eyes stare into mine, strong and steady. He smiles encouragingly and nods at me to go ahead. I hold my left hand out towards to my family and the diamond shines brightly under the ceiling light.

"Charlotte!" Mom screams and grabs my hand so hard she yanks me on the table. "You're engaged?"

"Eleanor, calm down, dear. Remember your heart." Dad touches Mom's shoulder gently to remind her to take it easy. He turns to us and smiles proudly. "Congratulations, Charlotte, you too, William."

"Thanks, Dad." I pull my hand away from Mom and stand up from the table. There's a glob of mashed potatoes on my chest where I was pulled into my dinner plate from Mom's exuberance.

"You're engaged?" Mom repeats her excited question as she tries to process the news. "This is wonderful!" She comes around the table and hugs me tightly. "I'm so happy!" She hugs William next and he kindly allows her to squeeze him to her heart's content.

"Edward!" Mom releases William and quickly walks over to Dad. "Our daughter is getting married!" He wraps her in his arms and she starts crying happy tears.

Eddie and Nick also congratulate us with big hugs and bigger smiles. Rob stands up and shoves his chair in roughly before walking out of the room.

"I'll be right back," I say to William as I gesture to Rob. William nods and keeps talking to Eddie and Nick while I make my escape.

"Hey!" I call out to Rob but he doesn't turn around. Instead, he walks down the hall and into his old bedroom. I race to the door before he can slam it in my face. "Let me explain."

"You said that weeks ago and you never did." His anger is warranted. Guilt rises from my stomach and into my chest. "What gives, Char?" He moves from the doorway and lets me in the room.

"It's such a weird situation and I had to figure it all out before telling anyone about it. I meant to tell you everything right away, but..." I gesture at the air around me as if trying to pull the rest of my sentence from an invisible plane. "I'm sorry. I have no real excuse." I shrug in defeat and hope he'll forgive me.

"Tell me everything, right now." Rob's eyebrows slant down so sharply I worry he'll poke his own eyes out with them.

"Okay," I begin. "A few weeks ago, Lizzy went on a date with William..."

"So, you got sloppy seconds?" He raises his hand to stop me from going any further.

"No, let me explain! He told her he needs a wife to keep his job at the church and she was on a list of women his boss picked out for him to choose from. Lizzy didn't want to date him, much less marry him, so she told me about him and I told him I would marry him."

"Are you crazy?" He interrupts me, his voice loud and accusatory. "You can't marry a guy you don't know!"

"First of all, no, I'm not crazy. Second, I can do whatever I want, and that includes marry a stranger." It's not the best defense and Rob knows it.

"Is this because of Mom and how she keeps pressuring you to get married?" His eyes soften and his frown lessens.

"Yes and no. I do want Mom to be happy and that is part of it, but I want to be married. I want this. William is a really good guy and I think this can work." I place my hands on my hips in defiance and give Rob a hard stare.

"Char," he pauses and shakes his head. "This is crazy." He thinks for a moment. "If I told you I think he's no good, would you listen this time?"

"Yes, of course." I ignored Rob's sixth sense last time. That won't happen again.

"Fortunately for you, I'm not getting any bad vibes...yet," he admits. "If this is what you want, I'll support you on one condition."

"What?"

"I want some one-on-one time with William. I want to figure out if he's worthy of you." He crosses his arms and towers over me, trying his best to be intimidating. Even though he's the youngest, somehow, he ended up the tallest of all of us and he uses that to his advantage.

"That can be arranged. Thanks, Rob!" I pull him into a big hug. I'm relieved to have Rob's (conditional) support and to have someone else who knows what's really going on with William and I.

"Crushing...my...lungs!" Rob pretends to suffocate so I let him go. "I think we've left your fiancé unprotected with the family long enough," he jokes.

As we head back to the dining room, I take a moment to enjoy the sight of everyone getting along so well with William. I don't think William is actually having a good time; however, he's doing a really good job of pretending he is. If he can pretend this well with my family, how can I ever know his true feelings about us? Fear chills through my chest like a winter wind. I get that our marriage is basically a PR stunt for his church and I have a certain image I need to present to make that work. However, I want whatever relationship or friendship we develop behind the scenes to be real.

William waves me over to join them. I shake off my worries and smile tentatively as I enter the fray. Mom is already scrolling through Pinterest and saving various wedding related pins. Eddie and Nick are warning William to respect me or they'll "kick his ass."

"Sorry for leaving so rudely earlier," Rob apologizes and shakes William's hand. "Welcome to the family!" His polite smile hides his previous frustration well.

"Thank you. I know it was unexpected for you all. No harm, no foul." William looks past Rob at me and a shiver runs through my body. He's got to stop doing that, especially with my family all around us. He gently tugs me close to him so we're perfect happy couple we're pretending to be.

As his arm wraps around my hips and his hand slides down my ass where no one can see, there's one real feeling he can't hide when it comes to us: he wants me. And Lord help me, I want him, too.

Chapter 10
William

It's not that I never wanted to get married, I just never gave the concept much attention before Cat made me. Hilltop has been my life, my focus for the past five years. Even before Dad passed away four years ago, I was busy working towards my doctorate so that, one day, I would lead his flock. I had two serious girlfriends between high school and now. Since neither was willing to accept my dominating nature in the bedroom, marriage was off the table.

And now, now I find myself committed to a woman I barely know who is mine for life, and instead of being overwhelmed with the sense of dread I should, I'm cautiously optimistic. She's easy to talk to and she fits the image the church needs. It doesn't hurt that she also fits my body's needs.

It's rather annoying how often I've been thinking about her in my bed. The image of her underneath me invades my thoughts at the most inconvenient times, like right now.

Outwardly, I'm giving another excellent, life-altering sermon. Inwardly, I'm fucking Charlotte with my tongue. I grip the pulpit to ground myself and focus on the words in front of me. Fortunately, I'm at the conclusion. Next comes the big announcement.

"Before I send you out into the world this Sunday, I have something to tell you all." I pause and survey my patient flock. "I have spent many years asking the Lord to guide me in my quest for a wife." This isn't remotely true, but Cat wrote this, so I'm stuck relaying it. "Recently, he has seen fit to bless me with one. She has entered my life seemingly out of the blue, and I could not be more thankful. Won't you all join me in welcoming my fiancé, Charlotte Lucas, to our church family?" I gesture down to where Charlotte is sitting in the front row, all prim and proper in her light blue pantsuit, heels crossed, hands folded in her lap.

Applause fills the church as Charlotte rises and awkwardly waves around the sanctuary. I hate drawing attention to her; this has got to be making her anxiety skyrocket. She smiles politely and sits back down. After I give the closing prayer, church members swarm around Charlotte and she's quickly hidden from view by the massive throng. Instead of walking to the back to shake hands like usual, I stride over to Charlotte's new fan club and force myself through the people to stand at her side.

I quickly grab her hand and clasp it with my own. Her fingers are a little twitchy and her palm is quite sweaty. I want to let go and wipe my hand on my pants, but I don't for two reasons. One, we need to look the part of a happy couple madly in love with each other. Two, if I let go, she might bolt. She was very detailed in her notebook regarding her anxiety and the best thing I can do to help her is keep her grounded. Even though this might be a fake relationship, that won't stop me from supporting her and caring for her like a husband or fiancé should. I owe her that much.

"Oh, Charlotte! We're so happy to have you here, even happier that Reverend Collins is settling down after all these years!" Eula Morris gushes effusively all over Charlotte.

"I'm happy to be here," Charlotte keeps her words and tone cordial and sweet as each person greets and congratulates her in turn. After what must have been the hundredth person, I cut the welcome wagon short.

"Thank you all so much for your warm welcome!" I use my preacher voice to get everyone's attention. The crowd goes silent. "Charlotte will be here every Sunday, so if you didn't get a chance to meet her, you will another day. Have a blessed week!" I excuse us and pull her out of the crowd before anyone else can start talking to her again. We've been at this for about half an hour; that's a lot even for someone without anxiety.

We walk quickly to my office to escape the well-meaning congregants. Once we're in the room, I close the door so we're in a cocoon of silence.

"Are you okay?" I ask, reluctantly releasing her hand. Is my touch comforting right now or too much? She welcomed it at dinner with her family, but a hand on a leg is different from a hand clutching a hand.

"Yeah," she nods. "Thanks for helping me escape." She smiles weakly. "I suppose I should get used to such attention."

"They'll only be like this for a week or two. Once you've established yourself as my fiancé and they have all met you, they'll give you your space."

"Okay." Her breathing slows to its normal pace as she looks around my office. "Is that your dad?" She points to the portrait hanging behind my desk.

"Yeah, that's him, Reverend Arthur Collins." I stare hard at the portrait, my expression carefully neutral.

"How long was he the pastor here?" She approaches the portrait and lightly traces the solid wood frame with her fingers. I can't help noticing how delightfully snug her pants are against her delicious ass. I want to grab her, spin her, and pin her to the wall. Instead, I swallow hard and try to ignore my hardening cock.

"He died when I was 28, so 28 years." I sigh heavily. He took over as head pastor the year I was born, thus making clear early on his preference for the church over his family.

"Wow. That's a really long time." She turns back towards me before sitting down in my desk chair. "You don't really talk about your mom," she points out, looking up at me with clear, bright eyes. "Did she pass away, too?"

"As far as I know, she's still alive." I shrug my shoulders and walk around the desk to her.

"As far as you know?" Her eyebrows raise as she tries to process my odd response.

"She left when I was a teenager. I haven't seen or talked to her since I was sixteen." I sit on the corner of my desk and put my hands in my pocket.

"Oh! That's awful. I'm sorry to hear that." Charlotte's soft green eyes are filled with so much compassion it's almost painful to take in. She tentatively lays a hand on my leg to comfort me. Her touch is warm and tender, reminding me of our night together two days ago. Even all covered up, I'm aroused by the curves of her body, the way the blue fabric stretches tautly across her waist and thick thighs, the slight dip around the collar of her shirt where it lays lightly against her small breasts; it's all tempting me terribly. I physically shake myself a little to help me focus on our very serious conversation.

"It used to bother me that I had no idea where she was or if she cared about me anymore. In time, I grew to accept her decision. Closure is overrated anyway." I try to sound nonchalant, though I'm not fooling Charlotte. She's smart enough to see through my façade.

"You don't have to pretend it doesn't hurt. If this is going to work, we need to always be honest with each other." She chides me for my white lie. I pull my hand out of my pocket and lay it over hers.

"You're right." I sigh and gently squeeze her soft hand. She tenses slightly at my touch, as if surprised by this small piece of intimacy between us. I lift her hand to my lips and lightly kiss it. If she was tense before, she's a stone wall now. "Relax, Lady Charlotte. As your fiancé, I'm allowed to touch you. Besides," I pause, placing her hand on my hardening cock. "I think we are way past just touching, don't you?"

"Yes," she whispers, her eyes focused on the floor as her cheeks grow rosy.

"Look at me," I command, my voice a low growl. Immediately, her head snaps up and her eyes lock with mine. "Good girl." Ever since I had a taste of her, I've been dying for more. It could be the fact that I was celibate for so long, or it could be the simple fact that fucking her is my new favorite past time.

"Stroke my cock." I watch as her hand starts moving back and forth over my covered erection. Her fingers dance up and down my shaft forcing a deep, guttural moan from my chest. I close my eyes briefly and surrender to her touch. Leaning down, I firmly grasp her chin and kiss her hard, forcing her lips apart as my tongue searches for hers. She responds in kind, her hand still teasing my cock. Suddenly, she grabs my tie with her free hand to pull me tightly against her face, kissing me even deeper and harder than before. She's ravenous for me; the feeling is mutual.

Grasping her hand and forcing her to release my tie, I pull back from her kiss reluctantly.

"Who said you were in charge?" As much as I'm enjoying the moment, I need to remind her I'm the dominant one here. Now that we've established she is the submissive one here, she can stand a little punishment. I can't say where my need for control comes from; it's just part of who I am.

Ever since I was a teenager, I knew I was meant to be in command, both in my future job and in the bedroom. Unfortunately, this became a problem in my romantic relationships. Along with not wanting to be a preacher's wife, my previous girlfriends were less than appreciative when I tried to correct their bratty behavior. Charlotte was so deliciously submissive last time, I thought for sure she would always give me full control.

Granted, this is all very new to her and our relationship is in a weird place between desire and compulsion, so I'll use this as a teaching moment.

"Um," she pauses, "no one?" Her lips are reddened from the force of my kiss. An idea strikes me. I stand up from the desk and move in front of her.

"On your knees," I order. She gets a little flustered for a moment before complying. Seeing her on her knees in her new pantsuit, a pantsuit she bought specifically for today, for me, has me straining painfully against my pants. "What's your safe word?"

"Waffles," she says as stares up at me.

"Take off my belt." Her hands move deftly as she unbuckles and slides my belt through the loops. "As part of your penance for yanking my tie earlier, you will suck my cock. Understood?" I stare down at her and watch hungrily as she silently pulls down my pants and underwear until nothing is left between us. "Since you won't be able to speak, tap my leg if you need to stop. Understood?" I snap.

"Yes, Sir William," she nods and maintains eye contact as she slides my cock into her warm, wet mouth. I grip her shoulder to keep my balance as my body is overwhelmed with pure bliss. She wraps a hand around my base and slowly, languidly, rolls her tongue over and around my shaft. Giving the head a quick flick of her tongue, she grins up at me, her green eyes practically glowing with need. Before I can order her to continue, she does, with vigor, taking me completely, deeply, without hesitation.

"Damn, you're so fucking pretty with my cock in your mouth, Lady Charlotte," I moan, grabbing the bun her is wrapped into and pulling it loose. I fucking hate when her hair is in a bun. She's doing it to appear formal and put together, to be "the part" she's playing for the church members. I don't want her to be like them; I want her to be herself. "That's better. Never wear your hair like that again." She nods rapidly which adds to my pleasure, both physically and emotionally. With one hand on the back of her head, I force her to increase her rhythm. "That's my good girl, my good little slut."

She holds onto my thighs for stability as she moves back and forth, alternating between licking and sucking until I want to scream for release. A deep growl starts low in my throat when I notice her hand move from her side to her waist where it sneaks down under her pants to reach her needy pussy. I lean down and roughly pull her hand out of her pants.

"You don't get to come, not today, not until you learn your lesson." I slap her hand back on my thigh and resume thrusting deeply into her mouth. Her expression changes from hungry to angry instantly. Good. I want her to be mad. I want her to remember this and know that she must always submit to me or there will be consequences. Small tears run down her face as she gags herself on my cock with even more force and energy now. She's being vindictive and I'm loving every second. I slam my cock into the back of her throat, making her gag.

My climax builds and builds, threatening to burst with each thrust. "Just like that. Good job. Yes, keep going!" I encourage her as she maintains her speed, her tongue wrapping and unwrapping around my shaft with just the right force and momentum. She digs her short nails into my thighs in retribution, but she doesn't know how I get off on the pain. I burst forcefully into her pretty mouth causing her to choke as she abruptly pulls back from me, releasing her hold on my legs.

I can tell she's about to spit out my cum, so I quickly grab her face, squeezing her cheeks so she can't open her mouth.

"Swallow."

With her eyes full of malice, she forcefully swallows my seed.

"Good girl." I rub my thumb down her cheek and across her soft lips. "Now, tell me who is in charge." I keep my voice soft and encouraging, removing all the anger and power that filled me earlier. I want her submission, not her hatred.

She looks up at me and stays quiet, her mouth firmly closed, her eyes watery and resigned. For a moment, I worry I went too far. My stomach backflips repeatedly as I reflect on what just happened between us. I punished her for her willfulness, that's all. She didn't use her safe word, so I shouldn't feel guilty. Her out was there the whole time and she didn't use it. I never felt guilty after punishing the other women, so why is this any different?

Right as I'm about to speak, she says harshly, "You are, Sir William."

Regret rolls through my body at her words. I pull up my pants and make myself look presentable again. "You can get up now." I extend a hand to help her, which she takes reluctantly. Standing in front of me, she erases any emotion from her expression and grabs her purse from my desk. Grabbing a tissue, she wipes her eyes wordlessly; her hand shakes a little, like after-shocks from an earthquake.

"Charlotte, I'm..." A knock at the door cuts off my apology. "Who is it?" I call out as we both turn and face the closed door.

"Josiah," he answers. I hold my hand out to tell Charlotte to wait a moment before opening the door.

"Hi, Josiah," I greet him politely though I'm perturbed at his importune visit. "What brings you by?"

"I came to meet your fiancé," he explains, a friendly smile graces his face as he turns his attention to Charlotte. "I'm Josiah Hall, the Youth Pastor here at Hilltop. I was at a Youth Group meeting right after service so I couldn't greet you immediately. I'm glad you're still here. I thought for sure I would have to wait until next Sunday."

"Nice to meet you, I'm Charlotte Lucas." She smiles charmingly at him and extends a hand, a hand that moments ago was gripping my thigh in frustration. Either she's genuinely happy to meet him or she's a really good actress. If it's the latter, I've severely underestimated her.

"William told me about your, uh, situation," Josiah hedges, glancing at me to confirm it's okay to talk about this. I nod and he continues. "You're a very brave woman for signing up for this."

"I wouldn't say I'm brave, maybe foolish." She side-eyes me for a second and my face reddens in embarrassment over my recent treatment of her. "Either way, I'm in it to win it, as they say."

"Good to know," he laughs jovially.

"I have to go. It was nice meeting you. I'll see you next week." Charlotte smiles meekly at Josiah before quickly walking out the door. I don't blame her for wanting to leave as fast as possible. I have some major damage control to do with her now, but it will have to wait. As she goes, I clock Josiah's eyes checking out her ass as she disappears from my office.

"Ahem," I clear my throat, bringing his wandering eyes back to me.

"Sorry, man," he says, though his tone is not apologetic at all. "She's got a nice ass." He grins devilishly.

"Well, that's my ass, thank you very much," I remind him.

"Okay, okay," he holds out his hands in surrender. "Speaking of, have you and your fiancé consummated your engagement?" He raises and lowers his eyebrows suggestively.

"Not that it's any of your business, but yes," I admit somewhat arrogantly.

"Wow." He shakes his head and gives me a funny look. "I was partially joking. I thought this was going to be a marriage in name only."

"What gave you that impression?" I cock an eyebrow at his statement.

"The fact that Cat made you do it in the first place. I've never heard you talk about marriage and we've been friends for years." He crosses his arms over his chest and raises an eyebrow. "You're not taking advantage of a vulnerable woman, are you?"

"You know me better than that!" I bark back. "I didn't assault her, if that's what you're implying." The space between us sparks with tension. I'm extra on edge right now because of my guilt over being rough with Charlotte. Just because he's my best friend doesn't mean I won't punch him.

"Calm down, William, my bad. I didn't mean it like that." This time, his tone and apology are sincere.

"This whole situation is a mess," I say, taking a deep breath. "I doubt if she'll actually make it down the aisle."

"Why do you say that?" He sits down in the chair across from my desk.

"Do you remember why Stephanie and Caroline broke up with me?" I sit in my desk chair and place my head in my hands.

"Yeah..." he thinks for a moment then it clicks. Josiah is my only friend who knows about that part of my life. It's impossible not to share everything (whether you mean to or not) with your college roommate of four years. "William! You've got to control yourself, man! You need her. You can't scare her away like you did the others."

"I know, I know." I run my hands through my hair and sigh heavily. "I'm going to fix it. I have to."

"The sooner the better." He wags a warning finger at me before breaking out into a mischievous grin. "Though, if things don't work out, I wouldn't mind taking a crack at her myself."

"Asshole," I say, throwing a pen at him and missing horribly. He's right. I need to talk to Charlotte and apologize before this whole thing blows up in my face. I need to control my dominant streak and learn when to stop before I go too far. I need my fiancé.

Chapter 11
Charlotte

Oh God, oh God, oh God!

I run to the nearest bathroom and vomit violently, heaving up my breakfast and my dignity. How dare he treat me like that! And how dare I...like it? What is wrong with me? He was so demanding and cold, yet my pussy is still pulsing from being denied. If Josiah hadn't arrived when he did, who knows what I would have let him do to me next.

I flush my shame and take a hard look at myself in the mirror above the sink. My eyes are red and watery. Who am I? How can you like being controlled and bossed around like that? The way his eyes burned into mine as I sucked his cock sends a shiver to my center even as my cheeks burn with self-loathing. I could have tapped out at any point, so why didn't I? He even called me a slut and instead of getting mad, I'm getting flustered. I fidget with my engagement ring and remember how it glinted under his office lights as I squeezed his strong thighs. Taking an old planner out of my purse, I frantically fan myself. I wonder if Josiah could tell what we were doing before he arrived.

And then there was Josiah... his handsome face has my stomach full of butterflies; he could be Mason Gooding's twin. Guilt quickly washes over me and effectively drowns my butterflies. I can't be attracted to another man; I'm engaged! It doesn't matter that my fiancé and I are not in love with each other and our upcoming marriage is just for show. My head is spinning and my stomach is swirling; this is all becoming too much!

I shake my head and grip the sink firmly. No. I'm not attracted to Josiah. I'm just pent up and super horny from William denying me my orgasm. Putting my hair back up in a bun and ignoring the dampness in my panties, I head out of the bathroom and back home.

I'm fine. This is all fine.

***

Arriving home, I'm immediately beset by Lizzy.

"Everybody loves you!" She exclaims, giving me a tight hug.

"Awesome," I respond half-heartedly, unbuttoning my jacket and tossing it over the back of the sofa. Kicking off my shoes I bypass Lizzy and head to my room to change.

"You don't sound very excited," she says, pouting and leaning against my door frame. "Hang that up!" She points to my discarded suit and stomps her foot. "You need to take better care of your clothes, especially expensive ones for church."

"Yeah, yeah, yeah," I brush off her advice and slide into my comfy weekend clothes.

"What's wrong?" Her tone changes from judgmental to concerned. "What happened after I left?"

"I can't tell you," I admit, turning away from her and sitting down at my desk. I ignore her annoyed stare and open my laptop to grade student work.

"Yes, you can. We tell each other everything! Spill!" She snaps her fingers at me like a I'm a misbehaving puppy and plops herself on my bed.

"Fine!" I cave to her demand and give her my full attention. "William is dominant... very dominant."

"Okay..." she waits for me to continue before giving her two cents.

"Like, with sex. He punished me today for making an unapproved move on him and I..." I avoid eye contact with Lizzy and take a deep breath. "I liked it."

"Tell me more!" Lizzy's eyes light up as she gets more comfortable.

"He punished me by making me give him a blow job and he was rough about it." The warmth rising to my cheeks at the memory is impossible to hide. "At first, I was mad at him for treating me like that, but then..."

"Then you started to enjoy it."

"Yeah. It was like nothing I've ever experienced before. And the worst part is he wouldn't let me have a good time, if you catch my drift."

"Sounds like a proper dom." Lizzy smiles playfully at me. "What's the problem?"

"What's the problem?" I repeat, dumbfounded. "That's messed up! I'm messed up!" My voice increases in volume and my hands clutch at my chest, trying to push down the rising panic.

"No, you're not messed up!" Lizzy emphatically assures me. "You're not messed up at all. It sounds like you have a submissive kink. I've read about it a lot in my romance books. I'll give you a few to read for educational purposes." She winks at me and I roll my eyes. "People have all kinds of proclivities when it comes to sex. Do what makes you happy."

"It's weird because I liked him being dominant the first time we had sex, but that was more about control. This was...demeaning, so it took a while to figure out if I liked that or not." I pause for a moment. "I guess I'm far kinkier than I ever knew, it seems."

"I love that for you!" Lizzy giggles.

"Other than that, I actually do feel guilty because after we, um, you know, Josiah came in and I was immediately attracted to him and that's wrong. I'm engaged to William. I shouldn't have attraction towards other men." Now that I've confessed all my "sins" to Lizzy, a burden lifts from my shoulders.

"Charlotte," Lizzy says, slowly releasing me from her embrace. "Josiah is hot. You'd have to be gay to not be attracted to him. Besides," she bends down and scoops up a very meowy Cleo. "Your engagement is based on a predetermined arrangement, not real feelings. You have nothing to feel guilty about." She gives me a compassionate smile and places Cleo in my lap. Not to be ignored, Tony purrs around my ankles impatient for attention.

"Thanks, Lizzy." I pet Cleo and take comfort in her soft purrs. Lizzy is right. Some people are turned on by things that others find disturbing; I guess I'm just one of those people. Sighing, I relax my tense shoulders and wipe away my scattered tears.

"Anytime." She stops before completely exiting my room. "It's a good thing he ended up with you and not me. I'm definitely not submissive." Laughing, she adds, "At least your man is screwing you. I can't get Darcy to go past second base." Rolling her eyes, she leaves me with my thoughts, one thought in particular: I'm so unbearably horny.

Closing the door to my room, I open my nightstand drawer and pull out Veronica, my bullet vibrator. William may be able to deny my pleasure when I'm with him, but there's nothing he can do to stop me from helping myself when I'm alone.

I take off my ridiculous church costume and lay down on my bed, naked from head to toe. Breathing deeply and closing my eyes, I recall the feeling of gagging on William's cock in his office. Instead of the shame I felt earlier in the moment, I feel unbelievably empowered. I turn on Veronica and trace the buzzing toy over my nipples, slowly, before trailing it down to my eager pussy.

William's words echo in my mind: "You're so fucking pretty with my cock in your mouth." A sharp gasp escapes my lips as the vibrator slides across my swollen, needy clit.

When he came in my mouth and forced me to swallow it, the tears I cried weren't from pain or from shame; they were from the agonizing need to come growing inside of my pulsing pussy. William's fingers gripping my cheeks as he stared into my soul with his powerful, sexy blue eyes is all I need to focus on before I'm coming so hard I can't breathe.

"Shit," I mutter to myself as my heart tries to return to its normal beating pattern. Ragged breaths are all I can manage as I come down from my much needed release. Take that, William! I smile to myself and drift off to sleep wondering what William would do if he knew what I just did.

I'm rudely awoken from my accidental nap by a loud ding from my cell phone about an hour after my explosive orgasm. It's a text from William.

Sir William: *Hey, I'm sorry about earlier. I took things too far. It won't happen again.*

I'm touched by his apology. Even though I don't need it, I appreciate his thoughtfulness. A pang of disappointment races through my body at his last sentence: It won't happen again.

I text back: *I appreciate your apology, but I'm totally fine.* I stand up from my bed and wrap myself in my fuzzy bathrobe.

Sir William: *There's no excuse for my behavior. I pushed you too far.*

Me: *No, I...*

I pause typing when another text comes in from him.

Sir William: *In fact, it might be best to pause all further sexual interactions until we're married.*

"What!?" I exclaim out loud making Cleo and Tony jump from my bed. My shriek makes Lizzy storm into my room.

"What? What happened?" She's holding a spatula in one hand, ready to defend against whatever foul beast has caused me to cry out. Looking from the spatula to me, she explains, "I was making cookies."

"William wants to stop having sex until we're married. He feels bad about what happened and doesn't believe me when I say I'm okay with it." I walk over to my bed and fall face first onto it. With my face crushed against the pillows, I release a muffled scream of frustration.

"Well, crap." Lizzy sits down next to me, the mattress dipping to the side and making me roll towards her. She lays her hand on my back and absent mindedly rubs my shoulders. "Maybe the next time you see him, you can convince him to change his mind."

"You act like I'm some sort of slinky seductive woman," I say, sitting upright next to her.

"You could be, and I can help." She grins broadly and gives me a conspiratorial wink. "Leave it to me." Despite my hesitation, I listen to her dastardly plan.

***

After another exciting week of teaching in which my students interrogated me repeatedly about my engagement and new fiancé, I'm so ready for a night to myself. Lizzy is out with Darcy and I have complete reign over the TV tonight. Originally, I had plans with William, but he cancelled at the last minute to go console a family who lost a loved one today. That's fine with me. I wasn't really excited about our date anyway.

Since he's cut me off from sex, I honestly don't care if we ever go on a date again. If I didn't have to put on a show at church every Sunday, I wouldn't bother seeing him again until our wedding day. In his place, he emailed me his own version of my About Me notebook. After pouring myself a glass of wine, I make myself comfortable on the sofa and turn on some braindead reality TV. While the crazy people on the screen argue over whether or not her boyfriend did or did not cheat on her, I open William's document and start reading.

The table of contents section proves to me what I already knew about William: he is organized. Unlike my hot mess of a notebook, his version is in chronological order, starting with his childhood and ending with the present. Each section is broken into subsections with bulleted lists and charts. I imagine this is the type of skill that helped him get his PhD; it's honestly impressive and a little sexy. He even has a family tree in the first chapter that goes back four generations! Hovering the cursor over his mom's name, Melanie Collins, I wonder what her story is, why she left, and why she hasn't come back.

Things must have been really bad for her to leave her only child and never return. Was William's dad beating her? Emotionally abusing her? I won't push William for answers on such a touchy subject, at least not yet, not until we know each other better. Glancing up the tree, I notice he's named after his grandfather on his dad's side. I'm not shocked at all to learn that his grandfather was also a pastor. I wonder if he chose to be a pastor or if it was just something expected of him, a sort of destiny he couldn't wriggle out of.

I'm drawn to the section on "Likes and Dislikes" and I can't help chuckling when I read "coffee" under "Dislikes." The first thing I do every morning is make a pot of coffee and fill up my thermos for the day. Coffee and teachers, name a more iconic duo. Scrolling down the list, there's thrillers, chess, pumpkin pie, and video games under the "Likes" section. A pastor who plays video games. That's certainly not what I expected, though I'm not mad about it. I like my men a little nerdy.

Calling William "my man" is so surreal. I fidget with my engagement ring, spinning it around my finger a few times. I haven't had a man to call mine since Brad Dillon took my love and ran it through a paper shredder two years ago. I gag involuntarily at the memory of our relationship. I'd rather be in a fake marriage with an uptight pastor than risk my heart anymore out in the real world.

Skimming through his "Education" section, I lose track of all of his academic awards and achievements. He was definitely the guy in school everyone hated because they were so jealous of his success. To other people, William's list of accolades would seem like bragging; however, they are just statements of fact. He's smart and he shouldn't have to be humble about it.

Intelligence is attractive, far more attractive than physical appearance, though I can't deny that William has the best of both worlds. The way he effortlessly hovered over me while he thrusted into me so powerfully, his strong arms holding firm on either side of my body has me aching for more. He's not ripped, per se, more so strong and lean, muscles taut and ready for action at a moment's notice. The way his broad shoulders fill out his suit jacket and his forearms strain against his shirt sleeves have my heart pounding every time I see him.

Taking off his glasses before devouring my pussy was the hottest thing I've ever seen a man do. It was like watching Clark Kent switch over into Superman, but instead of saving the world, he licked and pleasured me into the next realm of existence.

My phone buzzes, pulling my attention away from my naughty day dream. Picking it up, I roll my eyes before clicking the message.

Mom: *Are you pregnant????*

I almost spit wine all over myself. What is she going on about now?

Me: *NO! Why would you think I am?*

Mom: *Cat said the wedding is in June. That's only three months from now!*

Part of me regrets connecting Mom with Cat for wedding planning. The other part of me knows it was the right thing to do. I don't have any preferences when it comes to the wedding itself aside from what I wear, so giving Mom and Cat control was really easy. Anxiety balloons in my chest as I realize this is only the beginning of many complicated and crazy conversations Mom and I are going to have until the wedding is over.

Me: *That doesn't mean I'm pregnant. We just don't see the purpose in dragging things out and having a long engagement. I'm thirty, Mom. I kind of just want to be married already.*

The truth behind those words is heavier than I want it to be. It's why I'm marrying William in the first place. It's why I agreed to play the role of dutiful pastor's wife every Sunday. It's why I decided to increase the stress levels in my life and give my heart a workout every time I see William or get a message from him. Reading his "About Me" document has twisted and tangled my feelings for him, relieving me of some of my concerns but also creating fresh questions.

Mom: *And here I thought I was about to be a grandma!*

Me: *One thing at a time, Mom.*

I can't even bring myself to think about that topic. Kids with a man I married for convenience? Kids at all? I've always been a bit of a fence sitter when it comes to the idea of being a parent. Could I do it? Yes. Should I do it? I like kids, that's why I'm a teacher. However, the idea of spending all day with 70+ teenagers and then going home to take care of my own children is so overwhelming.

That's definitely something William and I need to talk about, though as long as he's taken sex off the table, I guess it's not worth mentioning. Besides, shouldn't people be in love before they decide to have a family? We're not in love. We're just two strangers using each other to get what we need. He needs me to keep his job, and I need him to make my mom happy. That's all. Love isn't part of what we have; hell, sex isn't a part of what we have unless I can make Lizzy's evil plan work.

Closing the document, I drain the rest of my glass as I try to erase all memories of William's body on mine, his tongue on my pussy, and his cock in my mouth. I'm going to need more wine.

Chapter 12
William

As I look around the ornately decorated banquet hall, all I can think is: this is really going to raise Charlotte's anxiety. Cat and Eleanor have spent all day preparing for this "engagement social" as they dubbed it.

"It's not a party," Cat assured me with a furtive grin. "Just a little get together for the church to celebrate your impending nuptials."

I had my doubts from the beginning about this "little get together," and seeing the absurd amount of time and money spend on this room alone, I was right.

"You're not supposed to be here yet," Eleanor says, her eyes full of excitement. "You and Charlotte will make a grand entrance later, remember?"

"Yes, of course. I just wanted to take a moment and appreciate your hard work. It looks splendid." My compliment has her blushing with pride.

"Enough with the compliments, young man. Off you go," she playfully shoos me away with a warm smile. I got lucky in the future in laws department it seems. Both Eleanor and Edward are kind people who have welcomed me into their lives with open arms, despite the suddenness of my insertion into their world.

When I return to the sanctuary to wait to be retrieved, I'm surprised Charlotte is already sitting in the first pew. As the door closes behind me, she gives me a wary smile. Her chocolate hair is in soft waves around her face. I can't know for sure if she changed her hair because I told her to; regardless, a trill of pleasure rolls through my body at her change. Instead of a pantsuit, she's wearing a knee length rose pink dress with white flowers dotted throughout. The dress matches the color of her lips and I'm reminded of what I made her do with those lips the last time I saw her.

"Hello, William." Her tone is friendly, any malice she may have for me is nowhere to be found. She claimed she was okay with what we did, yet I'm unsure about where we stand in our "relationship" now.

"Hi, Charlotte." I remain standing stiffly between the door and the pew.

"I'll be glad when this is over with," she admits, sighing heavily. Her body is hunched forward with her hands gripping the pew seat. Her anxiety has got to be sky high right now. I slowly walk toward the pew and sit down next to her.

"Sorry for all the fuss. This is just one of those things that come with the job." The urge to soothe her anxiety is strong and I resist placing my hand over hers. I have no idea if my touch is welcome at this point.

"I understand." Her face the picture of wary impatience.

"We won't stay the whole time, I promise, just long enough to talk to the big donors and get photographed a little." At this, her expression relaxes, though her body remains tense. "I'll be with you the whole time. It will go by so quickly."

"If you say so." She carefully pries her hands from the edge of the seat and attempts to relax her shoulders. "Mom is so happy. All she talks about is the wedding. My brothers are so tired of hearing about it." Charlotte smiles to herself and runs her fingers along the pearls around her pretty neck. The movement sends me back to the memory of our first night together and I'm itching to pull her close for a kiss. Heat quickly floods my face and my groin. I glance away before she can detect any hint of desire in my eyes. I told her sex wasn't happening until we're married, and I'm determined to stick to that resolution.

"I assume she's the main reason you're marrying me?" The question rolls off my tongue without much thought. I sound accusatory, like her wanting her mother's happiness is some kind of betrayal when we both know we're in this for selfish reasons.

"You have no right to be offended when you're marrying me to keep your job!" She snaps back, straightening herself up, all semblance of nervousness gone from her body. The anger in her eyes is justified. I want to shrink into myself and disappear.

"I meant for that to be a clarifying question," I explain. "It wasn't my intention to come off so aggressively." Reaching for her hand, I give it a quick squeeze. "I'm sorry."

She doesn't immediately pull away and slap me, so I take that as her accepting my apology. We have so much to learn about each other, not just our like and dislikes, but also the ways we each handle tough situations and speak about touchy subjects. There's a short knock on the side door before Eleanor enters.

"Come on, you two!" She waves us eagerly over to her. "Don't you both look so lovely!" The smile on her face puts the New Year's Eve ball to shame.

We follow her to the party for our grand entrance. When Eleanor turns to open the door, I quickly grab Charlotte's hand. She's surprised at my action, though understanding quickly dawns on her face. This is for show, she thinks, and she is partially correct. What she doesn't know is that I'm doing this for me, because I want to. I want to hold her hand and keep her steady. Charlotte is quite the paradox at times and as I learn more about her, I realize she's more fragile than she wants to let on.

The moment we enter the room, Charlotte's face assumes a false cheerfulness as she slips on her public mask with a polite smile. The irony of this isn't lost on me as I, too, put on my preacher persona and accompanying mask. We make our way around the room, greet the necessary people, stopping at various spots to be photographed. I introduce Charlotte to our biggest donors and she's so charming that they immediately promise to fund any church events or causes she is in charge of. Cat will be pleased.

Speaking of, every so often, I spy Cat in my peripheral vision keeping track of our movements. She's hovering and I hate it. I wish she would trust me more with public events like these. I've been in charge now for two years and she still insists on being my shadow when it comes to my public image. She forgets that I watched Dad play the game all my life; therefore, I know the rules just enough to bend them when necessary.

Charlotte leaves my side to talk to the Bennett sisters. She almost runs to them like they are water and she is dying of thirst in the desert. Funnily enough, my hand seems empty without hers to hold. I watch her with her friends, genuinely smiling and laughing for the first time since she arrived. My solitude doesn't last long as Cat sidles up beside me, a pleased grin on her wrinkled face.

"She's perfect, William, the ideal preacher's wife." Cat comments, nodding at Charlotte. "How are things going between you two, by the way?"

"Fine, just fine," I respond a little too quickly and she raises an eyebrow.

"That's reassuring," she says sarcastically.

"It's...complicated," I explain vaguely. That's putting it mildly.

"Uncomplicate it," she commands under her breath. "A false front will only hold for so long."

"Of course," I respond as if what she's asking is as simple as tying a knot. No one tells Cat De Bourgh no. That's how I got in this situation to begin with, after all.

"Keep up the good work." Patting my shoulder, she disappears into a group of church donors and I'm left a little deflated. Watching Charlotte laugh with Elizabeth, I marvel at God's plan for my life. When this began, I had my eyes set on Elizabeth as my future bride. And yet, here I am engaged to her best friend, feeling horribly guilty for letting loose my darker side during an intimate moment with her, eliminating what little rapport we had built in our short time together so far.

Once Charlotte and Elizabeth are alone, I walk over and join their giddy conversation.

"I can't help but assume I'm the object of all this laughter," I comment.

"And what if you are?" Elizabeth replies, placing her hands on her hips in mock defiance. "We were actually just talking about how this could have been my engagement party if I had taken your offer." Her jovial smile lights up her beautiful face and I let my eyes linger on it a little too long before turning to Charlotte.

"Are you having regrets, *Miss* Bennett?" I ask out of curiosity, realizing too late how Charlotte might interpret my question.

"No, no. Everything has worked out the way it was meant to. Life is just funny sometimes." She giggles and wraps Charlotte in a quick hug. Even though she hugs back, I can tell Charlotte isn't as into it as Elizabeth is. As Elizabeth walks back to her family, Charlotte looks at her sharply, almost slicing her down with her emerald eyes. Then, it's gone just as quickly as it appeared. Charlotte resumes her placid, polite expression and takes my hand into hers almost forcefully. Her strong grip startles me and I try not to think about it too much as we make our way around the room.

After an eternity at the party (which is really just two hours), I gather everyone's attention to give a speech in which I thank everyone for attending and notify them that Charlotte and I are leaving. As I'm speaking, Charlotte stands next to her mother who is all but openly sobbing with happy tears. Charlotte keeps handing Eleanor tissues from her purse; she was prepared for this moment. A pang of grief hits my heart as I wonder where my mom is and whether or not she would approve of Charlotte as my wife. Some days I hate Mom, and other days, like today, my heart aches with missing her and pondering all the "what ifs."

Once the crowd's applause dies down, Charlotte takes my hand and we exit the party, leaving everyone under the impression that we are very much in love and we can't wait to be alone together. When we reach the parking lot, Charlotte's mask falls and she sighs heavily with relief.

"I'm so glad that's over," she says, her eyes scanning the cars in the lot and then frowning. "I guess I have to go back and help clean up. I rode here with my mom so I'm stuck here anyway."

"Cat has people to put the room back in order. You're not stuck. I can give you a ride." My offer hangs in the air between us, an olive branch of sorts. She gives me a hesitant glare before nodding slowly.

"Okay. I would appreciate that." When we reach my car, she stops suddenly. "This is your car?" Her tone is full of surprise.

"Yeah?" I open the passenger door for her and she slides in.

When I start the engine, she says, "The Rolex was one thing, but a Bentley? I drive an eight-year-old Toyota with a finicky battery." Her voice is awestruck and I smile proudly as she takes in the shiny interior of my car.

"I work hard for my money. I deserve to have nice things." My explanation is simple and honest. Some people may call me too materialistic considering my occupation; those people are just jealous.

"Would it be rude of me to ask how much money you make? As your future wife, that's something I should know." She crosses her arms across her chest and gives me an inquisitive look.

"My salary is based on church donations and member tithes, so it can fluctuate," I say, both answering and not answering her question at the same time.

"That's a political answer and you know it. Are they okay with you spending their money like this?"

"You make it sound like I'm some sort of scam artist or con man. This car, my suits, everything about me, is a reflection of Hilltop. I have to project a certain image, the same one you're expected to project as my fiancé."

"Geez, defensive much?" Adjusting her seatbelt, she seems to realize something. "Do you know where I live?"

"Yes," I reply, a little amused at her expression. I've been driving for about five minutes and only now is she concerned where I'm taking her. "For now, you live with Elizabeth. Later, you'll live with me. The question is, which place do you want to go to right now?" I'm aware of how suggestive my question is, so I clarify. "What I mean is, I have some prep for tomorrow's sermon to do; however, you're welcome to come over and get used to the place in the meantime."

"Okay, that sounds good." There's an odd expression on her face that I can't quite place and I become a little uneasy.

After we arrive, I give Charlotte a brief tour of the house, intending to hide away in my office for the next few hours when I'm done. However, when I bid her adieu, she walks right behind me into my office.

"We need to talk," she begins, walking toward me, determination set firmly in her green eyes.

"Alright," I respond, caught off guard by Charlotte's forwardness. "About what?"

"This whole no sex thing you put into effect." Reaching out, she runs her hands up and down my tie, gently tugging it with each touch. "I don't agree with it."

"It's for the best, really," I assert, taking a step back from her exploring fingers. Not missing a beat, she comes with me, firmly pressing her body against mine, causing my somewhat involuntary erection to make itself known.

"Your body seems to disagree," she practically purrs causing a corresponding growl to begin low in my throat.

"You don't set the rules here," I remind her, trying very hard to ignore my hardening cock. My hands clutch into fists at my sides, but I resist pushing her away. If I touch her, I will lose control.

"That's not going to work." Her hands reach up and drape daintily around my neck. Her fingers slide up and thread through the hair at the base of my scalp causing shivers to run down my spine. She's playing dirty and she just might win at this rate.

"I was too rough on you, Charlotte. It's better this way." I swallow hard, my pulse pounding loudly in my head. Keeping my breathing steady, I reach up and remove her hands from my body.

"What if I told you I liked it that way?" Her hands slide down the front of my pants and skim over my painfully stiff cock. A small whimper escapes my throat and she smiles wickedly. "What if I told you I got myself off that day thinking about your cock shoved down my throat? What if I told you all I can think about is you punishing me right now for being such a commanding, disobedient brat? What if I said I wanted you to bend me over your desk and spank my ass so hard I can't sit for days? What if I..." Before she can finish speaking, the demon inside of me takes hold.

I spin her around roughly and shove her against the wall. A small "oof" falls from her lips when she hits the hard surface, her hands pressed against the wall to soften her landing. Yanking her hands down, I force them behind her, restraining them with one hand. I press my lips to her ear and whisper, "You don't tell me what to do, Lady Charlotte."

As my mouth moves from her ear to her collarbone, my teeth snag on her damn pearl necklace. "I hate this fucking necklace. It doesn't suit you."

"It's part of the look I'm supposed to have," she protests, her cheek a bright red from pleasure or pain; I don't know which and I don't care.

"Fuck that!" I growl and rip the necklace from her neck with my free hand. Shimmering pearls fall around us like pretty shrapnel. "Much better," I moan as my lips find purchase on her naked neck. Heat courses through my fingertips when I reach around Charlotte and pinch one of her nipples hard.

"More, Sir William," Charlotte begs, pressing her sexy ass against my cock.

I chuckle darkly. "Be careful what you wish for."

Chapter 13
Charlotte

Somehow Lizzy knew that me being a brat would make William change his mind about not having sex with me. I have a sneaking suspicion it came from those romance novels she reads and I'll never make fun of her for reading them again after this.

Pressed hard against the wall in William's office, his strong body molded to mine, his teeth at my throat, and his hand tortuously teasing my nipples, I'm in heaven. The moment he tore the pearls from my neck, my pussy convulsed so violently I thought I would come right then and there. The way he wants to control me, my actions, my appearance, should appall me, should send me running to the hills, and yet, I'm still here, begging for more.

I wasn't lying earlier when I told him I wanted to be punished, to be slapped, spanked, borderline abused by his hands. My body is putty in his hands, waiting to be molded and manipulated any way he sees fit. Pushing aside the fact that this whole thing is for show and we're simply using each other for our own selfish means, what we have can work, at least for a short time.

Suddenly, William pulls my dress up and over my hips. I gasp at the rush of cool air on my thighs and ass.

"Shit, Lady Charlotte," William moans, his hand caressing my bare buttocks. "No panties? I see you were pretty confident I would cave."

Releasing my wrists, he whips the tie out of his collar. "Hold still." He makes quick work of tying up my hands, the silk fabric of his tie soft and strong against my skin.

Placing his hands on my hips, he forces one of his knees between my legs, causing them to spread apart. "Wider, Lady Charlotte," he orders. I spread my legs as far apart as possible without losing my balance. As I'm getting situated, William removes his suit jacket and hangs it carefully on a hook by the door. Moving back to me, the sound of his belt sliding through the loops has my legs quivering in anticipation of his next move.

"Now, what was it you said earlier about being spanked so hard you can't sit down?" Out of the corner of my eye, I watch him fold his belt in half and rear back his arm. I brace for impact, but it doesn't come. Placing a soft hand on my back, William leans forward and kisses my cheek gently. "It stings less if you relax," he whispers. "Breathe."

Following his advice, I take a deep breath to steady myself. After I exhale, the belt bites into my ass with a quick slap. "Ah!" I cry out, aching from the pain, yet eager for more. I'm so wet right now it's dripping down my inner thighs.

"Don't forget your safe word, Lady Charlotte," William reminds me. "Just say the word and I'll stop." Another slap of the smooth leather across my ass and upper thighs has me whimpering like a sad puppy. "You take my punishment so well. Good girl." The belt hits the floor with a small thud followed by William quickly unzipping his pants. His knees hit the floor and he peppers my ass with soft kisses; each one erases the damage of his belt and soothes the soreness away.

"I love your ass," he moans between kisses. "It's so big, so perfect."

"Thank you, Sir William." I may not like much about my body, but I am quite proud of my very round butt. "Now, are you going to fuck me or not?" I throw a good bit of sass into my question, hoping to rile him again.

"Tsk, tsk. Someone's being a major brat today." As he stands up, his expensive pants fall to the floor. "You really are a glutton for punishment." Kicking off his pants, he walks briskly to the door and says, "Don't move." In his absence, I'm tempted to relax or at least stand up straight so my face isn't smushed against the wall. My neck is starting to ache and I wonder if I'm too old for rough sex. How disappointing would that be if I finally have someone to have regular sex with and my body isn't up for the task?

Before I can spiral further, William returns. He's removed his shirt so now he's completely naked except for a condom snug and secure on his ready cock. I was dripping before from the anticipation and the punishment, but now, with his naked body and his erection aimed at me like a powerful missile, my pussy is a heavy waterfall. Every nerve in my body is aching for release, aching for his body on mine, aching for his cock to send me to another plane of existence.

He strides over to me and grips my hips so firmly they'll be bruised tomorrow. "Now, where were we?" Sliding his cock between my legs and against my soaked entrance, he says, "Oh, I remember." With a solid thrust, he enters me. I inhale sharply as he fills me completely and stretches the taut walls of my pussy.

"Breathe, Lady Charlotte," he commands in my ear as he slowly and tenderly pushes and pulls himself in and out of me. My legs are threatening to break at this point, both from pleasure and from pain, not to mention the fact that my face is squished against the wall and my neck feels forever stuck at a 90-degree angle.

As if reading my mind, he says, "Walk with me," guiding my steps backwards with his cock still inside me. He backs us up until he reaches the chair at his desk where he sits down, yanking me with him so I'm sitting upright on his lap. "Much better," he says, sliding his hand around my waist and under my dress where he begins to strum my clit.

The fact that I'm dressed and he's completely naked is wrong and dirty, yet so hot at the same time. I'll never be able to look at this dress the same way again. Moaning at his touch, I begin to slowly rise up to the point where only his tip is in my entrance. Before he can complain, I slam myself back onto his cock, impaling myself on his mighty sword.

"Fuck!" William shouts. I'm still surprised he curses, and I love making him do it. Gripping my hips with all his might, he helps lift me up and down, making the job easier on my out of shape legs. "Milk my cock, Lady Charlotte!" His order has me almost to the edge of coming.

"Yes, Sir William," I stutter out between thrusts, my breath short and fast from arousal and exertion. Now that his hand has left my clit, I want so badly to reach down and help myself, then I remember his command from our first time together: *You will come from my touch and my cock alone.* As eager as I am to climax, I'm not eager for another punishment. The only way I'm able to ignore my sore ass right now is by focusing on William's pleasure.

"Just like that, good girl. You fuck so well, Lady Charlotte, so well!" His praise washes over me and my pussy vibrates with pleasure. "I'm almost there. Keep going!" He picks up the pace with my hips to the point where I'm no longer in control of the speed or rhythm: it's all him, his power, his control, his need. Without warning, he slides a hand to my folds and gives my needy clit all the attention it was longing for.

Within seconds, I'm there. "Yes!" The world recedes from view for a moment as my eyes roll back and all sensation in my body is turned up to eleven.

"Shit!" William groans with pleasurable agony as he comes shortly after me. I lean back against his shoulder as we revel in our joint climax. Once his breathing returns to its normal rate, he kisses my neck softly and sweetly, the complete opposite of what we just did. He kindly unties my wrists and my shoulders sigh with relief once back in their normal position.

While he's vulnerable, I turn my head to his handsome face and repeat my question from earlier, "So, now will you tell me how much money you make?"

He responds not with words, but with laughter, deep, full-bodied laughter. It's the laughter I've been wanting to hear from him since we met. As the sound rumbles down my back, it reaches into my chest and squeezes my heart. It's beautiful.

"You're really persistent. Has anyone ever told you that?" The smile on his face warms my soul.

"Yes, and it's been a very useful trait in my life." I smile back at him, enjoying this moment of post-sex clarity.

"I really thought you were lying when you said you were okay with how I treated you last time. You looked so angry, so downright furious."

"I was mad, just not at you." I turn my head away to break the spell his blue eyes have cast on me. Staring straight ahead, I exhale and continue. "I was mad at myself because I liked it. I started feeling conflicted and confused. I'd never had a man demean me like that before. I was ashamed of how pleasurable it was." There, I said it.

William wraps his arms around my stomach and gives it a light squeeze. "I, too, felt ashamed when I first realized I got turned on by, let's say, not being a gentleman. It felt wrong at first, like I was going to accidentally turn into an abusive person. It didn't help that for most of my previous relationships my kink was a deal breaker." Kissing my shoulder gently, he continues, "In time, I learned to accept that part of myself. God made me this way and He made you that way too, it seems."

"It's a lot to process. Also, I was worried you would think less of me or something." My face heats as I wait for him to confirm my fear.

"Charlotte," William says, turning my face back to his. His eyes are full of compassion and sympathy. "You have nothing to feel embarrassed about. Never feel like you can't be yourself with me, like you have to hide who you are when we're together. Our engagement may be for show, but I promise to always be real with you. I expect you to do the same." His kind words are like a cozy blanket on a snowy day. How can he be so commanding and powerful when it comes to sex, yet so kind and caring when it comes to my feelings?

"Is that an order, Sir William?" I smile cheekily at him.

"It's an expectation," he replies, lifting my chin up and kissing my lips. Pulling away reluctantly, part of my brain reminds me that unless I want an UTI, I need to get to the bathroom soon. Sliding myself off his lap, I make my way to the bathroom he showed me earlier.

When I return, he's bent over his desk typing on his laptop, already hard at work. That doesn't surprise me. What does surprise me is that he is wearing gray sweatpants and a white t-shirt. I stand in the doorway, mouth agape, speechless.

"What?" He notices my expression and gives a sexy grin.

"I've never seen you in normal clothes before," I admit.

"Did you think I wear a suit at home?" Chuckling, he raises an eyebrow and walks towards me. Even under his shirt, his lean physique and bold tattoo is apparent. Without intending to, my eyes wander down to his crotch and my pussy clenches at the outline of his cock, somehow already hard again.

"Since you'll be living here in a few months, you might want to consider moving some of your belongings in ahead of time so it's not too much all in one day. Keeping some clothes here, for example, would be a good start."

His hand reaches up to my chin and tilts it up at him. "Though you're perfectly welcome to walk around here naked."

I swallow hard and gather my thoughts. "I'll bring some stuff over next weekend," I say, almost too lost in his icy blue eyes to think correctly.

"I'll get you a set of keys to the house so you can come and go as you please." He kisses my lips lightly, teasingly. Despite just having had sex, I'm dying for more.

"Okay," I respond, my brain not at all focused on anything besides his body right now. The ringing of my phone pulls me reluctantly back to reality. It's Mom.

"Hi, Mom."

"Are you still at Reverend Collins' house?" Mom asks.

"Yeah, he was giving me a tour." He was certainly giving me something, I think to myself, blushing deeply.

"Well, don't forget you have to try on the dresses at some point. Cat gave them to me and I'll keep them at my house until you can come by. She said you have to pick one by Tuesday or it won't be ready in time." Her voice is almost giddy. As per Cat's original instructions, she chose five dresses that she deemed "appropriate" for the wedding and I'm to pick one from the group. I'm picturing very conservative, full coverage dresses that only leave my face exposed, and even then, there's going to be a long, ridiculous veil to cover that.

"Okay. Do you want to come see the house and then I'll come home with you?" She's going to want a house tour eventually, so I may as well get that over with today.

"That sounds fantastic! Be there soon!" The eagerness in her voice fills my stomach with guilt. Pushing it down and hanging up the phone, I text Mom the address and give William a remorseful look. "I forgot that Cat was giving the wedding dresses to Mom today."

"Wedding dresses plural?" His confusion is well warranted.

"Cat gave a couple of wedding dresses to Mom for me to choose from." I twist my engagement ring around my finger and sigh lightly.

"Whichever one you choose, you will be lovely," he assures me.

"Whichever one I choose, I'll look the part," I counter. "I doubt I'll look lovely covered up from head to toe in old lady lace."

"I guess I'll just have to be the pretty one, then," he teases. We laugh and I'm once again surprised at easy it is to talk to William, how effortless and uncomplicated our conversations are despite our weird and tangled situation. At this point, I guess we're friends with benefits, benefits I'm so glad I put back into place.

After Mom arrives, William gives her the grand tour just like he gave me. She *ooos* and *aaaas* at the size of the house, the number of bedrooms and bathrooms, and the modern kitchen.

"We'll have to have Thanksgiving at your house this year, Charlotte. There's so much more room than our house!" As she examines the cabinets, the pantry, and the fancy dishwasher, a sense of panic invades my veins. The thought of my whole family, parents, brothers, aunts, uncles, cousins, grandparents, etc. in William's house makes this whole thing suddenly so real, so undeniably inevitable.

How many Thanksgivings will I be able to put on the façade? How many events at the church will I have to present a whole new persona? Will this get easier with time? Will *preacher's wife* become my new identity for real at some point? Why didn't I think this through? My fingertips are buzzing and I'm trying really hard not to slam them into something to make it stop.

"Alright, Mom. I think we've bothered William enough. Let's get going so I can pick a dress for Cat." I want to get out of this house fast without causing some kind of panic induced bad decision. Mom is thanking William profusely as I practically drag her from the house.

After dinner with the family, Lizzy comes over so she and Mom can be my dress judges. Five dresses are hanging in the closet of my old bedroom, the same closet that held my prom dresses and graduation robes. Choosing one at random, Lizzy slips it over my head and begins buttoning the back.

"As your maid of honor, I hope you don't choose this one. I don't like all these buttons!" She complains as she loops the last one into place. Fluffing out the skirt, I stare at my reflection in the floor length mirror.

When I was younger, I watched a lot of shows like "Say Yes to the Dress" and hoped to one day have my own exciting dress moment. I couldn't wait to see my family and friends' reactions when I chose "the" dress. I would look like a princess and everything would be magical.

That is not how I'm feeling right now. I feel ridiculous in this white, poufy, lacey nightmare. This is so wrong and I don't know if it's because the dress is ugly, or because my wedding is going to be a sham. Guilt bubbles in my stomach over what I'm undertaking. Most days I can forget that my marriage is based on convenience, though on days like today, it consumes me. Lizzy is smiling over my shoulder, though her face falls when she sees I'm crying.

"Char! What's wrong?" She grabs tissues from her purse and starts dabbing at my cheeks and eyes. "There are four more dresses to choose from. Don't worry!"

"It's not the dress," I begin, snagging a tissue and blowing my nose loudly. "And it's not William either." Crumpling to the floor, the ivory tulle poufs up around me on all sides and makes a weird crunching sound when I lean over to throw the tissue away. "I'm lying to God, Lizzy. The irony of a fake marriage to a pastor is obscene. He's going to strike me down dead when I walk down the aisle." I'm not an overly religious person, but I do take my relationship with God very seriously. I really should have consulted Him before I proposed my plan to William. Ironically, when I decided to marry a pastor, God wasn't part of the equation.

"No, Charlotte, that won't happen." Lizzy sits down next to me and pushes aside the dress so she can see my face better. "Do you at least like William as a person or as a friend?"

"I think so. He's been really great through all of this and the sex is out of this world," I confess.

"Well, that's a good place to start, I think," she points out. "Aren't wives supposed to be friends with their husbands?"

"Aren't wives supposed to love their husbands?" I counter, fresh tears rolling down my face.

"Oh, Char-Char," Lizzy sighs and wraps her arms around me. "Maybe you will love him one day. If you're really worried, maybe you should talk to William about it. He's both your fiancé and a God expert, so to speak." Releasing me from her embrace, she stands up and holds out her hand to help me up. "For today," her tone switches from compassionate to inspiring. "You're going to be strong and pick a dress, put on a smile, and make your mom happy." I use her hand to get off the floor and she starts unbuttoning the dress. "This dress definitely isn't it, though. Let's put on another."

With Lizzy's moral and physical support, I dry my tears and I try on each dress. With a smile on my face, I show them off one by one to Mom's delight. Fortunately, the others are less hideous than the first. We collectively decide to go with the least hideous dress, an A-line silhouette with lace sleeves and an illusion, sweetheart neckline. Is it the dress of my dreams? No. Is William the man of my dreams? I don't know. Am I glad to get home and cry into my pillows? Yes.

Chapter 14
William

"How are things going with your future wife?" Josiah asks as he absent mindedly thumbs through the stack of flyers in between us.

"Pretty well, I think." I place a pile of folders next to the flyers.

"I assume you got the whole control issue figured out?"

"I did, actually. In fact," I pause for dramatic effect. "She's not like Caroline or Stephanie at all when it comes to that."

"Really?" His eyebrows raise at my unexpected statement. "Maybe she's the right woman for you after all."

"Maybe," I shrug and try to contain a grin.

"I think it's more than a maybe," he comments, nodding at my not-so-subtle smile. "Are you developing feelings for her?"

"I don't know," I run my hand over my face and through my hair. "Between all the engagement nonsense with Cat and trying to keep on top of everything here, I haven't had time to think about it like that."

"If you have to think about it, you don't have feelings for her," Josiah responded. "When you know, you know." He places his hands over his chest dramatically and sighs.

"Uh huh. Is that why you're still Mr. Bachelor?" I playfully swat at his arm with a folder.

"You got jokes, huh? Keep it up and I'll be Mr. Steal Your Girl." We laugh loudly and start putting a flyer in each folder for Bible Study. Part of me gets a little riled at the thought of Josiah dating Charlotte, but I let it go and focus on why I asked Josiah to help me in the first place.

"Thanks for your help with this. With Sierra on leave, I really appreciate the help." I stack the completed folders on the desk and slide them into a tote bag. "Aside from just enjoying your company, I had an ulterior motive for asking to see you today."

"I knew something was up when you asked for my help with such a small task." Josiah puts his phone down and gives me his full attention.

"Are you busy June twelfth around five p.m.?"

"Since that's my best friend's wedding day, you could say I'm going to be very busy." He smiles mischievously. "Are you asking me to be your best man?"

"Who else would I ask?" I hold out my hand and he grasps it firmly with his own. Pulling me in for a half hug, he gives me a hearty slap on the back.

"I'd be honored," he says, releasing me from his mighty embrace. "I won't have any strippers at the bachelor party, I promise." He holds up his hand as if he's taking an oath of office.

"There better not be," I warn. I hadn't even thought about a bachelor party up until Josiah mentioned it. And if I have a bachelor party, that means... "I should probably tell Elizabeth no strippers at Charlotte's bachelorette party, too." The idea of other men looking at my fiancé in any sort of lustful way fills me with rage. I may not be madly, deeply in love with her, but she is mine, now and forever.

"You're already telling her what she can and can't do? Seems a bit much, don't you think?" Josiah's questions rub me the wrong way, like touching velvet backwards.

"It's only fair," I explain. "In fact, maybe we should do a joint bachelor/bachelorette party? Those are a thing, right?" That way I can keep an eye on things on both sides so nothing gets out of hand. Hilltop can't afford a PR nightmare, especially one involving me and scandalous entertainment.

"I guess," Josiah shrugs, all the excitement drained from his face. "I'll talk to Lizzy and see what she thinks."

"Excellent!" I clap my hands together. "Now, if you'll excuse me, I have a date with my fiancé."

***

From the moment the waiter takes our order, I can tell something's worrying Charlotte. Her polite smile fades once he leaves our table. She's holding tightly onto her napkin and slowly tearing it to pieces while avoiding eye contact. Sure, the paintings on the restaurant walls are lovely and deserve notice, but there's more to her gaze than art appreciation.

"Rough day at work?" I ask, slightly leaning forward to better hear her answer. The instrumental music playing overhead is a bit on the loud side, which is annoying, though not a deal breaker.

"What?" Finally looking at me, I take in the deep worry in her eyes, not to mention the slightly dark circles underneath them. "Work is fine," she assures me, nodding repeatedly for emphasis.

"What's wrong?"

"What's right?" she counters, completely putting me off guard. Dropping the remnants of her napkin on the table, she sighs heavily. "Do you think God is okay with what we're doing?" she asks suddenly.

"Um, what do you mean? Where is this coming from?" Her concern is completely out of the blue. The last time I saw her, she didn't seem to have any qualms about our marriage. Although, the last time I saw her we spent more time fucking than talking, so there's that.

"Technically, our marriage will be based on a lie. Lying is a sin! It's one of the ten commandments!" She glances frantically back and forth between me and the ceiling, which I guess is representing God in this situation.

"Charlotte," I reach out and take her hand so she'll stop picking at her cuticles. "This, us, is His plan, albeit a plan I never saw coming, but His plan nonetheless."

"How can you be so sure?" Her green eyes cut into mine as her eyebrows furrow deeply.

"Faith."

"Faith? Okay, that answer might work on your church members. It's not going to work on me." She huffs and pulls her hand away.

"Okay, what about trust? I have always trusted God with my life and I'm where I'm supposed to be, doing what I'm supposed to be doing. When I was in seminary, I had a million doubts. I worried I was becoming a pastor simply because that's what I was expected to do. I thought God would know my heart wasn't in it and He wouldn't speak through me. I thought I was making a huge mistake because I hadn't even considered being anything else." I pause for a moment and take a deep breath. "In the end, I decided to trust Him and everything worked out. Why should this be any different?" I want Charlotte to have the same trust in God that I do, though why would she? I was literally born into the church, molded by it, guided to adulthood through it. For me, trusting God is as easy as breathing.

"So," she begins, "you think this," she gestures to me then to her, "is okay because you trust that this is part of God's plan for your life?"

"I will admit, I was hesitant about it all at first. It's not exactly how I saw my life playing out. However," I hold up a finger briefly as a pause point. "After some prayer and reflection, I was reminded that I need to trust in Him as always and everything would work out."

"Your trust is much stronger than my own," she confesses.

"Are you changing your mind?" My tone is unexpectedly threatening. Why do I care so much if she does? This is a business arrangement, not a real relationship. I clear my throat and hide my concern with a large gulp of ice water.

"No, I just want to be sure we're doing the right thing, that I'm not somehow defrauding the church by marrying you without loving you."

"Defrauding the church? No, you're not doing that." I can't help chuckling at her fear. "Though I am glad to know you have a strong moral compass." That gets a small smile out of her and the tension between us cracks.

"Speaking of moral things, I did want to ask what exactly my job as a preacher's wife entails. Do I go with you to visit sick people? Will I have to lead a Bible study group? Am I in charge of anything important?"

"Well," I try and think for a moment about all the things Mom did for the church before she left. "The main expectation is that you help out with things involving the women's group, children's activities, and the occasional fundraising event. Obviously, you can be more active if you want to be. I'm not going to tell you that you can't do something that will make you happy and benefit the church."

"In that case, I think the church should do a blood drive." Charlotte sits upright in her seat and smiles proudly at her declaration.

"A blood drive?" Now it's my turn to be doubtful and worried.

"Yes. The Red Cross is always in need of donations and since you have hundreds of people at Hilltop, it could help a lot of people."

"We've never held a blood drive before. Typically, we stick to mission work and international ministry. Dad was always a staunch believer in spreading the word of God around the world. He believed that America could handle America's problems. Hilltop's focus is mission work; it has been for over thirty years."

"No time like the present to start something new!" The excitement in Charlotte's eyes is a welcome change from her previous worry and fear. Since I just said she can do what she wants for the church, I can't very well tell her no.

"Very well. I'll let you and Cat work out the details."

"Me and Cat?" Her face falls at my directive. "She's very intimidating. Can I work with someone else?"

"If you really want it done, Cat's the person to talk to." Part of me hopes she'll let this go since she's terrified of Cat. I'm not a fan of change, especially change to something so important in my life.

"Okay. I'll talk to Cat." Charlotte sighs and pulls a small planner from her purse. "We should probably do it after the wedding, that way there aren't two events being planned at the same time at the church. Maybe the end of June or early July." She looks up from her calendar to me and smiles broadly. "Thanks for letting me do this. I really appreciate it."

My chest clenches at her happy expression and kind words. Allowing her to do something at Hilltop that's never been done before makes me highly nervous. I hope this is the last time she'll request something like this, though I have a feeling this is just the first of many changes she wants to enact in her new role. I hate to use Cat as some type of barrier to Charlotte's ideas, although I'll take any scapegoat, honestly.

"Of course. Hilltop is your church, too." I return her smile and check the time on my watch.

"You do that a lot," Charlotte points out, nodding at my wrist.

"I like knowing what time it is," I reply. "Time is very valuable after all." My comment seems flippant, though there's more to it than she knows.

"It makes it seem like you'd rather be somewhere else every time you check your watch," Charlotte says, a worried frown appearing on her pretty face. For the most part, Charlotte puts on a brave, confident face for the world. I've noticed that the more time we spend together, the more vulnerable she allows herself to be with me.

"Maybe I'm just making sure every minute we have together counts." A flirty smile dances across my lips at my super cheesy line. I'd do almost anything to alleviate her worry when it comes to our unique situation. I need her...for my job, that is.

"Smooth, real smooth," she concedes as her frown disappears and her eyes light up with laughter. Our food arrives, thus bringing it with it a safe topic change. "I assume Josiah said yes to being your best man?"

And with that, we're back to our typical easy banter. Over the past month, I would say Charlotte and I have been become good friends, albeit friends with benefits. Josiah's question about whether or not I have feelings for Charlotte pings around my mind as we eat. Yes, I enjoy spending time with her; being with her isn't a chore, which is a huge relief.

Her question about our marriage being a lie to God completely surprised me. Initially, I, too, had that same worry. Her concern would certainly remove any of Cat's qualms about Charlotte being some type of secret gold digger. In all our time together, I've never asked Charlotte about her relationship with God, and perhaps I should have early on, yet ever since I first met her in that coffee shop, I somehow knew she was right with God.

"Have you thought anymore about moving some of your belongings to my house before the wedding?" I ask as I hand the waiter my credit card and he scurries away.

"I have. I'll bring some things over this Saturday, if that's alright."

"That works for me. I have some church matters to attend to, so I won't be there." I reach into my pocket and pull out a copy of my house key. "It's your house, too, so here's a key."

"That's very thoughtful of you," she says, taking the key from my hand and placing it on her own key ring. "It's a good thing my lease runs from August to June. It would be very annoying to pay rent for a place I no longer live at." She holds the keys in her hand for a moment, her brow furrowed. "I do feel bad about moving out and leaving Lizzy behind, though."

"I'm sure she'll be fine." I wave away Charlotte's concern. "If you're worried about your half of the rent, I can pay it until she finds another roommate or moves out."

"That's, that's very generous." Charlotte's eyes widen. "I can't ask you to do that."

"You're not asking," I point out. "I'm offering. Besides, she might turn me down."

"It wouldn't be the first time," Charlotte says, trying her best to hold back a mischievous grin and failing miserably.

"Ha ha. Very funny," I say, taking her teasing in stride. I appreciate Charlotte's sense of humor and her willingness to poke fun at me. I come off to everyone as a very serious person; Charlotte sees right past that façade.

Part of me worries that she can see all of my secrets, fears, and dreams without me ever verbalizing them. The way she looks at me with her bright green eyes so full of curiosity and interest every time we meet is both sultry and unnerving.

Even now, as she watches me drive away from the restaurant, I worry I'm in too deep. So far this has been a mutually beneficial friendship with the occasional sexual episode. However, I can't deny our chemistry or how easy it is to be around her and not feel the slightest bit awkward. This is all just for show, isn't it? Isn't it?

Chapter 15
Charlotte

As I unlock the door to William's house, I'm struck by the fact that soon this will be my house, too. This is the door I'll unlock every day when I come home from work. This is the door I'll open when family and friends come to visit. This is the door I'll hang a wreath on for each season.

"Hurry up, Charlotte! This box is so heavy," Lizzy complains from beside me.

"You're the one that decided to carry the heaviest box in first," I point out, opening the door and entering the foyer.

"Wow!" Lizzy follows me in and stares around her at the huge interior, temporarily forgetting about her heavy burden. "This is so fancy! There's a chandelier up there!" Her excitement reminds me of my own when I first entered the house.

"Yeah, your church must be very generous in your offering for him to live this sort of lifestyle." Even if the house has been part of his family for generations, the property taxes on it must be outrageous.

"I can't speak for everybody else, but I know my parents do give a sizeable chunk of change every Sunday," Lizzy admits. "Now, where do you want this thing?"

I lead her past the kitchen, living room, dining room, two bathrooms, and finally to the last room on the right: a guest bedroom William showed my mom when she came to tour the house. He had said that would be where she could stay if she ever wanted to be an overnight guest. For now, this will be my room.

"Oof!" Lizzy slightly drops the box on the floor by the dresser. I place the smaller box I'm carrying on the bed. We head back out to the car and bring in four more boxes. After unpacking them and putting things both in and on the dresser, we flop down on the queen-sized bed.

"Thanks again for your help with this," I say, gesturing at the boxes sitting all over the floor.

"Sure thing!" Her smile turns from eager to mischievous. "Now, about that favor…"

"Already?! You're full of diabolical plans, aren't you?" I rest my hands on my hips and shake my head. When I told Lizzy I owed her a favor to thank her for helping me move some things to William's house, I had no idea she'd cash it in so soon.

"Yes, yes I am!" She clasps her hands together and wiggles her fingers like an evil mastermind. "So, you know how Hilltop has a house band for our worship songs?"

"Yeah," I respond hesitantly. "What about it?"

"Mariah is going to be stepping away temporarily while she goes on tour for a few months. The band needs a new lead singer, and I thought…"

"Don't you even finish that sentence!"

"But you're a great singer!" Lizzy pleads for me to listen to her crazy argument. "It's just for two months and it's over the summer so it doesn't impact teaching at all."

"Overhearing me sing in the shower does not mean you know whether I can or can't sing. No."

"Will you at least audition for it? Please? It would mean a lot to me, plus it would probably earn you some brownie points with Cat." She dangles that carrot high above my head and I'm so tempted to reach up and grab it.

"No. I can't. My anxiety..." I try to justify my hesitancy and use my anxiety as a scapegoat. Lizzy is undaunted.

"Anxiety, smanxiety! Lots of singers have anxiety and they are able to be on stage in front of people all the time." She waves her hand in front of my face as if erasing my anxiety away. I wish it was that easy.

"Lizzy..."

"Will you at least think about it? Please? Auditions aren't until next week." The hope shining in her eyes is too much to quash right now.

"Fine," I sigh, surrendering to Lizzy's plea. "I'll think about it."

"Good." She appears relieved by my acquiescence for a moment and sighs loudly.

"What's wrong?"

"I have to admit I'm a little jealous of you, Charlotte."

"Jealous? Of me? Why?" I've always been the one jealous of Lizzy. She's far prettier than I am and she has a natural ease when it comes to handling leadership roles at work. If she's ever been anxious or stressed out, she's really good at hiding it.

"I know your relationship isn't a romantic one and I know this is all for convenience's sake, but I can't help being a little sad I'm not getting married, too." She stares down at her hands as if afraid to look me in the eyes.

"You will get married one day, of that, I have no doubt. Who knows? Maybe Darcy will propose and you'll ride off into the sunset together!" I want to paint a pretty picture of her future, despite the fact that I can't imagine Darcy smiling, let alone making Lizzy happy for the rest of her life.

"I hope so," Lizzy sighs. "Jane says she thinks Charlie is going to propose to her any day now."

"They just met like two months ago? That's crazy!" The irony of my statement isn't lost on me; however, I highly doubt Jane is marrying Charlie because he needs a wife to keep his job.

"Really, Char?" Lizzie says, immediately noticing my hypocrisy. "Be that as it may, between you getting married and Jane possibly getting married, I can't help feeling a little left behind." Lizzy lays down on the bed and stares hard at the ceiling.

"You're not behind. You're just the only one of us with good sense," I tease. This brings a small smile to her face.

"That's true," she laughs lightly. "Besides, teaching keeps me too busy to even think about planning a wedding. How are you doing it?"

"The truth is, I'm not. Mom and Cat are in charge of everything. Occasionally, they ask my opinion on something small like the font on the invitations or the vases for the centerpieces. I just have to show up the day of in the dress I picked." Part of me is a little miffed at how little of my input is being used for my own wedding. However, my anxiety is very relieved to have someone else in charge of the wedding chaos.

I've seen enough reality TV shows revolving around weddings to know about the negative effects all that stress and planning has on the brides. Plus, the wedding is basically a huge PR stunt for Hilltop, and that's Cat's job anyway; I'm glad to let her take charge.

"Wow." Lizzy shakes her head in disbelief. "I'm too much of a control freak to let someone else plan my wedding. I don't even use the general lesson plans for English we have at school. I'm too particular."

"Little Miss Type A." I poke fun at her as I lay down next to her and place my hands on my stomach.

"It's amazing we haven't gotten on each other's nerves more than we have being roommates, Little Miss Slob," she laughs at her joke.

"I think we complement each other nicely," I admit. "Who else would clean up my disasters and keep the kitchen organized?"

"I guess that will be William's job in a few months." Lizzy's comment brings me back to my impending reality. I nod in agreement, though my heart isn't in it.

"Will you replace me, Lizzy?" I ask, bringing the conversation back to just us and away from William's role in my future.

"I'm not sure. We still have a few months left on the lease and I could ask my parents to help pay your half until I can move into a one-bedroom apartment." She shrugs and appears unconcerned.

"I can help with that." William's voice startles both of us as he enters the room.

"I don't think pastors are supposed to eavesdrop, Reverend," Lizzy says, sitting up and scolding him immediately. We're both completely caught off guard; he was supposed to be gone all afternoon. The clock on my phone reads 5:00 and it's no longer afternoon.

"Fair point, Elizabeth," William concedes, the corner of his mouth curling up slightly. He's wearing a navy blue suit that hugs tightly to his lean yet muscular frame. The collar of his shirt is unbuttoned as if he just removed his tie, making me think back to how he used a different tie to restrain my arms the last time we had sex. I can't hide the blush creeping up my face, and it only worsens when we make eye contact. "My statement still stands. I can help with your rent after Charlotte moves out."

"I can't accept such generosity," Lizzy protests, though faintly.

"I can afford it," William assures her. Lizzy looks at me with relief on her face. Despite her statement earlier, it would kill her pride to ask her parents and there's no way she can afford it on her own.

"And would the church approve of you using their money this way?" I can't help asking. He throws money around like it's nothing, probably because to him it is. I've pointed out to him many times how crazy it is to me that he has to have the appearance of wealth to lead a church. He assures me I'll understand after we're married and I've assumed my role as his wife/the other half of the Hilltop "image."

When Mom panicked over how much everything was costing for the wedding, he assured her the church had it covered. She and Dad wouldn't have to pay a dime. To make things easier on the budget, I chose the cheapest dress out of the options Cat gave me, and it was still over $5,000. She claims she can write almost everything off as a business expense which raises all kinds of red flags to me, but William just does what she wants. I gave up on that battle, though I still fight him on it when I can.

"Charlotte," William begins, shaking his head like I've disappointed him. "Elizabeth is a church member. There are funds for helping members with housing and other basic needs. You worry too much." His smooth smile tells me the conversation is over. "Take the help, Elizabeth."

"I suppose it would be rude to refuse help from a pastor. Thanks, William." She smiles genuinely and gets up to give him a quick hug. He's uncomfortable and a little embarrassed in her brief embrace.

"Sure thing." He says, now free of Lizzy's grateful arms. "How are your parents, by the way? Your dad said his diabetes was acting up the other day." The way he switches from regular guy to pastor mode fascinates me. It reminds me of how easily I alternate between regular Charlotte and Ms. Lucas with my students. We both have two identities to manage, and by becoming his wife, I suppose I'm adopting a third. Yeah, I definitely need to increase my anxiety medication dosage.

"He's doing better. The doctor put him on a different type of medication and that's helped balance his insulin so that's not a problem now."

Lizzy maintains a polite tone with William, not too superficial, but nothing more than a friendly acquaintance. I can definitely see why their date did not go well; they have negative chemistry.

"Good. And your sisters? Are they well?" William's knowledge and concern for Lizzy's family touches me deeply. I wonder if he is this caring and intimate with all of the members of his church. There's no way he keeps up with the personal lives of over two thousand people, or does he?

"Mary is graduating from college next month, so we're pretty excited about that. Kitty won prom queen and that made her whole life." Lizzy laughs. "And Lydia finally decided what college she wants to go to. Mom and Dad are not happy at the price tag, though. She had the audacity to pick a private college." Lizzy rolls her eyes as she speaks. She doesn't include an update on Jane and, fortunately, William doesn't ask about her.

"What exciting times for the Bennet family!" William smiles at Lizzy's family update and I can't ignore the tinge of sadness in my heart for him. He has no family to give an update on. No one can ask him how his parents are. All my life, I've taken my large family for granted. Much like Lizzy, I grew up with busy, active siblings and there's always been something to talk about or something to do as a family. William didn't have that experience and my heart breaks for him.

"There's never a dull moment at our house." Lizzy looks over and me then back to William before saying, "Well, I have dinner plans with Darcy so I'm going to head out. Charlotte, think about what I asked okay?" She gives me a hug and William offers her a handshake as she walks out.

"What did she ask you?" William steps closer to me and takes stock of the slightly cluttered dresser.

"She said I should audition to be the temporary lead singer of the church band. I told her I would think about it, but I'm probably not going to do it." As much as I appreciate Lizzy's unwavering belief in me, I don't have the confidence to sing in front of hundreds of people, even if it would help me get on Cat's good side.

"Do you sing well? You didn't mention that in your notebook." He picks up a small porcelain cat from the dresser and inspects it thoroughly.

"I'm okay. I'm not Lauren Daigle by any means, but I'm not terrible."

"Then you should give it a shot." He sets the cat down and turns his attention back to me. "I'd love to hear you sing."

"Oh, um..." The way he's looking at me has my palms sweating. "Right now?"

"No," he laughs loudly, "not necessarily right now. If you audition, I want to be there." His laugh does something to my heart, something comforting yet thrilling. I want to please him. I want to sing for him.

"Maybe." That's my compromise. Maybe I will and maybe I won't. We'll see how my nerves hold up by the time audition day rolls around.

"You've got quite a lot of literature here," he notes, gesturing towards the three stacks of books on the floor by the bed. Picking up one of the books on top of the pile, he thumbs through it. Furrowing his brow, he says, "This isn't what I expected you would read. I thought most women read those silly romance books."

"First of all," I take a step forward and jerk the book from his hands. "There's nothing wrong with romance books. Second of all, are you surprised in a good way or a bad way?"

"A good way. There's a lot of nonfiction here that I wouldn't mind borrowing if you don't mind. I've always wanted to beef up my knowledge of U.S. history, particularly all the stories that get ignored in the mainstream history textbooks."

"In that case, you'll want this one." I carefully extract a book from the Jenga book pile and, fortunately, it remains intact. "I read this one in high school. As long as you don't mind highlighting, it's still readable." I hand him the worn-down book. I don't lend my books out lightly to many people, especially those with so much sentimental value, but I can trust William with it.

"*A People's History of the United States* by Howard Zinn," William reads the cover and carefully opens the book. "Wow. You weren't kidding about those annotations." After flipping through a few pages, he sets it down on the dresser and turns his attention back to me. "Have you ever thought about getting a Master's degree in history?"

"Oh, um, yes, actually. Unfortunately, it takes so long and only adds $2,000 to my yearly salary." If only the general public knew how little advanced education for teachers was valued in the education system; the irony isn't even funny anymore.

"I see." He takes off his suit jacket and hangs it on the corner of the open door. "If neither time nor money was an issue, would you do it?" His expression is genuinely curious. Any time he's like this with me, I start to sense a bond strengthening between us, something maybe more than friendship. I like this side of William, the comfortable, relaxed side; it's the preacher persona I could live without.

"Probably." I shrug noncommittally. William "hmmms" to himself as if deep in thought. I almost ask what he's thinking, but then he looks back at the dresser and notices one of the framed photos I have laying haphazardly on the corner.

"Is this you and Alex Trebek?" He picks up the picture and points at it in surprise.

"Yeah. I met him while I was there for one of the college bowl weeks. That was so long ago." Even though I was the runner-up and only got to participate because the actual winner got sick that day, it's still a major achievement for me. "Mom and Dad were so proud." The memory of them sitting in the audience to support me brings a huge smile to my face.

"Of course they were proud. I'm proud of you, too." His icy blue eyes make me shiver. "Not a lot of people can say they've been on Jeopardy. That's quite an accomplishment." William's praise wraps around my heart like a hug.

"I'm just lucky like that, I guess." I refuse to read too much into William's compliment or the way he's looking at me like...nope. Impossible.

"Smart. The word you're looking for is smart, also dedicated, motivated, and hard-working. All of which are traits I admire about you, Charlotte." The gentle hug around my heart has evolved to a full-on squeeze. He admires something about me? Flutters of long suppressed emotions burst through my body against my will. Shut it down, Charlotte. He's just a nice guy giving you a compliment. Do not read too much into it. Do not break your own heart.

William sets the photo back on the dresser and stands it up next to a photo of my family. A twinge of guilt runs through me as I notice him checking out the family photo with a bit of sadness in his eyes. It occurs to me that, since we are getting married, my family is now his family, too, and that gives me an idea.

I step towards him and place my hand on his strong chest. I can't help myself; he's hot. "What are you doing for dinner?"

"Well, I hadn't expected to be back home until later on, so I have no dinner plans." He squints at me suspiciously and tries to guess my intentions for dinner.

"Every Saturday, my parents have a family dinner. Will you come with me? Mom won't mind. She loves you. Any chance to see *the reverend* brings her so much joy. Besides, she always makes way too much food."

"I would like that," William admits, a hesitant smile on his face. "As long as I'm not intruding or causing extra work for your parents," he cautions.

"They think you're amazing. You could never intrude." I move to walk towards the door, but he grabs my hand to stop me.

"Before we go, I just have one question."

"Shoot."

"Why did you put your things in the guest room?" He looks between me and the messy dresser with a confused expression.

"I didn't think you'd appreciate me invading your space with all my junk. Besides, putting my stuff in your room implies that I sleep there and we haven't really talked about that." I'm just making excuses for my own uncertainty and trepidation.

Claiming space in his bedroom is so personal and intimate. Sure, we have sex occasionally and we get along well, but sleeping in the same bed as someone all night is a different story. That implies a romantic, emotional bond that, as far as I know, we don't have. Yes, I want to strip him naked and let him fuck me in every position imaginable. Yes, I want him to degrade me and use me for his sexual pleasure. As for sleeping in the same bed all night and cuddling together? That's a no, or at least a not yet.

"If you want to use this room as a storage space, you are welcome to do so. However," he pulls me toward him and tilts my chin up. "If you want me to keep fucking you, you'll sleep in my bed once we're married." His words send a rush of warmth to my center and I can't deny my sudden need to have him inside of me. Damn, he's good.

He kisses my lips softly and I can't help whimpering embarrassingly in response. "Use your words, Lady Charlotte," he commands, his voice a low, deep timbre.

"Please, Sir William." I'm so weak for this man.

"Please, what?"

"Please fuck me."

"Lay down," William orders, and, without thinking, I do as he says. He leans over me and begins unbuttoning my jeans. In the back of my mind, I know we need to get going or we'll be late to family dinner. In the front of my mind, I know if he doesn't fuck me right now, I'll explode. I'm practically panting with anticipation by the time he tosses aside my pants and underwear.

"Since we have dinner plans, I only have time to give you one orgasm. My apologies," he says, a sexy smirk on his handsome face as he runs his hands up my inner thighs towards my pulsing pussy.

Right as I'm about to ask, "What did you say?" he slides a finger smoothly inside of me and I forget what words are. His thumb moves up and swirls around my clit in a perfect circle of pleasure. An "oh!" escapes my lips, followed by a low moan that comes from my very core.

Glancing down at William kneeling between my thighs, I have to fight the urge to reach down and pull his face closer to my waist. He stares into my eyes and pulls his hand away from my pussy. While maintaining eye contact, he takes the finger that was just inside me and licks it clean. "Damn, you taste heavenly." His words roll through my body and set my legs shaking at a dangerous rate. I'm trying so hard to be patient, so hard to be good.

He stands up and walks over to the nightstand. After fishing a condom out of the drawer, he removes his pants and returns to my waiting, needy body. Heat pervades every inch of my skin as I watch the condom glide onto his hard, beautiful cock. My legs are dangling off the end of the bed and I wonder if I should scoot upwards so he has room to climb on top of me.

He stands between my legs and gives a dark chuckle before grabbing my hips and pulling me towards his waiting cock. The moment our waists touch, the sensation of him inside of me is almost overwhelming. Involuntarily, my legs wrap around William's strong body as he thrusts into me. The way he's handling my body has me limp like a ragdoll, like I'm only here to be used for his pleasure, my own be damned. God, it's so hot!

"You feel so good, Lady Charlotte, so fucking good!" William moans each time he re-enters me, and I can't help but do the same. "Touch yourself!" Instead of following his demand immediately, I give him a puzzled look. The last time I tried to do that, William pushed my hand away. Is this a trick? If I do it, will he punish me?

"Did I stutter?" William's voice increases in volume as he stares down hard at me. His eyes are wild with lust and he's in domination mode. I quickly take my hand and move down to my pussy, touching my fingers to all the right spots. I'm so charged up, between my hand and William's continual movement inside of me, I'm climaxing almost immediately. Waves of pleasure scatter throughout my body, causing me to writhe on the bed like a woman possessed.

"Fuck!" William cries out. His hold on my hips increases, almost painfully so, while his climax rocks through him. I'll be shocked if I don't have bruises there tomorrow. His breath is ragged as he pulls out of me. There's a slight sheen of sweat on his brow which he wipes away with the sleeve of his shirt. He kisses my pussy before standing up and leaving the room. My body is too tingly, too sensitive, and too overstimulated to get up quite yet. I just want to lay here in the afterglow of my orgasm for a little longer; however, an alarm on my phone reminds me I have places to be right now.

After a quick bathroom visit, I put my underwear and pants back on. As I check my hair in the mirror, I take a few deep breaths and fan myself to cool down. It's only the fourth time we've had sex, and I'm convinced I'm engaged to some kind of sex god.

William returns to the guest room in a pair of khakis and a light blue button up shirt. How does he make business casual so sexy? "Shall we go?" He extends his hand to me with a smile and my heart does a jumping jack in my chest.

Reaching out towards him, an unexpected sense of calm, almost peace, enters my soul. For a second, a still, small voice echoes in my mind: *Trust.*

Without question, I do as the voice says and take William's hand.

Chapter 16
William

Like any other Saturday, I'm stuck in my office at Hilltop worrying over the final revision of tomorrow's sermon. As usual, Cat has the final say and the final proofread. For now, it's still in my hands, still 100% what I want to say. Next Sunday's sermon will be almost verbatim what it was for last year's Mother's Day, which means I'll have more free time next Saturday than I do today. Eleanor insisted that I come to every family dinner from now on since I'm almost family. She even said she would move it to Friday nights if that made it easier for me.

I can't lie. The warm welcome the Lucas family gave me last week when I showed up unexpectedly healed a broken part of me, a part I thought was a lost cause. Eleanor reminds me of Mom, at least how Mom was when I was a kid. On the other hand, Edward is nothing like Dad. Where Dad was reserved and stoic, Edward is outgoing and not afraid to express his emotions. Growing up with those loving parents must have been such a blessing.

Meanwhile, my own childhood was a blending of sporadic maternal affection and constant paternal rejection. Nothing I did was ever good enough for Dad. I thought for sure if I became a pastor, he would be proud of me. And he could have been for all I know, but he never said the words to me. Even after his death, I'm still seeking his elusive approval.

Leaning back in my chair, the top of his painted head slides into my line of sight behind me. Some days I want to pull the picture off the wall and set it on fire. Some days I want to stare at it for hours and wallow in grief over what could have been. Today, I'm torn between both options.

"I spoke to Charlotte about her blood drive idea," Cat says, jarring me from my inner thoughts, her tone oddly cool. She's standing in the doorway of my office looking perplexed.

"I'm guessing you told her no?" There's no way Cat approved Charlotte's blood drive idea. That's not the type of thing Hilltop does.

"That was my original plan. However," she crosses her arms. "She has good intentions and she had a very impressive PowerPoint presentation. There really wasn't a way for me to tell her no."

"Huh," I say, leaning forward and placing my head in my hands. "That's not what I expected."

"She went on and on about community and people in need. It's not a fundraiser for Hilltop, though it could be a good PR opportunity to gain more members and increase our donations down the road." There's the Cat I know, always looking for something to take Hilltop to the next level.

"I suppose. What date did you two settle on?"

"July 1st. We're going to have an Independence Day theme with lots of red, white, and blue decorations and Uncle Sam hats for those who donate. That was Charlotte's idea. I could care less if this thing has a theme or not." Cat shrugs her shoulders.

"Well, she teaches history, so that theme makes sense," I point out.

"Speaking of that," Cat walks towards my desk and puts her hands on her hips. "When is she quitting?"

"I haven't talked to her about it yet," I admit, avoiding eye contact with my very stern, old-fashioned boss. The truth is, I don't have the heart to tell Charlotte that Cat wants her to quit her job. Cat thinks that a pastor's wife's job should be to tend to the church and its many needs, not to mention have a lot of children and stay at home to raise them all. I mentioned to Charlotte when we first met that she wouldn't have to work anymore. I didn't say she couldn't work anymore.

"William Arthur Collins," Cat practically thunders at me. "If you don't do it soon, I will, and I won't be as nice about it."

"I will, I will," I assure her, inwardly groaning at her threat.

"Good. Are you almost done with tomorrow's sermon?" She reaches for my laptop and I quickly close all the non-sermon related tabs. In between edits, I was watching a clip I found of Charlotte on Jeopardy. It didn't have a ton of views, but it was there and I was enjoying watching her in competition mode.

She looked so cute in her college sweatshirt and matching headband. She was usually the first to buzz in for any category that wasn't related to science or math. The way her eyes lit up when she got a question correct was, quite frankly, adorable. Watching her in this clip makes me want to watch her teach. If she's this into random trivia knowledge, I bet she's even more animated in her classroom.

"It just needs a few more edits, maybe another half an hour?" I hate handing my sermons over to Cat. It's like giving a piece of meat to starving lion.

"Okay. After you finish, I'll be in my office so we can go over it." Placing my laptop back on my desk, she turns and exits my office. I sigh heavily once she's gone. People think that because I'm the head pastor, I run Hilltop. The truth is, without Cat and her insane micromanaging, this place would fall apart. Dad appointed her when he founded the church and she was integral to Hilltop's growth over the years. She used to say that Dad was the face and she was the hands. They worked well together, with only a few disagreements between them. My relationship with Cat isn't one of equals working side-by-side. It's more like a boss and low-ranking employee situation. I'm not overly thrilled with it; however, it's been working so far and I see no need to rock the boat.

Glancing back down at my screen, the words go fuzzy. Rubbing my eyes, I stand up and leave my office. After getting a scolding from Cat, I need a break from work. I give casual hellos to the various congregants and employees around the building as I wander around, no set destination in mind. As I approach the main sanctuary, the soft strains of music reach my ears. Glancing at my watch, I take note of the time and frown. Band practice was this morning, so why is music playing right now?

I quicken my pace to hurry up and satisfy my curiosity. As I round the corner, I spy the band members posed on the stage with their instruments. A woman is walking off the stage and taking a seat on the right side with about twenty other women. Mariah Calloway, the lead singer of the band, and her husband, Rich, the music director, are sitting in the front row watching the stage intently.

"Next up, Charlotte Lucas," Mariah's voice rings out loud and clear. My attention is immediately drawn to the stage where I'm shocked when Charlotte starts walking towards the microphone in front of the band. The last time I asked her about auditioning for the band, she was still unsure. If I hadn't needed a brain break, I would her missed her audition entirely. Despite being so far away, I'll be able to hear her perfectly through the state-of-the-art sound system that hangs from the rafters above. Though I would prefer to be closer, if she sees me, she'll lose her nerve. I slide into the back row and hope no one notices me and interrupts Charlotte's audition.

"Whenever you're ready," Mariah coaxes Charlotte from below the stage. Charlotte nods and looks behind her at the band. Even from here, I can tell her hands are shaking as she clenches the microphone.

I want to shout encouragement at her and let her know she's got this. I want her to know that whatever happens, she's done her best and I support her. We're a team, not just for show, for real, whether she knows it or not.

Jeff starts strumming his guitar and the familiar strains of Lauren Daigle's "Trust in You" fill the sanctuary. Charlotte closes her eyes and opens her mouth to produce the most beautiful sound I've ever heard. By the time she reaches the chorus, I'm lost in her song.

"When you don't give the answers, as I cry out to you, I will trust, I will trust, I will trust in you!" The passion and faith in Charlotte's voice wash over me with such force it takes my breath away. God is speaking to me through the words of the song, reassuring me that my trust in Him is well founded. A sense of overwhelming joy fills my soul. It's a feeling that the word "happy" is too small, too inept to describe.

As Charlotte sings, the stained-glass window behind the stage is flooded with early afternoon sunlight. The vivid reds, blues, greens, yellows, oranges, and purples of the glass have an ethereal glow to them, framing Charlotte perfectly in a resplendent rainbow of light. She finally opens her eyes when she finishes the chorus and my heart ceases to beat for a moment.

This woman, randomly inserted into my life and into my world, is now inserted into my very soul; this is the moment. Josiah's words ring in my ears: "When you know, you know." He was right. Every conversation, every intimate encounter, every moment with Charlotte plays through my mind with a new lens. The love that I thought I felt for Caroline and Stephanie pales in comparison to how I'm feeling about Charlotte. What I thought was merely an easy friendship with benefits is so much more. I'm somewhat caught off guard by this overpowering love for Charlotte, but at the same time, it makes so much sense. I'm so foolish for not realizing it before now. My desire for her so quickly, my willingness to trust her with who I really am, the way every little thing she does intrigues me, and the way I'm so quick to anger when I think another man is interested in her: its' clear now.

By the time Charlotte finishes the song, tears are coursing down my face. I quickly wipe them away and thank God for helping me realize what he knew all along.

She was always meant for me.

Chapter 17
Charlotte

My hands tremble as I release the microphone. I can't believe I actually did that. Without looking at the people in the pews, I quickly walk off the stage. Ignoring the other women who auditioned before me, I awkwardly half-jog past them towards the back of the church. I want to be out of here, right now, so I can do some undisturbed deep breathing. I was crazy to do this.

All of those women sounded so much better than I did. Why did I let Lizzy talk me into auditioning? She had begged to come listen, but I told her if she came, I wouldn't go through with it. I'd rather sing for strangers than people I know.

As I approach the back exit, I freeze. William is walking my way. What is he doing here? I didn't tell him I was going to be here. Did he hear me sing? Is he going to end the engagement because I sound terrible?

"I didn't know you were watching," I stammer out as William takes long strides towards me. His expression is intense, like a man possessed. "Are you okay?"

Instead of responding, he grabs my chin and crushes his lips to mine. I immediately melt into his kiss. It's different than usual, less lusty and desperate, more tender and emotional. His tongue deepens the kiss as it runs around my lips and into my mouth. A small moan escapes my throat as his hands slide from my chin to the back of my neck. As his fingers move into my hair, my knees go weak. I've never been kissed like this before. My mind goes absolutely blank as I surrender to William's desire.

When he breaks the kiss, he asks, "Why did you pick that song?" His blue eyes stare deeply into mine.

"I thought about what you said about trusting God. That's what I'm going to do, so the song made sense to me." "Trust in You" has always been one of my favorite contemporary Christian songs, so when it came time to pick one, it was in my top three. When I remembered what the voice said to me at William's house, it was a no-brainer.

"I…" He stops speaking and looks at me with such sincerity, yet there's a slight nervousness about him, like he's afraid of what he might say next. "You sing very well," he says, composing himself finally.

"Thank you. You kiss very well." I'm still not over the way he kissed me. It's such a cliché, but he literally took my breath away. He kissed me like…like he loves me. The thought sends a light shiver through my body that I shake off immediately.

"It's not hard when I'm kissing you," he confesses, a flirty smile on his lips.

"You're so cheesy." Like usual, when our conversations get too close to real emotions, I turn to humor to deflect. I'm trying to keep things light between us despite the hammering in my chest. Does he love me? He's never said so and it's only been six weeks since we first met. This is all business with benefits; love isn't part of this, or at least that wasn't the plan.

"Only with you," he responds, tucking a piece of hair behind my ear. It's such a gentle, caring gesture. Between coming down from the anxiety of singing in public and William's unexpected appearance/amazing kiss, I'm at a loss for how to respond. What is even going on right now between us? This is different, not in a bad way, though, just different.

"You probably didn't want me here, but I was taking a break from work and I heard the music so I wandered in here. I didn't even know you were auditioning." He looks a little hurt that I kept my audition a secret.

"I didn't mean to hide it from you. Honestly, I wasn't even sure I would go through with it. I was afraid I would step on the stage and run right off of it without singing a single note. I'm sorry I didn't tell you," I apologize.

"It's alright," he says, smiling gently. "It's sort of funny how I just happened to be walking by right before you sang. I think God wanted me to hear you sing."

"It does seem that way," I admit. The circumstances of his random appearance are too coincidental to ignore. William's perfect timing proves to me without a doubt that it was God's voice whispering "trust" that I heard last week. Now I know for sure that God won't smite me on my wedding day, which is a huge relief.

A blonde lady with very round glasses pokes her head into the sanctuary. Once her eyes land on William, she briskly walks over to us.

"Reverend Collins?"

"Yes, Janet?" If he's annoyed that we've been interrupted, he doesn't show it. This man is Dr. Jekyll and Mr. Hyde when it comes to his job.

"I've got a member who would like to speak to you about officiating her wedding. She and her fiancé are here in the hallway. Do you have a moment?" She nervously looks behind her then back to William.

"Of course. I always have time for my flock." He turns to me with an apologetic smile and says, "Duty calls." Taking my hand, he gives it a kiss before we follow Janet out to the hallway.

"Charlotte?" A man's voice stops me in my tracks. That can't be him. There's just no freaking way. Taking a deep breath, I turn to the voice and sure enough, there's Brad Dillon. He's just as handsome as the day he broke my heart. He's holding hands with a tall, curvy woman in a red blouse and black mini shirt. She's gorgeous; of course she's gorgeous.

"Brad," I breathe out slowly, still in denial that he's here of all places. "It's been a while." My skin tingles and my fingers twitch as the impending anxiety attack makes its first move.

"Yeah, it has," he agrees, looking awkwardly between me and William. Extending a hand toward William, he says, "We haven't been introduced yet. I'm Bradley Dillon. You already know Katie, my fiancé."

William slowly shakes Brad's hand and glances at me out of the corner of my eye. "Nice to meet you. Hi, Katie. I was wondering when you'd bring this guy around." William's teasing gets a smile out of both Katie and Brad.

"I figured it was time you two met. He's thinking about joining Hilltop and it's only right that we get married here," Katie responds. Knowing that Brad will be here at my new church, my new home, makes my stomach lurch. I have to leave. Now.

"Excuse me," I say, unceremoniously interrupting their impromptu meeting. Without looking back, I brush past William and power walk to the parking lot. Once I'm outside in the fresh air, I take several deep breaths and try very hard not to throw up.

I refuse to have this strong of a reaction to seeing him again. It's been two years! No, I don't care about him in a romantic way at all. That's not what this is. This feels like a trauma response, something akin to PTSD, though I wouldn't call it that exactly.

My thoughts are fuzzy and my mouth is dry as a cotton ball. I manage to make it to my car and slump into the driver's seat. The urge to vomit has been replaced with pounding in my chest.

"Walrus, seal, dolphin, starfish..." Placing my hand on my chest, I try very hard to bring my anxiety down from a ten. "Sea turtle, whale, coral, sting ray, jellyfish…" After a few more deep breaths the world is a little less overwhelming.

Gripping the steering wheel, I grab my phone and call Lizzy. I'm not leaving this parking lot for a little while longer. My nerves are still too rattled to drive.

"Hello?" The moment Lizzy's voice comes through the phone, I burst into tears. "Char! What's wrong? Where are you?"

"It's Brad. I saw Brad!" I admit between choking breaths.

"What!? Where?" Her alarmed tone matches my current level of anxiety, which is saying a lot.

"At Hilltop." I take my hundredth deep breath of the afternoon to calm down. "Apparently, his fiancé is a member there."

"I had no idea. I'm so sorry, Char! Did he say anything to you?" Her tone is all concern and compassion.

"He said hi and then he started talking to William, so I ran away as soon as I could." Is running away from one's ex the mature thing to do? Probably not, yet that's exactly what I did.

"You left William there with him?"

"Yeah, he actually came by with his fiancé to talk to William about officiating their wedding." The words are like gravel in my mouth. She must have no idea about his past dating history, either that or she's far more forgiving than I am.

"Oh, okay. Wow. Of all the places, huh?" She pauses for a moment. "Do you think William could tell he was your ex?"

"I have no idea. He was in preacher mode, so if he noticed anything weird, he kept it to himself." I exhale slowly and dab my eyes with a tissue from my purse.

"That's so crazy. It's been, what, two years since you broke up?"

"Ten months, fifteen days, and eight hours. So, yeah, two years give or take." Does anyone ever really forget the day their heart shattered?

"The fact that you are still holding on to that day is unhealthy, Charlotte," she lightly scolds me. "Well, Hilltop is a huge church. It's unlikely you'll have to interact with him ever again." This fact helps relieve the remaining echoes of my Brad-related panic.

"True," I admit, sniffling lightly. "Sorry to interrupt your Saturday grade-a-thon." I feel so silly for getting so worked up over this asshole. He shouldn't still have any effect on me after all this time, and that stops right now.

"Don't be sorry. I needed a break. Besides, I was going to call you soon anyway to ask how the audition went."

"Um, fine, I think. I won't know anything for a few days. There were a lot of people auditioning."

"I bet you were the best one!" Her encouragement is flattering and helps take my mind off of my romantic past. "I wish you had let me come hear you sing."

"You've heard me sing before," I point out. "However, speaking of that, William was there. He wasn't supposed to be; I didn't even tell him I was auditioning. He just showed up right in time."

"Weird! What did he say afterwards?"

"He said I sounded good and he kissed me..." I leave off the rest of that thought. Before I tell Lizzy my suspicions about William's feelings, I want to get a better read on them myself.

"How sweet! I told you that you sing well, see?" She laughs to herself. "You've had quite the eventful afternoon. Are you coming home before you go to your parents for dinner?"

"I'm going to head straight there now that I've calmed down. Thanks for listening." I knew talking to Lizzy was the right call (literally).

"Of course! What else are best friends for?" There's a smile in her voice. "So, the question is, will I see you tonight or in the morning?"

"I'll be home late, but I'll be there." Despite William's sexy demand that I sleep in his bed, that only applies when we're married, and I still have three weeks before I have to give in. Until then, I'll sleep in my apartment with Cleo and Tony curled up next to me.

After hanging up with Lizzy, I head to my parents' house and start helping Mom with dinner. I don't tell her I ran into Brad, her almost son-in-law. They really loved Brad. They thought he was the human embodiment of perfection. He had us all fooled. Well, except for Rob. He told me something was off when they first met. I wish I had listened to him.

Just as I set down the last dinner place, the doorbell rings. My brothers race to the front door like excited puppies. Rob isn't as eager as the others. His promised interrogation time with William is coming up soon and I hope that makes up for my initial mistake of not telling him the truth of our relationship before we got engaged.

And now? What's the truth now? Is this still a relationship based on convenience, or is it becoming something more? Remembering the way William kissed me earlier today has my chest humming, and for once, that humming isn't anxiety.

"Charlotte," William's voice cuts through my brothers' chaos to reach me in the dining room. "May I speak with you for a moment?"

"Sure," I say, shooing everyone out of the room. Once it's just us, William steps towards me and leans down for a kiss. It's soft, sweet, and too short.

"How do you know Katie's fiancé, Brad?" He cuts right to the chase.

"He's my ex-boyfriend," I confess, sighing heavily. It's better to get this over with now, I suppose. Cat may not have found any skeletons in my closet, but my relationship with Brad is definitely something I'm ashamed of.

"How long ago?" William's eyes narrow and I can't tell if it's with jealousy or curiosity.

"About two years." I try to sound casual, as if my time with him was no big deal.

"Why did you break up?"

"What is this, twenty questions?" I snap back, a little meaner than I intended.

"He wasn't in your notebook. Why did you break up?" William's intensity is scary and a little hot at the same time.

"He cheated on me. A lot." The admission itself wouldn't be so bad if it didn't also bring back a flood of memories with it. Every late night working at the clinic to help with emergency cases, every veterinary conference out of state, and every time he quickly grabbed his phone before he left a room. I still remember their names: Lily, Tory, Emma, and Rebecca. Just like me, they were all pet parents who got hypnotized by Brad's way with their fur babies, not to mention his laughing eyes and flirtatious smile. We all thought we were the only woman in Brad's life. We all thought wrong.

"Charlotte," William says, slowly and almost too deliberately. "You didn't deserve that. No one deserves that. I'm sorry he did that to you. If I could take away all the pain he caused you, I would." He places a hand on my cheek and looks deeply into my eyes. "I will make you forget he ever existed."

"That's going to be hard considering he's joining Hilltop," I point out, trying very hard to keep my thoughts together when all I want to do is melt into William's gaze.

"I have final say on all new members. He's denied." There's a fire in William's eyes I've never seen before.

"Just like that?"

"Just like that." His deep voice warms me from the inside out.

"Must be nice to have all the authority," I tease. Leaning into him and resting my hands around his neck, I say, "Thank you, Sir William." Until now, I never questioned the fact that touching William, even a casual touch like this, felt natural, felt right. I thought it was all part of our act to convince others that we were a real couple. When did the charade start to falter?

"The pleasure is all mine, Lady Charlotte," he replies, his voice low, almost a murmur against my ear. "Now, how fast can you eat dinner?"

"Um, pretty fast. Why?" The fire that was in his eyes earlier is still burning. This time, however, it's a fire fueled by lust, not anger.

"Because I want to take you home and have you for dessert." His words take my horniness level from six to ten immediately. I've never eaten lasagna so fast in my life.

Chapter 18
William

If I wasn't trying to get on his good side so badly, I would be really pissed at how many times Rob's beaten me already. I promised Charlotte I would be myself with Rob, but I don't think she understands what that means when it comes to gaming.

"Take that, preacher man!" Rob shouts enthusiastically as he knocks my character off the platform for the third time this match.

"You know, when I invited you over to play *Smash Bros.*, I was really hoping you were bad at it," I admit as **GAME!** lights up the TV screen. After talking to Charlotte, it seems Rob is the main brother she wants me to bond with, and there's no quicker way to get to know another guy than kicking his ass in a video game.

"Unfortunately for you, it's my favorite game." He leans back against the sofa. "What does that make? Ten for me and three for you?" His smug grin is almost too much to bear.

"Yeah, yeah. Did you ever consider I'm letting you win?" I'm not, but he doesn't need to know that.

"Sure, you are." Rob rolls his eyes before getting a serious expression on his face. "Now, let's get to the real reason you invited me to play games. When Charlotte asked you to hang out with me, I assumed you gave in to get on her good side. Then, I realized you wouldn't care about that since you're just using her to keep your job." His words cut me to the core. Ouch.

I wasn't surprised Charlotte told Rob the truth about our situation, yet hearing it phrased like that makes it sound so much worse than it actually is.

"Whoa, now," I say, setting down the Switch controllers and holding up my hands like I'm surrendering in a duel. "Using is a strong word. It's a mutually beneficial relationship." My explanation does not please him.

"How romantic. Is that how you swept her off her feet, by being all formal and logical?" His eyes narrow as they shoot daggers into my own.

"I don't know why she took me up on it, I really don't. You know as well as I do that she propositioned me first." I'm trying so hard to keep an edge out of my voice. Staying calm is the best way to reassure Rob that I'm not some kind of evil villain bent on stealing his sister's innocence.

"Either way, it's all very weird and I don't trust you, no matter how many family dinners you come to or how much everyone else fawns all over you. She's been hurt before by someone the family trusted." His anger is well warranted. I wouldn't trust me either if I were him.

"I assume you're talking about Brad," I respond. He looks at me like he's seen a ghost. "She told me about him last weekend," I explain.

"Yeah," Rob shakes his head and sets down his controllers. "Fucking Brad Dillon."

"Is he the reason you wanted to talk to me, to make sure I'm not like him?" I ask.

"Pretty much," Rob begins. "I knew from the beginning he was trouble. Charlotte wouldn't listen. She thought I was just being a typical over-protective brother." He sighs deeply. "Did she tell you I was the one that caught him?"

"No, no she didn't." Ah, that explains why Rob is extra defensive about me.

"I was out at a bar with my friends and I saw him all cozy with a woman who was not my sister. When I asked him about it, he straight up lied and said I was imagining things." Rob clenches his hands into fists and then slowly releases them. "I wish I had beat his ass right then and there." He looks like he still wants to beat Brad to a pulp and I don't blame him; I want to, too. "When I told Charlotte, she didn't believe me. She thought they would get married one day. She thought he was 'the one.'"

"How did you convince her you were telling the truth?" I can't tell if talking about this is cathartic for Rob or if I'm reopening old wounds. I don't want to pry, yet I'm compelled to know more about this bit of Charlotte's past.

"I saw the same woman at the bar on a different night and I asked her about it. She said she and Brad had been dating for months, so she was not happy when I informed her that he was also dating Charlotte. She gave me her number and told me to give it to Charlotte." His expression goes from hard to devastated. "After talking to Brad's side piece, Charlotte realized I was telling the truth. I'll never forget how she looked when she found out." He rubs his hands over his face before placing them in his lap. "I can't have her go through that again. She won't survive."

"I understand," I reply. Rob turns to me and give me the most intense glare I've ever seen.

"Do you? Do you understand?" He lifts his hands as if he wants to grab me and shake me then thinks better of it.

"Yes," I assure him. "I'm committed to Charlotte. I'm not going to marry her just for show and then run around on her. This is what God wants me to do. This is who He has chosen for me."

Rob thinks for a moment before extending his hand. "You're a man of God, and I respect that. There's nothing I can threaten you with that's worse than Hell if you're lying."

"I'm telling the truth," I respond, grasping his hand and giving it a firm shake. "I love Charlotte. I would never hurt her." Shit. I had not meant to say that part out loud.

"You...you love her? I thought this was all for show?" The incredulous look he gives me is well deserved; that was the original plan, after all.

"Please don't tell Charlotte I said that. I haven't told her yet. I only recently realized it myself." My words pick up speed and start tumbling from my lips. "Yes, this originally was to keep my job and that was it. Something changed along the way. I will love and cherish her as long as she'll let me, even if she never feels the same way I do in return."

"Wow," Rob blinks slowly and shakes his head. "I'm sorry for coming in so hot earlier. I had no idea."

"I don't blame you. I would've done the same thing if I had a sister in this weird situation." I exhale deeply and my shoulders lighten. It feels nice to tell someone how I feel about Charlotte, even if it isn't Charlotte herself.

"Normally, I don't like to keep secrets from my sis, but this time I'll make an exception." He gives me a wry smile and we're all good now. "With all that seriousness out of the way," he picks up his controllers and presses a few buttons. "Let's get back to kicking your ass."

"Oh, it's on!" I joke, the mood between us much lighter than when he first arrived. With Rob's trust in me, I'm that much closer to winning Charlotte's heart.

***

It's a regular Tuesday afternoon in my office and I'm rolling through my tasks of the day. Since its late-May, currently most of my job is making sure all of our summer plans are in place. I just finished coordinating the leaders for our upcoming Vacation Bible School and approving the budget for this summer's mission trip. The only thing left on my agenda for today is meeting with Josiah to discuss the annual Youth Group Summer Spectacular.

A loud knock resounds on my office door. Assuming its Josiah, I cheerfully call out, "Come in!" Unfortunately, it's not Josiah. Its Brad fucking Dillon.

"Hello, Brad. I wasn't expecting you." I've never been more grateful than in this moment for my ability to flip the switch between William and Reverend Collins.

"Yeah, and I wasn't expecting to be denied membership," he seethes. "What gives?"

"Based on your application, you don't seem to be a good fit for Hilltop." My answer is purposefully vague for legal reasons. While I do have all say on new members, Cat is always worried about potential legal action on the part of those I refuse.

"What the fuck does that mean?" Brad's anger is getting the better of him and it gives me just what I need to fire back.

"That. That right there. Your temper and your foul language break two of our membership rules." Are these rules legally binding? No. Does he know that? No.

"That's bullshit!" Brad clenches his jaw and gives me a murderous glare. "This is about Charlotte, isn't it?"

Despite my inner rage, I don't respond and I do my best to keep my expression neutral. How dare he say her name! He lost that right when he broke her heart.

"Katie told me you two are engaged," Brad sneers. "Figures."

"What does that mean?" Crap. His bait worked.

"Well, preachers usually have plain wives, just like Charlotte!" His sneer turns into a malicious grin.

"I'm going to give you two options," I say, rising to my feet, my head pounding with unbridled contempt. "You can leave here of your own accord and on your own two feet, or you can be kicked out on your ass. Your choice." Most days, I find our security team a waste of funds. Today, they are worth every penny.

"Okay, I get it," he says, holding his hands up and turning towards the door. "I just have to ask one question before I go."

"You can ask. I'm not going to answer," I reply, my hand poised over the emergency button under my desk.

"Is Charlotte still a tiger in the bedroom?" He laughs at my shocked expression. "Hell, she may not be pretty, but Goddamn if she wasn't good in the sack."

"You son of a bitch!" I run around my desk and lunge at Brad's smug face. He dodges before my fist can connect with his jaw. Grabbing my arm, he throws me to the ground and kicks me hard in the ribs. I manage to turn on my side so I can curl up and protect my stomach right as another kick comes my way.

When the third kick comes, I grab his foot, twist, and yank him to the floor. I get to my knees and rear back my arm. Before he can roll away, my fist connects with his cheek. A satisfying smack reverberates through my hand. I hit him again, hard, my fist bloodying his nose, but before I can get in a third hit, Josiah comes running into the room.

"Whoa! Whoa!" Josiah pulls me away from Brad and pushes me against the wall. "What are you two doing?" His eyes are wild as he glances from me to Brad and back to me again.

"Let me go!" I push back against Josiah's arms, but it's no use. He's always been stronger than me, even before we started working out together.

"No, not until you calm down." His tone is firm and reasonable. I hate it. Normally, I'm the logical one. What is wrong with me? Cat is going to lose her shit.

"Enjoy your bitch, Reverend Collins," Brad says as he gets up from the floor rubbing his jaw. "I know I did." Laughing, he leaves my office.

"Josiah, if you don't let me go right now, I will break your arm!" My threat is empty and Josiah knows it. Even with all this adrenaline coursing through me, the worst I can do is maybe give him some bruises.

"Breathe, William, breathe." He's right, so I do as he says until I've gained back my self-control. "Better?"

I nod and he lets me go. Once I'm sitting in my chair, I'm reminded of the kicks to my ribs. An "oof" escapes as I try to lean forward and rest my arms on the desk.

"Explain," Josiah commands, standing over me like Dad did whenever I was in trouble.

"He's Charlotte's ex. I refused his membership. He insulted her. I let my emotions get the better of me," I confess.

"I see that," Josiah says, his hard expression softening as he sits down across from me. "Since when do you let that happen? You're always Mr. *Cool as a Cucumber*."

"Turns out, when it comes to Charlotte, I'm not as logical as I'd like to be," I admit.

"I thought this was all business?" Josiah asks, raising an eyebrow.

"Can't a man be protective of his assets?" I argue, knowing full well Charlotte is my soul mate and not an object.

"You love her, don't you?" Josiah sees right through my nonchalant attitude; he always has. I can't hide the slight blush that comes to my face at his question. "I knew it!" He jumps up and pumps his fist in the air. "I knew it before you did. Ha ha!"

"And you didn't tell me because...?"

"It was more fun watching you figure it out for yourself," he replies, grinning like a kid who just won a game at the county fair.

"If you say so," I say before I begrudgingly thank him for saving me from myself earlier.

"It's a good thing we had a meeting at three today. If I had come later, I'd hate to think how much worse it would have been. Cat is going to eat you alive when she finds out." Josiah's fearful expression on my behalf would normally have me worried. However, I'm still riding high from fighting with Brad.

"Whatever she says is warranted, but also worth it. I can't let that asshole go around saying that shit about Charlotte without any consequences." I wince as I stand up.

"Maybe that defense would fly in an eighteenth-century duel. However, this is the twenty first century so you better hope he doesn't sue Hilltop for all its worth," Josiah counters. His words are serious, though it's clear he's proud of me when he smiles in spite of himself. "Now, I suggest you go home and put a bag of frozen peas on your injuries. We can talk about the Spectacular tomorrow."

"Fine," I admit defeat and head home. As expected, by the time I'm home, Cat has called me three times. Thank God for the "Do Not Disturb" feature while I drive. I take off my shirt and place a bag of frozen corn on my ribs while I lay on the couch. Cat's angry voicemails are literally insult to injury as she berates me for my "thoughtless aggression" and my "foolhardy actions." Instead of letting her words sink in and sow the seeds of guilt, I delete her messages.

The only opinion that matters to me is Charlotte's, and I'm not looking forward to that conversation.

Chapter 19
Charlotte

There's nothing quite like the empty quiet once all the students have left school for the day. Any other day, I would wallow in the silence and take my time getting ready for tomorrow. However, since my students have their statewide assessment in two days, this is no time to relax. I've been pushing them, and myself, harder each day to prep for this test. My anxiety is in maximum overdrive this time of year and it's made worse by the fact that I ran out of my anxiety meds three days ago. I thought I had enough to get through the rest of the school year. Boy, was I wrong.

As I place all the final study reminders in each student's folder, the pounding of feet in the hallway gets closer to my door. It's only after the feet have entered my room that I look up to see who they belong to.

"Hi, Claire," I say, trying to not sound annoyed at her sudden appearance. Her mom teaches math two halls down and her favorite thing to do is bother her teachers after school.

"Miss Lucas, I have a bone to pick with you," she starts, her tone indignant. The urge to roll my eyes is strong. Claire always has a bone to pick with someone.

"Go ahead, pick the bone," I tell her as I quickly glance over my students' review games for tomorrow.

"Are you quitting?" Her question gets my full attention.

"Am I quitting? No, why would you think that?" Guilt for my initial frustration at her interruption rises in my chest. She's just a kid; she doesn't deserve the brunt of my anxious aggravation.

"Brianna told me you have to quit because you're marrying her pastor," Claire explains, her eyes beginning to well with tears. "You can't leave! I'll be so sad!"

"Oh, sweetie!" I get up from my desk and hand her a tissue. "I'm not leaving. You don't need to be sad." She grabs the tissue and pulls me into an awkward hug.

"I love you, Miss Lucas. You're my favorite teacher!" Claire says as she releases me from her tight grip.

"Thank you, dear. I appreciate that." I sit back down at my desk and sigh. "Please tell Brianna that I'm not leaving and she should stop spreading rumors."

"Okay. Bye, Miss Lucas!" Claire waves cheerfully before leaving me alone once more. I wonder how many students now think I'm leaving because of Brianna's accidental misinformation. Ugh. I don't need this extra stress right now! My fingers tremble on the keyboard as I draft out a message to send my principal in case rumors have reached his desk.

I can't deny that the thought of quitting teaching is appealing some days, especially the days when the students make me want to step into the hallway and scream or when the principal is guilt tripping teachers over low test scores that we have zero control over. And yet, much like with William and preaching, I know in my heart this is what I'm meant to do.

When a student shows me a picture of their cat, jumps up and down with excitement over a high test score, makes a unique connection between history and current events, or tells me they love my class, that's what I live for. Besides, I don't want to help run Hilltop and this job is an excellent way to avoid having to do that.

As I'm driving home, I remember what William said about me not having to work once we're married. I took that to be an option, not a requirement. What if I was wrong? He can't expect me to quit my job and be a kept woman (though it does sound appealing on a day like today). I worked hard for my education and my career. Lizzy didn't find anything in the pre-nup about me leaving teaching, therefore that can't be a requirement, can it? My pulse pounds in my wrists and makes its way to my head before too long.

I feed Cleo and Tony then head directly to my room. I'm too stressed to eat for myself. When William calls, I almost don't pick up.

"Yeah?" My voice is tense and tired. I can't muster the energy to pretend I'm in a good mood.

"Are you okay?" William is immediately concerned and I would be touched if my mind would stop taking my thoughts and tossing them like wet noodles on to a wall.

"No," I admit, my voice choking up as tears come to my eyes. I've been so overwhelmed and on edge all week, it was only a matter of time before my stress turned to sobbing.

"How can I help?" He's trying to be sweet and that just makes the crying worse. "Take a breath, Charlotte, in and out." Listening to his words, I manage to calm myself down enough to finally speak again.

"Unless you have a secret stash of anti-anxiety meds, there's really not much you can do," I joke, wiping my tears away with my sleeve.

"Who's your doctor?" That's not the response I expected.

"Um, Dr. Lewis at the family clinic. Why?"

"I'll call you right back." Click. What the what? I'm staring at my phone like it called me horrible names. Did he just hang up on me? Why did he ask about my doctor?

Groaning, I roll onto my side and cuddle Tony to my chest. Cleo has already claimed my back. Cats aren't medication, though they do help some. About fifteen minutes later, William calls me back.

"You'll have pills soon. They were just called into the pharmacy you go to." His voice is solid, though I'm having a hard time understanding his words.

"What? How did you do that?" I sit upright, accidentally jostling Cleo and Tony in the process. They *mrow* in protest and jump from my lap.

"I know people," he replies, his voice sounding slightly like a Batman impression.

"Did you threaten the Joker or something?" I say, letting out a sharp laugh.

"Sort of," he pauses and I can sense his smile through the phone. "When is your students' test again?"

"Friday." Of all the days for a state assessment, they chose a Friday. "Why?"

"Come over for dinner Friday night. I have a surprise for you." From his tone, he almost sounds pleased with himself.

"Do I get a hint?" My curiosity is overriding my anxiety for the moment.

"The hint is you'll like it," he responds, teasing me with his deep, bedroom voice.

"Then I will definitely be there," I assure him.

"Good. Now, go get your meds and eat something before I tell Elizabeth to take charge," he teases.

"Okay, okay. Thank you, William." I hope he can hear the gratitude in my voice. I don't know what he did to get me more medication or why he cares so much if I'm anxious or not; I'm just glad he did. I've never had a man be this concerned about my well being before. Maybe he does love me...or maybe I'm just reading too much into it.

***

After the world's longest, most stressful week, its finally Friday. I sent up several prayers while my students tested, but sadly I won't have the results until Monday. Now that I'm back on my medication, I can handle the wait much easier than I could have a few days ago. Even with that, though, I still find myself picking at my dinner.

"I'm sure they'll all pass," William says, jolting me from my swirling thoughts.

"Am I that transparent?" I ask, laying down my fork beside my plate.

"I like that you care so much about your students," he replies, evading my question. "It shows what a good teacher you are."

"Speaking of that, am I supposed to quit my job?" By the startled way he drops his utensils, its clear I've caught him off guard.

"Who said anything about quitting your job?" He's stalling.

"That doesn't answer my question," I point out, giving him a pointed stare. He's not wriggling out of this conversation.

"Yes and no. Cat wants you to quit. I don't. I want you to do what makes you happy, and teaching seems to make you happy." His explanation makes sense. Of course, Cat wants me to quit. She probably envisions me as some sort of old-fashioned housewife, meant to serve her husband, pop out kids, and have no life other than what's at home. Fuck that!

"It does. I'm not quitting. She's just going to have to deal with that." I nod firmly. To my surprise, William laughs. "What's so funny?"

"You're cute when you're stubborn. That's all." William's compliment causes me to blush from head to my toes. Wait... can toes blush? Either way, I'm all hot and bothered now.

"Oh, um, thanks?" I tuck my hair behind my ear like a nervous teenage girl. How does he do that?

"Come with me," William stands up and leaves the dining room. I follow him without question. Is this about the surprise he promised?

We enter the master bathroom and I'm surprised at the transformation. The only light in the room comes from at least a hundred tea lights scattered across the sink, window ledge, the back of the toilet, and all around the base of the freestanding bathtub. William turns on the water and adds some type of reddish-pink liquid that immediately creates tons of foamy bubbles. It smells like cherries. How did he know my favorite scent?

Turning to me, he says, "Take off your clothes."

"Yes, Sir William." I quickly toss my shirt, pants, bra, and panties to the floor in front of the sink. Once I'm completely naked, his eyes rove over me hungrily. It's been about a week since we had time for sex and I'm horny as all get out.

"Get in the tub," he commands. I gingerly step into the warm, foamy water, careful not to splash any outside of the tub. I lean back against the tub and drape my hair over the edge so it doesn't get wet. William turns off the water and disappears. I close my eyes and let the warmth surround and soothe my anxious body. When he returns a few minutes later, he has a cup of hot tea in his hand and there's instrumental music playing from his phone.

He sets the cup on the counter and moves behind me. Suddenly, he's on his knees and his hands are in my hair.

"What are you doing?"

"I'm helping you relax, Lady Charlotte." His fingers move up and through my hair, massaging my scalp slowly.

"Mmmmmm," is all I can get out before my eyes close and I let William take control of reducing my stress. The scent of cherries pervades my senses as I slowly sink further into the white foam. Between the candles, the music, and the bath itself, I finally relax and let go of all the stress that built up over the past week. William's hands leave my head and I'm a little disappointed. When I open my eyes, he's putting my hair up into a very sloppy bun.

"I thought you didn't like my hair up like that," I remind him.

"I'll allow it this once," he says, leaning forward to nip my collarbone with his teeth. "Your neck is so sexy," he breathes over my shoulder. "All of you is so sexy." He kisses my earlobe and moans into my ear. I can't help letting out a small whimper of desire.

"Not as sexy as you," I counter.

"Shall we compare?" And with that, he stands up and starts taking off his clothes. Oh, hell yes! "Scoot forward." I slide up and some water sloshes over the side extinguishing a few candles. William steps in the tub behind me and slides down so my back is to his front. With me between his legs, I'm very aware of how hard he is right now.

He places his hands on my shoulders and begins massaging them. Oh, I really needed this. His fingers knead and press all my stress away in muscles I didn't know I had back there.

"What did I do to deserve such pampering?" I ask, my head slumped against my chest as I surrender to his strong fingers.

"You've had a hard week. Let me spoil you, Lady Charlotte." He kisses my shoulder and resumes the massage.

"Before I lose all consciousness and drown in the most relaxing bath of my life, I have a question," I say in between grateful moans.

"Ask."

"How did you get me more anxiety medicine?" I've been dying to know all week and now seems like a good time to find out.

"I called your doctor and said my wife needs more medication and they called it in." The words *my wife* coming from William's lips sends a shiver of delight through me. I'd given up hope of ever being anyone's wife after Brad destroyed my heart. Being claimed by him as his wife before we're even married is intoxicating.

"I'm not your wife yet," I point out. Each day the wedding gets closer, and each day I'm falling more and more in love with this man despite my brain warning me against potential heartbreak.

"You are my wife in everything but name," William murmurs into my ear, causing pleasurable tremors to coast through my body. His hands move from my shoulders to my breasts. The water ripples as his fingers twirl around my hard nipples.

"Oh!" I moan and lean back, pressing hard against William's chest.

"Have I told you how sexy your tits are?" He gives them a gentle squeeze as he speaks.

"No, I don't think so. I figured they were too small to be sexy," I explain. I've always been self-conscious about my small bra size. Brad always made fun of me for it and suggested on more than one occasion that I get a boob job.

"They're perfect," he growls and bites my neck. The mix of pain and pleasure has me writhing in anticipation of what comes next. I don't even care that I've knocked so much water and so many pretty bubbles over the sides of the tub. "They're perfect little handfuls and they fit so nicely in my mouth. Just the right size to hold, squeeze, and suck." He places emphasis on the "k" and my body tingles at the thought of him doing just that.

"I'd like that," I murmur in response. His fingers pinch my nipples, causing me in suck in a breath. "I don't think teasing me is helping me relax," I point out as my body writhes against his for release.

"I won't apologize for being unable to keep my hands off of you," he says, continuing to play with my breasts, forcing my body so close to the brink of orgasm, yet not quite there. I fight the craving to reach down and touch myself to end this delicious purgatory. Instead, I sit here, moaning and whimpering, completely at William's sexual mercy.

Once he thinks I've suffered enough, he stops and says, "Let's get dried off. I still have to give you your surprise." He stands up and leaves the tub to get us towels. While he does that, I stand up abruptly from the warm water in hopes that the cool air will decrease my throbbing need. The only thing it actually does is make me cold, thus making my nipples painfully hard.

William wraps his towel around his waist and then proceeds to dry me off, smiling mischievously at my perky, hard nipples. I choose to ignore his glee and instead melt into what has to be the softest, yet most absorbent towel I've ever experienced.

As he's standing in front of me, I can't help noticing purplish-blue bruising along his ribs. I reach out and gently touch it.

"That's new. What happened?" His smile droops a little then resumes as he finishes drying my shoulders and arms.

"I'll explain later. Here." He hands me a navy-blue bathrobe. I slip into the world's comfiest robe as he changes from the towel to a pair of gray sweatpants.

"You better!" I threaten, though my threat is hollow. If I had known he was bruised there, I wouldn't have leaned against him in the tub. I grab the cup of tea, take a sip, and allow William to lead me to his bedroom.

Chapter 20
William

Once Charlotte and I are in my bedroom, I place her in front of the full-length mirror.

"Stay," I order and she does. I grab the two small boxes from my dresser and bring them back to her. Standing behind her, I slide my hand up and around her beautiful neck. Lightly gripping it, I grin and say, "While this is my favorite necklace for you to wear, it's hardly proper to wear in public, so..." My hand disappears momentarily and returns with a silver chain from the first box.

"This seems more your style."

"How do you even know my style?" She teases me, a sly look in her green eyes.

"I'm a very observant man," I reply, my eyes roving slowly up and down her reflection. "You're not a pearl necklace kind of woman."

"You mean like Lizzy?" She asks as I lift the necklace and place it around her neck. "If you're expecting me to be the same kind of wife Lizzy would have been, you will be sorely disappointed." There's a hurt in her eyes that guts me to my core. "You forget I was there when you asked Lizzy if she had regrets at the engagement party," she reminds me and I curse inwardly that she remembers that moment.

"I don't want *Lizzy*," her name hisses through my teeth. "And I don't anticipate being disappointed by you in any capacity." My compliment makes her body tremble slightly. I kiss her neck softly. "Do my words turn you on, Lady Charlotte?"

"Yes, Sir William." Her voice is breathy as my hand reaches up and around her neck, clasping into place firmly, my thumb stroking the underside of her jaw carefully.

"Now this," I tap my finger on the pendant. "Is for the church…" the golden cross in the center of the silver heart gleams brightly. "But this," I reach behind me once more and grab a long velvet box. Opening it, I explain, "is for me." Inside is a dual strand pearl bracelet with a silver clasp. After I place it on her wrist, she lifts the bracelet close to her face and squints her eyes.

"It's engraved," she says, inspecting the little disk next to the clasp.

"What does it say?" I ask, watching her reflection's expression as she reads the engraving on the top side.

"Lady."

"Turn it over," I command, my breath warm as I whisper in her ear.

Turning it over, she reads, "Charlotte. Oh!" Her eyes light up with delighted surprise when she locks eyes with me in the mirror.

"In case you were wondering what happened to the pearls I ripped from your neck, I decided I liked them better on your pretty wrist." My hand wraps around her newly braceleted wrist and I give it a hard, possessive squeeze. "This way you don't forget who you belong to."

"Isn't that what this is for?" She holds up her left hand and wiggles her ring finger.

"This is more…personal," I explain. The ring was just the first step of making Charlotte mine. When I bought it, it was nothing more than an expected trinket, a basic symbol to the world of our impending nuptials. I wrap my arms around her waist and rest my head on her shoulder. We make quite the handsome couple, if I do say so myself.

"What's up with you being super romantic lately?" Her eyes flick up to mine in the mirror. I'm not ready to tell her the truth. I'm not ready to expose my heart to her. Not yet.

"Only you would question being spoiled by your fiancé," I reply, carefully answering and not answering her question at the same time.

"You're really good at deflecting," Charlotte says, moving my arms away from her body and turning to face me. "Talk." She points to my bruised ribs and taps her foot impatiently.

"If I told you I got them from defending your honor, would that suffice?"

"No. That would only pique my curiosity further." She crosses her arms over her chest and gives me a sexy glare. "When and why were you defending my supposed honor?"

Running my hand through my hair, I sigh and say, "I sort of got into an altercation with your ex."

"William! You didn't!" Her hands raise to her mouth in shock as her eyes widen. "Was this at Hilltop?"

"Yes," I admit reluctantly. "He came by to ask why I had denied his membership and then he started insulting you."

"What did he say?" Of course she wants to know.

"I'm not going to tell you. You don't need to hear that."

"Tell me right now." Her tone has switched from casual interest to intense determination. I don't want to tell her, but she won't give up until I do. "I deserve to know what that asshole said about me."

"Fine." I cave. "He said it made sense that you were marrying me because preacher's wives are..." I can't bring myself to say the last part.

"Are what?"

I sigh heavily and say, "Plain."

To my surprise, she calmly says, "I can't be mad at him for speaking the truth. I'm not exactly a knockout." She fiddles with her bracelet, flipping the charm back and forth. "I never could figure out why he was dating me. The other girls he was talking to were much prettier than me."

"Don't you dare talk about yourself like that!" I reach down and pull her chin up. Unshed tears glisten in her eyes. "You, Charlotte Lucas, are beautiful inside and out. Unlike those other women, you are more than just what people see on the outside. You are intelligent, driven, caring, hard-working, and more perfect than any man could ever deserve."

"You don't mean that," she slowly shakes her head as the tears roll silently down her cheeks.

"I do, I really do. I wouldn't be marrying you if I didn't mean it." This conversation is not where I saw tonight going at all, yet it's necessary. She needs reassurance that she's worthy of love. I hate that she was so broken by that asshole, though I will gladly take all the time in the world to heal her and prove to her I'm right.

"You just need a wife for your job," she sniffles.

"Fuck my job, Charlotte. I need you for me." It's as close to "I love you" as I'm willing to get right now and I hope it will be enough. "Look in my eyes. This may have started as a mutually beneficial plan where neither of us was invested emotionally, but I've grown to care for you. You are my wife." I lean down and kiss her salty, tear-streaked cheeks.

"I...I care for you, too." It's not an "I love you," but her meaning is clear. She's just as invested in us emotionally as I am.

"Now," I pull back, untie her robe, and push it off her shoulders to the floor. "Be a good girl and stand against the door." Her expression is understandably confused, though she does as I command. She places her back against the door and looks at me with complete trust. "Lift up your arms." Once she does so, I reach above her and wrap the door's restraints around her wrists, carefully sliding her bracelet out of the way first.

"You're so pretty all tied up," I murmur against her cheek as I give her a soft kiss. She smiles at my praise and damn if that doesn't go straight to my already hard cock. "Spread your legs." She complies immediately, without question. I kiss her from her cheek to her neck, then to her shoulders, her breasts, and her stomach before I drop to my knees before her. Her body writhes with what I can only assume is pleasure as I grip her hips and lift one of her legs over my shoulder.

"I need to taste you, Charlotte. I'm starving for you," I say as my mouth inches closer to her pussy. The heat radiating from her center draws me in as I bite and suck her inner thighs, causing her to moan deliciously above me.

"Please, oh please, please!" Charlotte begs, her breath ragged with desire.

"Tell me what you want, Lady Charlotte," I murmur against her sweet cunt, teasing her with the very tip of my tongue. She inhales sharply and whimpers loudly.

"I want you to eat me out," she states. "Please." She adds oh so politely.

"Your wish is my command." Tossing my glasses to the floor, I press my tongue deep between her wet folds and lose myself in her intoxicating taste. Even though it'll hurt my ribs, I lift her other leg over my other shoulder and grip her generous ass tightly.

"OH!" Her pleased surprise is evident as a rush of flavor invades my mouth. Fuck, she tastes so good! I gently nibble on her clit and slap her ass hard. "William!" She moans, her legs shaking around my neck and squeezing my head. I'm drowning in her pussy and I never want it to end.

"I'm, I'm...oh!" With a violent jerk, she presses her pussy against my face and I voraciously pick up my speed, making sure to lavish her entrance and her clit with forceful yet precise attention. Once the orgasm passes, her body relaxes and I reluctantly place her feet back on the floor. If not for the wrist restraints, I'm sure she would've collapsed entirely by now. Standing up, I cup my hand to her chin and admire her completely blissed out expression.

"Absolutely breathtaking," I whisper. Once her eyes flutter open, a sheepish grin appears on her blushing face. I reach up and release her wrists, kissing her neck as I do.

"Mmmm," she moans, whether from pleasure or from finally having her arms down where they belong, I'm not sure. "If I didn't know any better, I'd think you were trying to make me fall in love with you, Sir William." She looks up at me with half-lidded eyes and my heart slows for a beat.

"What if I was?" The hope in my voice is painfully blatant. Fortunately, she's too high on her climax to take me seriously.

"A girl could get used to this," she says, rubbing her wrists and smiling broadly. "I have an idea." She bends down to pick my glasses up from the floor. Handing them to me, she says, "You're going to want these."

The world comes back into focus once more as I follow Charlotte back to the mirror. With her back to the mirror, she places me in front of her and gets on her knees. My cock immediately goes from hard to painfully throbbing as I realize what she's doing.

"Do I need to remind you who's in charge here, Lady Charlotte?" I warn, my voice low and growly. Instead of responding, she reaches up and pulls down my sweatpants, freeing my aching cock, already glistening with pre cum.

"I know who's in charge, Sir William," she replies, looking up at me with her sultry green eyes. "I'm just getting you ready to serve you."

"What a thoughtful girl," I place both hands on either side of her face. "Open wide." The moment her lips part, I thrust my cock into her waiting mouth. I'm so pent up from touching and tasting her, this might be embarrassingly quick. Her hands reach up and grip my thighs, her nails digging into my body in the most deliciously excruciating way.

"Fuck!" Holding tightly onto her head, I pound into her perfect mouth over and over again as her tongue works its magic up and down and around my cock. When I take in our reflection in the mirror, her body on the floor serving me and my needs, her head bobbing back and forth on my cock, I can't hold back any longer.

"Shit!" I cry out and send my release down Charlotte's throat. After she swallows, she pulls back and gives my cock one last taste before making eye contact with me. Releasing my thighs, she licks her lips and stands up.

I'm speechless as I just stand there, panting like a dog on a hot day. Charlotte kisses my lips, grabs the robe from the floor, and disappears to the bathroom, I assume. I practically fall backwards onto the bed once she's gone.

I love you. I love you. I love you.

That's the only thought running through my mind when she returns wrapped in my robe. "Stay the night." The moment the words leave my lips, I worry I've made a mistake.

"William, I told you I'm not staying here overnight until we're married. Her words have more conviction than her tone. I might have a chance.

"Stay," I put more force into my voice so she knows I'm serious.

"Is that an order?" She raises her eyebrows at my boldness.

"It's not an order. It's a... hopeful desire," I say, standing up and walking over to her. I sigh with relief as I watch her expression switch from determination to resignation.

"Just this one time," she qualifies, holding up a finger for emphasis.

"Just this one time," I repeat. Once we're ready for bed, she looks at me warily.

"I don't have any pajamas. I don't sleep naked," she explains. As much as I want to order her to sleep naked anyway, she's already out of her comfort zone and I won't push it. I retrieve one of my gym t-shirts from the dresser and hand it to her. "Thank you."

Once she's dressed, she slides into the bed and buries herself in the comforter. "Good night, Charlotte." I turn off the light and crawl into the bed next to her. The urge to spoon her is strong; I resist. At some point in the night, she must have come over to my side because I woke up with her on my chest.

As the morning light streams in the window and lights up her face, she takes my breath away. Thank you, Lord, for Charlotte. I don't deserve her, but I will thank You every day that I have her. Amen.

Chapter 21
Charlotte

"Just think, a week from today you're getting married! You'll be Mrs. Charlotte Collins!" Lizzy claps her hands together gleefully, an enthusiastic smile lighting up her face.

"It's so surreal," I respond, looking around at all the women gathered here for my bachelorette tea party. They're all here to support and celebrate my upcoming marriage. Lizzy invited Mom and I wanted her to be here; however, she insisted this was something for younger women and she would be too emotional for us to have a good time anyway.

"Where are you going for your honeymoon?" Lydia asks.

"We're going to tour a few historical places in Europe I've always wanted to go to." I can't deny the perks of marrying someone with a big enough bank account for such a trip. I couldn't afford to study abroad in college, so I've only been to historical places in the continental U.S.

"That sounds...nice," Lydia comments, clearly feigning polite interest in my nontraditional honeymoon plans.

"I can't wait to be married," Kitty remarks while sipping her tea with her pinky out. "It's so romantic!"

"You're only eighteen!" Lizzy reminds her while rolling her eyes. "Besides, there's more to life than being married."

"Says the old maid." Kitty smirks at her older sister before wisely walking away and dragging Lydia with her.

"I blame Mom," Lizzy says, sighing dramatically. "All she talks about is us getting married. It doesn't help that Jane and Charlie got engaged last weekend."

"What?" I choke a little on my tea.

"Oh," Lizzy starts, realizing this is new information to me. "I thought I told you about that." She looks away at the other guests and nervously plays with her hair.

"No, you didn't." I take a deep breath. "Good for her. She deserves to be happy."

"That's not the response I expected." Lizzy raises an eyebrow and puts her hands on her hips. "What gives?"

"Why can't I be happy for Jane?" I shrug and take my tea to our reserved table. Lizzy follows me and immediately sits down next to me.

"Because you don't like Jane. Because you're mad at her for stealing Charlie." Lizzy's explanation tracks and I get why she's confused. I was mad at Jane for that. *Was.*

"I'm over it. She's happy. I'm happy."

"You're happy?" Lizzy squeals, causing all the other guests to give us a weird look. I smile awkwardly at everyone and glare at Lizzy.

"Shhh! Don't be so loud. People are going to think I was depressed or something." I take a bite of the tiny sandwich on my plate. Mom thought the tea party idea was weird. I thought it was perfect. I don't want strippers, phallic shaped food, or alcohol. Besides, I have a prim and proper reputation to uphold as William's future wife. While we're here, he and his friends are at his house playing video games. We're so wild and crazy.

"I kind of thought you were, to be honest," Lizzy whispers to me as Mary and Lydia pass by. "You've been so all over the place with William and how you feel about him, I wasn't sure if you were happy with everything. A few weeks ago, you were crying on the floor in an ugly wedding dress because you were worried you were defrauding God."

"A lot has happened since then." My response is unintentionally coy.

"Spill the tea, but don't actually spill the tea!" Lizzy demands, laughing at her joke.

"Do you remember last week when I ran into Brad at Hilltop?" I begin. Lizzy grabs a cookie and nods vigorously. "He and William had a bit of an altercation."

"No way!" Once again, Lizzy's volume brings unwanted attention to our table. At my embarrassed stare, she lowers her volume and asks, "They had a *fight*?"

"Yeah," I pause when I notice two of our colleagues heading our way.

"This is such a lovely party, Charlotte!" Angie says. "So much classier than mine." She laughs and gives Brittney a knowing nod. Much like Lizzy and I, they are best friends brought together by working in the high school trenches.

"I guess since you'll be a preacher's wife, strippers were out of the question," Brittney says.

"William was adamant about that," Lizzy pipes up. "Besides, Charlotte's not a stripper kind of gal." I bristle a little at her insinuation that I'm boring or a prude, but I smile politely and let it go.

"I'll be sure to have them at yours," I reply, causing the three of them to laugh lightly. After Brittney and Angie walk away, I resume telling Lizzy about Brad and William's fight.

"Brad came by to talk to William about why he rejected his membership application. It started off peaceful until Brad said some...unkind things about me." I won't repeat them to Lizzy. I refuse to gives his insults any more power over me. "William did not appreciate that, so he and Brad got into it."

"I can't picture Reverend Collins beating up anyone," Lizzy says, shaking her head. "Is he okay?"

"He's got some bruising on his ribs from where Brad kicked him. He says he's fine, though." It must not hurt too bad considering how easily he lifted me and ate me out the next day. My face colors bright pink at the memory.

"Wow. That's crazy!" She takes a sip of her tea. "That's also really hot."

"Hey now, that's my fiancé you're talking about," I jokingly chide her. "But yeah, I wasn't terribly mad about it." Someone needed to put Brad in his place; I'm just sad it wasn't me.

"Speaking of not being mad about it," Lizzy wiggles her eyebrows at me. "I couldn't help noticing you didn't come home the last time you went to William's for a date. Does this mean you caved and actually stayed the night?"

"I did," I admit. I hadn't planned on caving to William's desire that I sleep over that night. I hadn't planned on a lot of things in our relationship. Waking up next to him was actually kind of nice. I hadn't slept over with a guy since Brad. That level of trust, that willingness to be that relaxed and safe with a man, is something I never thought I would have again. And how could I say no after a massage and an incredible orgasm?

"So does that mean you love him?" She's hanging on my every word like I'm a suspenseful thriller.

"I..." I want to say yes, I want to admit to Lizzy what I can't admit to myself. William has worked his way deep into my heart against my will. He somehow snuck past the security guards and made himself right at home. He does seem to care for me, he admitted as much when he said he needed me for himself, not for his job. Ever since he came to my audition, he's changed, he's become more attentive, more involved, and more vulnerable. Does he love me?

"You do! I knew it!" She gives me a quick hug and squeezes me tight before letting go. "I knew even before you two met that you would be good together!" Lizzy squeals.

"How did you know that? Did God tell you?" I sound like a crazy person, yet I have to know how she knew.

"Um, I don't think so, but it was such a strong feeling, maybe He did." She shrugs. "Why do you ask?"

"I think God spoke to me. He told me to trust Him when it comes to William. Ever since then, things have been different." My admission is freeing, I can't lie.

"That's so cool!" Lizzy is practically bouncing in her seat. "I think that proves you're meant to be with William."

"What if...what if I'm wrong? What if he breaks my heart like Brad did?" My voice wavers at the thought of that possibility.

"William is nothing like Brad," Lizzy assures me. She puts her hand on my shoulder and looks me in the eyes. "It's going to be okay, Charlotte. It's like that song about letting love back in your heart, or something like that. You just have to let go and let God."

"Since when did you of all people become a relationship expert?" I joke, sniffing lightly to avoid letting a tear fall down my cheek.

"Well, I have been with Darcy for two months now, so I think that counts for something." She smiles sheepishly. "He's coming with me to your wedding. I can't remember if I told you that or not."

"You didn't. That's awesome, Lizzy! I'm glad things are going well with you two." I smile approvingly at her and glance around Hilltop's banquet room which Lizzy has transformed into a lovely tea party atmosphere, complete with fine China tea cups, bright pink roses, lace tablecloths, and snacks galore.

If someone had told me six months ago that I would be getting married this summer, I would have thought they needed a psychiatric evaluation. But now? Each day that passes, marrying William makes more and more sense. If only my stupid heart would get the memo and fully let me be happy.

"Lizzy." Kitty's voice interrupts my thoughts and my heart-to-heart with Lizzy.

"What now?" Lizzy's tone is annoyed and for good reason. She's done a fantastic job of throwing this party for me and her youngest sister has been a fly in the ointment the whole time.

"Mary is talking about the Marvel Cinematic Universe to your teacher friends and making everyone uncomfortable." Kitty gestures towards the wall where Mary has literally cornered Brittney and Angie. They keep glancing towards the exit, too polite to tell Mary to go away.

"Fine, I'll get her to stop." Lizzy groans and walks in their direction. Kitty takes her seat and sidles up to me.

"I guess your students will have to start calling you Mrs. Collins now," she says. Kitty was a student of mine two years ago and it was very hard for her to not call me Charlotte the whole time.

"Yeah. It will be an adjustment." I sigh and eat a dainty cupcake in one un-ladylike bite.

"I thought you might quit since Reverend Collins is loaded. Don't most teachers hate their job?" She crosses her arms and gives me a conspiratorial glance. "I know you do. My class was awful."

"Actually, I don't hate my job. There are hard days and difficult students, but it brings me joy. William's money is just a bonus, not a reason to throw away my years of education and experience."

"Sure," Kitty says, rolling her eyes. "If I married a rich man, I'd never work again. That would be so nice! I could just spend his money and be a pampered princess." She sighs and rests her chin in her hands.

"Oh, dear sweet Kitty," I shake my head at her youthful dream. "Does this mean you're not going to college?"

"I'm definitely going to college," she says, perking up. "Where else am I going to find a rich man?" We both laugh at her naïve confidence.

"What's so funny?" Lizzy returns to our table with Mary pouting behind her.

"Teenage dreams," I reply.

When the party ends, Lizzy insists that I go on home and leave her and her sisters to clean up. She literally shoos me out of the room when I start collecting the dishes from the tables.

Over the past week, I've moved most of my stuff out of our apartment and into William's house. The only things left behind are my bed, dresser, bookcase, and enough clothes for the last week of school.

When I start my car, I set the radio to my favorite Christian station and leave the parking lot with the setting sun in my rearview mirror. Right as I turn onto the highway, the song changes and I turn up the volume when I recognize the opening chords.

"You're shattered, like you've never been before..." It's the song Lizzy was talking about, the very song she referenced when she told me that everything with William is going to be okay.

"Tell your heart to beat again, close your eyes and breathe it in. Yesterday's an open door, you don't live there anymore..." By the end of the chorus, I have to pull over and park because my tears have made it impossible to see the road.

This is no coincidence. This is God.

I have long believed in the power of worship through song, and now that's come back to me twice. First in the "Trust in You" song I sang for the audition, and now in this song, this specific song that has the right words to reach inside of my heart and wiggle that last loose piece into place.

As I sit there, parked on the side of the highway, with the song washing over me, tears streaming down my face, I'm overcome with the love I was holding back for William. He is good, he is safe, he is right. He's healing me, not breaking me. I love him.

When the song ends, I wipe my tears away and text Lizzy. I won't be home tonight after all.

Chapter 22
William

After gaming for three hours, its' safe to say this has probably been the lamest bachelor party any of these guys have ever been to. Josiah and Charlotte's brothers have been good sports about the whole thing and haven't complained at all, which I appreciate. The lack of nudity and alcohol was disappointing to Nick and Eddie at first, but Rob and Josiah took it in stride.

"What time will the girls' party be over?" Josiah asks as he scarfs down more chips and salsa.

"I think she said it will be done around eight. Why?" I cringe at all the crumbs now littering my floor. Five guys demolishing snacks can be very messy.

"That way I know when to leave." He slurps his soda and burps very loudly.

"Nice!" Nick yells from the corner where he's playing *Mortal Kombat*. Despite being the oldest of Charlotte's brothers, he's somehow the least mature.

"She's not coming here tonight," I clarify. As much as I want to see Charlotte, I'm letting her choose how often she visits.

"Does she think you'll be too tired from all your nerdy activities today to hang out?" Josiah laughs and almost drops the guacamole.

"Maybe." I sigh heavily. "I think with the wedding next week she's just enjoying being away from me as much as possible." After telling Charlotte that I want her for me and all but declaring my love for her, I've hardly seen her. She claims the last two weeks of the school year are the craziest and I believe her, so I'm trying not to take her distance to heart.

"I'm sure that's not true." Josiah stands up and more chip crumbs fall to the floor. "Hey, Rob!"

"Yeah?" Rob appears from around the corner with a sandwich in his hands.

"You and Charlotte are real tight, right?"

"Yeah, I'd say so. What's up?" He enters the room and takes a seat across from us.

"What sort of vibe are you getting from her about how she feels about William?" Josiah's question has me sputtering in embarrassment.

"Rob, you don't have to answer that," I tell him, my eyes begging him to not respond. He knows for sure how Charlotte feels and if she doesn't love me, I'll be devastated. I'd rather live my life with her in ignorance than despair.

"As her future husband, you should already know how she feels about you," Rob says, both answering and not answering Josiah's impertinent question.

"You would think so. He's clueless for some reason." Josiah rolls his eyes at me.

"You're making me sound like an idiot," I retort. "I know she likes me to some degree; I just don't know if she loves me."

"She can be hard to read at times, I'll admit," Rob says, finishing off his sandwich. "And that's, you know, because of the Brad situation. Despite her saying she's only in this to make Mom happy and this is all some kind of weird arrangement, I think she's lying to herself." Rob's words douse my heart in hope.

"Why do you say that?" I can't help asking.

"When she tells us you're coming over for family dinner, she's genuinely happy. When she thinks no one's looking, she's looking at you and smiling. When Mom asks her wedding questions, she blushes and gets a little nervous." He glances between Josiah and I before continuing. "If she doesn't love you, she's doing a really great job of pretending that she is."

"There you go!" Josiah shouts like his team just scored a touchdown in overtime. "Now, we've been here long enough. Call your woman and tell her to get her fine ass over here so you can tell each other how you feel."

"Gross, man." Rob pretends to gag. "That's not how I would have put it, but I second Josiah's suggestion. Eddie, Nick, let's go." Eddie and Nick reluctantly leave their games and head out the door with Rob.

"Thanks, man." I give Josiah a quick half hug before he goes.

"Anytime. Sorry about the lame party," he says, gesturing back at my game room. "I didn't think Cat would approve of us having a real party, even if we went way out of town to have it."

"That's alright. You and I both know I'm not a stripper kind of guy." I shrug.

"The look on your face would have been priceless, though!" He laughs. "See you tomorrow."

I clean up the guys' mess before I sit back down and call Charlotte. I have a housecleaning service for weekly stuff, but that doesn't mean I'm going to live like a slob in the meantime.

"Hello?" Her sweet voice sends a shiver through my body.

"Hey, um…" Suddenly, I'm very nervous. I grip the phone tighter so my sweaty palm doesn't drop it. "How was the party?"

"It was nice. How was yours?"

"Good." This is way more awkward than it normally is. I know why I'm being weird, but why is she being so formal in response? Usually, she would have made a joke by now about how lame my party must have been.

"Good."

Silence.

"Is it okay if I come over tonight?" Her words take me completely by surprise. I was going to ask her to do that very thing.

"Sure, that's fine. When were you thinking?"

"Now. I'm actually in your driveway." She's *here*?

"Yeah, come on in." As difficult as it is, I somehow manage to keep my tone nonchalant. That doesn't prevent my heart from pounding when the front door opens and Charlotte's heels click on the hardwood floor.

"William?" She calls out.

"I'm in the living room." I wipe my gross palms on my pants to try and dry them off quickly. Why am I so nervous? I'm never nervous with Charlotte. Rob says she loves me and I know I love her. All that's left is to verbalize our feelings.

Charlotte enters the living room and all I can think is: *Fuck, she's beautiful.* Her deep brown hair is half up and the rest is wavy down her shoulders. My bracelet is on her wrist and the memory of when I gave that to her gets my cock rock hard. A white and gold sash hangs across her chest that reads "Bachelorette." Her dress is the same green as her eyes. I love how it hugs the top of her thick thighs before flaring out to reach her knees.

"Hi." She stands in front of me with a nervous smile.

"Hi." I move to rise from the couch, but she holds her hand out to tell me to stay seated. "I didn't expect you would want to come over tonight."

"I didn't expect it either," she says, her eyes shining as if she's been crying.

"Are you okay?"

"Yeah, I'm actually really, really good." Her smile turns playful and I'm hopelessly confused. "I know you didn't have strippers at your party, and I appreciate that," she says, a mischievous look in her eyes. "The only woman stripping for you should be me."

Before I have a chance to fully register what she means, she pulls her phone from her purse and starts playing a song. After setting it down, she shakes her hands as if to settle her nerves. Is she actually going to...oh, yes, she is!

Charlotte begins moving to the song in a very seductive fashion. Her hands run up and through her hair as her hips sway to the beat. One hand reaches behind her back and she turns around so I can watch her unzip her dress very slowly. I'm so close to reaching up and yanking it off of her, so it's a good thing she spins back around and finishes it out of view.

Her face is a deep pink and she's looking at me like a cheetah hunting its prey. When the song hits the chorus, she slides the dress off her shoulders and down to the floor. She steps out of the dress and struts towards me, her perky breasts lifted up high in a white lacey bra. I reach forward to touch her and she playfully smacks my hands away.

"Charlotte," I growl. "Let me touch you." My command has no effect. She simply smiles sweetly at me and turns around so her round ass is in my face. "Fuck!"

She lowers her hips until her ass is just grazing my restrained erection. As her hips swirl on my lap, I can't help grabbing her neck and holding her in place.

"I can't finish if you don't let go, Sir William," she informs me, her voice low and teasing. She pulls my hand from her neck and stands back up. I'm torn between taking her here and now and letting her finish her little striptease show.

As she bends over in front of me and reaches down to touch her toes, her panties ride up between her cheeks and I'm ready to explode.

She reaches behind her once more to unhook her bra. When she turns around to face me, her hands are holding her tits and she's stroking her hard nipples. My breathing is heavy, my hands are aching, and my pants are suddenly way too fucking tight.

Only after the last chorus does she hook her thumbs into the sides of her panties and slide them down her legs. She giggles as she throws them at me and then runs down the hall. Oh, she wants to play? I can play.

I run after her, stripping my own clothes as I do so. By the time I make it to the bedroom, I'm just as naked as she is. She's laying on the bed on her stomach with her chin in her hands and her feet up in the air.

"Did you enjoy the show?" She smiles all innocently as if she wasn't the cause of my intense need right now.

"Oh, Lady Charlotte, you can strip for me anytime." I grab a condom from my dresser and quickly slide it on. "Right now, I have to punish you for not letting me touch you."

"Oh no!" She pretends to be scared. "Not that! Anything but that." Her mischievous smile gives away her secret desire to be controlled, manipulated, and punished by me.

I reach into the nightstand and pull out a pair of nipple clamps. "What's your safe word?"

"Waffles." Her eyes light up as she eagerly sits up and gives me direct access to her tits.

"Good girl," I praise her eagerness and compliance. As each clamp grabs hold of her nipples, she lets out a sharp whimper and bites her bottom lip. "Turn around."

She does so quickly, pressing her chest to the bed and raising her ass high. Reaching back into the nightstand, I grab a padded leather paddle.

"What else do you have in there?" Charlotte asks, wide-eyed at my collection of toys.

"Is this not enough, Lady Charlotte?" I growl as I run the paddle lightly up her backside.

"It is if you say it is, Sir William." Her obedience has my cock aching to dive deep inside of her. But first, her punishment. I pull back my hand and gently tap her ass with the paddle. I repeat the motion, each time increasing my force. Her cries of pleasure and pain are almost too much to bear as I hold off on giving her what we both want.

"Your ass is so pretty when it's all pink for me," I compliment her and she moans in response. I grab her hips and run my tongue up her inner thighs. The way her body shakes and shivers in response is beyond delicious. When my mouth reaches her cunt, she's dripping with arousal. I lick and tease her clit until she's crying out my name, begging me to fuck her.

"Have you learned your lesson?" I ask, climbing onto the bed behind her and placing my ready cock at her soaked entrance.

"Yes, yes, sir," she replies, her voice tight and breathy.

"Now tell me something, Lady Charlotte. Who do you belong to?" When I called her earlier, my plan had been to confess my love for her and enter a new level of our relationship. Her stripping had put that plan temporarily on hold. So, for now, I'll settle for her acknowledging that she is mine and mine alone.

"You, Sir William. I belong to you." Right as she finishes speaking, I thrust myself into her and delight in her cry of pleasure when I've filled her up. With so much buildup, it's hard to not immediately let myself go. Instead of rapid-fire thrusting, I decrease my speed and focus on finding just the right spot inside her warm pussy to make her body implode.

"OH! There, there!" She cries out, her hands fisting the sheets as she screams into the mattress. "I'm, I'm..." And there she goes, her body shuddering around my cock, her walls squeezing me so tightly I end up coming right along with her. I grip her hips so firmly she'll bruise; fuck, I don't care. Right as I pull out, her lower body relaxes down onto the bed.

"You're so beautiful," I tell her, leaning down and kissing her cheek. She smiles at me and her face gets even redder before a small tear slides down her face. "What's wrong?"

"You've said that before, but I don't believe you," she says, rolling onto her back and sitting upright against the headboard. The heart charms on the nipple clamps dangle wildly from her perky tits, so I quickly unclamp them and toss them to the side.

Grabbing her chin, I turn her face towards me and kiss her lips softly. "You are beautiful, gorgeous, dazzling, ravishing, stunning, bewitching, and fucking irresistible." I take the corner of the sheet and wipe away her tears. "And you know what makes you so beautiful?"

"What?" She sniffs and looks genuinely curious.

"This," I point to her head. "And this," I say, pointing to her chest. "You are the whole package. God made no mistakes when He made you. And I thank Him every day that you are in my life, that I get to grow old with you, that I get to make you smile and laugh, that I get to have children with you..." Oh, that might be too far. We haven't talked at all about having kids. I clear my throat before I continue. "I'm so very blessed," I conclude.

"Thank you," Charlotte says. Her smile is tentative, yet I'm reassured that she believes all my praise. "While we're on the topic of how we look," she pauses and traces her finger over my chest tattoo. "This is hot, number one, but I know there's a story here. Will you tell me?"

She cuddles up next to me and I cover us both in the sheets. Might as well get comfortable. It's a long story.

Chapter 23
Charlotte

"Like I told you before, Mom left when I was about sixteen. Saying I was depressed after she left is an understatement. I was devastated. She was the loving one, the kind one, the one who asked me how my day was and listened to my problems. She was everything my dad wasn't, everything he couldn't be." William brushes his hand through his hair. "A week after she left, I wrecked my car, completely totaled it. By the time they got me to the hospital, they declared me dead."

"Oh!" I cover my mouth to hide my shock. This is not where I thought his tattoo story would begin. Instead of asking questions, I nod for him to continue.

"I was dead for seventy four seconds before they brought me back. When I woke up, I was surrounded by church members and Dad was praying loudly at the foot of the bed. A few people fainted when I began to speak. Dad said, 'It's a miracle!' and then I passed out. There was a lot of internal bleeding and some broken bones that needed healing, of course. I was in the hospital for almost a month."

"That's a long time." It sounds dumb, but it's the only thing I can think to say right now.

"I kept busy with school work and reading to pass the time, so it wasn't too bad. The worst part was how Dad never visited me by himself. He always had a group of people from church with him. I became his "miracle" and his proof that prayer works." He rolls his eyes. "Once he had milked my resurrection for all it was worth, his attention to me decreased." William shrugs. "There's only so long you can trot out your one trick pony before people stop caring."

"He used your accident to get donations for the church? Is that what you're saying?" I'm shocked and hurt on William's behalf. "That's cruel and wrong!"

"Out of all the things he did, that was the cruelest." William takes off his glasses and rubs his eyes. "Dad wasn't perfect, but boy did he pretend to be. It wasn't until Mom had been gone for three months that he finally told people about it."

"Where did they think your mom was all that time?" What kind of man uses his son's pain to make a profit? What kind of man lies about his wife's whereabouts for months? The kind of man whose wife leaves him, I guess.

"The excuses varied from visiting relatives to missionary work overseas. With her painted as the villain, he used personal tragedy to his benefit again. People felt so bad for the abandoned pastor, they gave even more money to the church." He puts his glasses back on and wraps an arm around my shoulders.

"Wow, I don't know what to say about that. Your dad doesn't sound like the most moral person, much less someone who should be a pastor." I feel so judgy for saying that, but it's the truth. No one is perfect, not even God's "employees," yet shouldn't they be setting the moral high bar for their people?

"And don't even get me started on all the sympathy sex he got from women at church. He didn't know I knew about that. He told me he was visiting all these single women just to pray with them." William shudders in disgust.

"Wow. That's...that's gross. I'm so sorry you had to go through that." As I'm piecing together William's story, something doesn't add up. "So, you got Lazarus tattooed on your chest because you came back from the dead like he did, right?"

"Yeah, pretty much," he nods and doesn't make eye contact with me as I scoot up to look directly into his eyes. "I know I check my watch a lot and that's probably annoying, but I do it because I feel like I'm on borrowed time."

"That's very poetic," I begin. "But I don't think that's the whole story. Lazarus was brought back by Jesus because it wasn't his time. How do you know that accident wasn't your time? Car accidents are a pretty common way for people to die."

"Because it wasn't an accident," he admits, his blue eyes finally looking back into my green ones. "I tried to kill myself."

I can't hide the gasp that escapes my lips at his admission. "Oh, William!" I wrap my arms around his strong chest and squeeze him tight. He rests his face on my shoulder and dampness seeps through my shirt as tears fall from his eyes. "I'm so glad it didn't work. I'm so glad you're here. I'm so glad you came back." Soon, I'm crying too and we're just a mess of tears and sniffles wrapped up in expensive cotton sheets.

"In my previous relationships," he whispers into my shoulder. "When they asked about my tattoo, I made up a story about being born again. You and Josiah are the only people who know the truth. And he only knows because he kept bugging me about it." He attempts a weak chuckle as he lifts his head.

With his chest bare in front of my face, I kiss each letter of his tattoo. "William, I..." I take a deep breath. "I'm so sorry about all that you've gone through. You're so strong and good hearted. I couldn't ask for a better man to have as my husband."

William smiles tenderly. "Even if it's all just for show?"

"It's not, not really," I admit. "At least not for me anymore." Here goes nothing, or rather, here goes everything.

He places a hand on my cheek and looks at me intently. "Charlotte, are you saying what I think you're saying?"

"Depends on what you think I'm saying," I try and joke to lighten the mood but he sees right through it.

"I love you, too." At his words, all the ragged edges of my heart smooth out. Everything clicks into place like the snap of lock on a chain link fence. He presses his lips to mine and I'm lost in his kiss. It's the same way he kissed me after he heard me sing. Is that when he knew? Has he loved me since then? His hands move down my body, caressing my curves with his fingertips.

Suddenly, he wraps his arms around my back and just holds me there, resting his chin in the crook of my neck. I'm so protected, so safe, so loved. There's nothing between us, neither physically nor emotionally now. He's healing me from Brad's mistreatment and I'm doing my best to give him the love he's been lacking in his life for so many years.

"So, kids, huh?" I ask, both to lighten the mood and discuss the thing we've been avoiding addressing.

William leans back and gives me a cheeky grin. "I said what I said."

"Well since you're the one giving birth, I guess you get to make that decision," I say, keeping my tone lighthearted.

"Of course," he replies, shrugging like it's no big deal to pop out babies. "But not yet. I want time with just you first. There's still so much we need to learn about each other before taking on the responsibility of parenting together."

"I agree." That's one of the things I like about William; he's practical. Even when emotions are involved, he's level headed. We just admitted we love each other. Kids should probably be later on down the road.

"Now, we have church in the morning, so we should probably get ready for bed," William says, sliding out of bed to dispose of the condom and clean up.

"What makes you think I'm staying over?" I ask as I watch his sexy body walk towards the bathroom.

He turns back and says, "It's not staying over when it's your house, too."

As he disappears into the bathroom, I fire back, "Not for seven more days!"

***

The next week drags by, which makes sense because that's how the last week of school always goes. Both teachers and students are just going through the motions to get to graduation day and onto summer break.

I spend the days corralling hyperactive teenagers and my evenings moving the rest of my belongings into William's, I mean, our house. Lizzy alternates between being happy for me and crying because I'm moving out.

By the time Saturday afternoon rolls around, my anxiety is the main thing keeping me from passing out from exhaustion. I don't know where Lizzy has gotten her energy from, but I wish she would share some with me.

"Okay, now that your hair is done, the makeup artist is next," Lizzy says, checking each step of the day off of her list as it happens. I'm sitting in a tall chair, wrapped in a pink robe with the word "Bride" on the back, my hair has been curled and coiffed to perfection, and it's taking all that I have to keep my cool. I'm not a girly girl by any means, so all this attention to my physical appearance is weird and uncomfortable.

"Do I have to have my make up done?" I ask Lizzy as I tap the arm rests of the chair with my freshly manicured nails. "I think I've suffered enough."

"Yes!" She looks at me utterly horrified. "Oh, good, here she is!" A tall blonde woman with legs for days marches over to me with cases and cases of torture implements. She opens one and pulls out jars and jars of skin colored paste.

"Relax," she tells me. "You're in good hands."

I close my eyes and start thinking of animals that live in the rainforest. Then I think about animals that live in the mountains. I've pretty much run out of animals when she finally says, "Done!"

I don't really recognize the woman in the mirror. When I blink, she blinks, so it must be me. Growing up, I always knew I wasn't the prettiest of my friends. Any attempt I made at using fancy make up failed, so I didn't bother with it all. I was always the "makeover" friend in high school. They enjoyed dressing me up, slathering me with make-up, and "improving" my overall appearance. I was their doll. At first, it was fun to see what they would do. Then I realized they were changing me so they weren't embarrassed to be seen with me.

I imagine this make-up situation is so that Cat isn't ashamed to have me as William's bride, the other half of the "face of Hilltop." Whatever. I just have to get through today and then I can be myself again.

Once the makeup artist is gone, Lizzy helps me get into my wedding dress. After she zips up the back, Lizzy peers around me to the full-length mirror in front of us.

"Oh, Charlotte! You look so perfect!" She really wants to hug me, but she doesn't want to wrinkle my dress. Instead, she grabs my hands and squeezes them tight. "William is a very lucky man. I hope he knows that."

"Thanks for all your help, Lizzy. If not for you, this day never would have happened."

"Who would have thought me going on a date with my pastor would lead to you getting married?" She laughs.

"God certainly works in mysterious ways," I reply. At the at moment, the door opens and Mom walks in.

"Oh, Charlotte!" She places her hand to her mouth and starts crying. Lizzy runs to her with a box of tissues. "Thank you, dear." Mom attempts to compose herself as she walks over to me.

"Hi, Mom." I smile affectionately at her and try not to cry myself. I do not want to have all this makeup redone.

"You look so lovely, and so very happy!" She dabs at her eyes with a tissue. "It's a bittersweet day when your oldest gets married. You're in good hands with Reverend William. I trust him to love and support you no matter what. You will be such a good wife, and one day, a good mother." Her smile reaches her watery eyes and I have to look away for a moment before I start tearing up.

"Mom, you're going to make me cry!" I laugh and pull her in for a hug. Wrinkles on my dress be damned.

"Okay, Mrs. Lucas, the wedding starts soon so go ahead and wait by the sanctuary doors. Remember, Rob is walking you in." Lizzy gently leads Mom out of the room before my tears can make a break for it.

The wedding march music begins, so Lizzy and I hustle to our spots in line. When I turn the corner and Dad is standing there waiting for me, I have to stop and take a deep breath. He has such pride and love in his eyes. To him, I'm still his little girl, the one who made him dress up like a princess for tea parties, the one who made sure his pants matched his shirt before he left for work, and the one who picked flowers for his work desk.

"Don't you look beautiful," Dad says, offering me his arm. The tears are welling up in his eyes as one of my own escapes down my cheek.

"Thanks, Dad. You look very spiffy yourself." This gets a huge smile out of him. We watch everyone walk in before us. Once Lizzy reaches the altar, it's our turn to walk down the aisle.

Chapter 24
William

The last person I expected to visit me in my dressing room before my wedding was Cat. Yet, here she is, tying my tie and looking unexpectedly emotional.

"I know how to tie a tie, Cat," I point out. She glares up at me and purses her lips.

"Good for you." She pins the tie to my shirt and steps back to admire her handiwork. "Josiah!" She hollers for him even though he's not ten feet away from us.

"Yeah?" He turns towards her, trying to hide his annoyance.

"Do you have the rings?"

"Yep," he says, patting his shirt pocket for emphasis.

"Good. Now, make yourself scarce. I need a moment with William." Cat's request catches us both off guard. Josiah looks at me like a deer in headlights, mouths, "Sorry!" and exits the room.

"Now, William," Cat begins. She places her hands behind her back and starts pacing in front of me. "This is a momentous day, not only for you, but for Hilltop, for all your father worked for."

I cringe when she brings up Dad. When I was younger, I used to wonder if the two of them had some type of romantic relationship. That thought didn't last long once I saw them yelling at each other one day over the new carpet in the sanctuary.

"As you know, I have no children of my own. And I know I've been hard on you, but that is because you are like a son to me." This is the closest I've ever been to hearing Cat get sentimental. It's weird. "This marriage will be good for you. Our membership applications have increased ever since you announced you were getting married three months ago. Imagine how much higher they'll be once you are actually married!" And there it is. Cat is all about the bottom line, and that's a good thing since the bottom line is her job. It's just not the part of Hilltop I like to think about that much.

"Yep. Good news all around," I reply sarcastically.

"You've done well so far with your image. Now is not the time to let it slip. Remember what's at stake." Her previously loving tone has turned sour. Just when I think Cat has a heart after all, she proves me wrong. Fortunately, Josiah returns right then to let us know it's time to go in for the ceremony. Cat nods at us and takes her leave.

"What was that about?" Josiah asks, looking very curious.

"Just reminding me that I'm the cash cow, that's all." I roll my eyes and rub the back of my neck.

"Like I've been telling you, man, it's time for a change. I don't know what it's going to take for you to believe me." Josiah and I walk through a side door into the sanctuary and take our places up front with Mateo, my assistant pastor. If Josiah hadn't been my best man, I would have asked him to officiate. Mateo is taking over while Charlotte and I are away on our honeymoon. He's a good guy, if a little bit condescending at times.

When the music starts, I turn my attention to the back doors. My heart is pounding in my ears and my palms are becoming a sweaty mess. After Lizzy walks over to her spot, Mateo motions for everyone to rise and the music takes on a different chord.

"Here comes the bride," Josiah whispers to me as he gives me a steadying pat on the back.

All eyes are on Charlotte as she and Edward walk down the aisle. She's smiling nervously; her anxiety must be bouncing around inside her like a wacky beach ball. When he places her hand in mine, she takes a deep breath as she steps towards me. Her lips are a bright, rose pink and her eyes are heavily made up, but she's still my Charlotte underneath.

After the ceremony and the thousands of posed pictures inside the church, outside the church, with family, with guests, with just us, we finally make it to the reception in the banquet hall. I haven't even had a chance to talk to Charlotte today other than our vows and every time I try to get her alone, someone comes along to congratulate us.

It's not until our first dance that we get some time to ourselves.

"How are you feeling, Mrs. Collins?" I ask as we sway on the dance floor, trying to ignore all the guests staring right at us.

"Anxious, but happy." She smiles at me and my heart melts. "I don't like being the center of attention," she admits.

"Just a few more hours and we can go home."

"Good," she sighs and rests her head on my chest. I kiss the top of her head and thank God for Charlotte, my wife, my love, my everything.

The only bittersweet part of the evening comes when Charlotte leaves my side to dance with Edward. At first, she wasn't going to have the traditional father-daughter dance since I can't dance with my mom. I assured her I would be fine and she should have her dance.

Now that I'm watching them together, my heart aches as I wonder where Mom even is. There's no way she doesn't know today's my wedding day. It was posted everywhere. The local news even did a story about it where they interviewed Cat, Charlotte, and I about it. It was another lovely PR opportunity for Cat to talk about Hilltop and seek "generous contributions."

As Edward spins Charlotte around, I can't help noticing the small tears in his eyes. Charlotte is close to tears herself; it's been a very emotional day. When the song ends, I hand her my pocket square so she can dab her eyes. The happy, grateful look in her eyes sets my heart fluttering like hummingbird wings. She grabs my hand and says, "I have a surprise for you."

She gives a thumbs up to the DJ and he starts playing another song, a very sappy song about mothers and sons.

"What's going on?" I ask as she gently drags me toward the middle of the dance floor.

"My mom is your mom." She gestures for Eleanor to come forward from the crowd. "You deserve a mother and son dance." Before I can protest, Charlotte walks away, leaving me standing awkwardly with Eleanor. She places one hand on my shoulder and the other in my left hand as she guides us through the dance.

"I'm so glad Charlotte found you, Reverend William. We were beginning to give up hope she'd ever find anyone, to be honest." Eleanor's words are punctuated with sniffles. Her eyes are red from crying happy tears all day.

"Sorry it took me so long to show up," I joke. "I appreciate you taking me into your family."

"What's one more son?" She laughs and pulls her hand away to dab a balled-up tissue to her weepy eyes. "Just call me Mom, no more of this Eleanor business."

"As long as you stop calling me Reverend, you have a deal." I smile at her amused expression. The song ends without her completely breaking down into tears, so that's a relief. After a very prolonged hug, she releases me and makes her way back into the crowd.

As Charlotte approaches me, I can't help pulling her close and kissing her deeply, much to the approval of the clapping and cheering guests.

"Thank you." I'm touched by her endless thoughtfulness and selfless actions. Her surprise means more to me than she'll ever know.

"Don't mention it."

The moment passes all too soon and we're right back to the schedule of events, resuming with toasts from Josiah and Elizabeth, which make both Charlotte and I misty-eyed. I smear only a little bit of frosting on her cheek after we cut the cake, and I grin wildly when she shoves her half all over my mouth.

The night rolls on with a constant barrage of inappropriate questions from guests about when we're having kids and awkward jokes about "enjoying the honeymoon." Eventually, we make our grand exit and arrive home around eleven p.m.

"You can't be serious," Charlotte says with a cute smile after I open the front door and hold out my arms towards her.

"I'm very serious," I reply, quickly reaching around her and scooping her up into my arms. The skirt of her dress drapes over my arms and almost to the floor. "What kind of husband would I be if I didn't carry my wife over the threshold?"

"A smart one!" She squeals as I step into the house and put her back on the ground. "I cannot believe you did that. You could have broken a rib or strained a muscle."

I step right behind her and start unzipping her dress. "It would have been worth it," I murmur into her ear. Her dress falls to the floor and I kiss her shoulders reverently. She leans back against me and sighs as her stress melts away. It's at this moment Charlotte's beloved felines decide to join us. They officially moved in with her last night and have made themselves at home very quickly. Tony warmed up to me immediately, but I'm going to have to work to earn Cleo's love.

They start purring around her ankles and rolling in the dress's abundance of tulle. "Hi, babies!" She says, laughing at their antics. Having cats in the house has been an adjustment for sure. I'm not anti-cat, but at this moment, they're not exactly wanted.

"Come with me." I take her hand and led her to the bathroom, leaving Cleo and Tony behind to play with the dress's fabric.

"Sit." She sits down on the closed toilet seat and awaits direction. I grab her face wash from the shower and a damp cloth. After squirting a little of the wash on the cloth, I gently start wiping all the makeup from her face. Her expression switches from confused to relaxed with each stroke. Closing her eyes, she allows me to wash all the powdery compounds from her face. Once I'm done, I say, "There's my girl."

Her broad smile makes my heart swell and fill my whole chest.

"Thank you, husband," she says, standing up and yanking my tie off. "You look so handsome like this, but I know you're not comfortable."

We walk to the bedroom where I shrug out of my suit jacket and hang it in the closet. Charlotte is perfectly fine leaving her dress in the living room; I prefer my things where they belong.

When I turn back around, Charlotte is there to unbutton my shirt. The moment it's undone, she slides her hands across my chest and down my back. I'm already hard from seeing her almost naked body, and her touch sends a throbbing sensation straight to my cock as I contemplate where else her hands could go.

"Are you tired?" She asks, looking up at me with half-lidded eyes.

"I can rally," I reply, sliding my hand up the back of her head and grabbing a handful of her wavy hair. "I need to make love to my wife."

"She would like that," Charlotte purrs. I pull her face to mine and kiss her fervently, with wild, reckless abandon. My free hand reaches behind her and unclasps her bra, freeing her perky tits so I can pinch and tease her gorgeous nipples.

I want to take it slow this time, show her how much I love and cherish her body, so when she reaches for my cock, I gently push her hand away. "Not yet," I whisper in her ear before trailing kisses down her neck and shoulder. "Get on the bed."

She steps around me and sits on the side of the bed. I bend down and kiss her so forcefully she falls backwards, landing on the soft bedspread with a slight, "oomph." "Let's get rid of these," I say, hooking my fingers into the sides of her panties and quickly sliding them down her smooth, generous thighs. I get on my knees and place her legs over my shoulders so I can kiss her inner thighs as I journey to her center. Each kiss and intermittent bite has her quivering and moaning around me. She's getting antsy for me to reach her pussy since she keeps trying to clamp her legs around my head and force me to hurry up.

"Patience is a virtue, Lady Charlotte," I remind her as I run my tongue up her thigh and give her clit a light kiss.

"If you don't get in there right now," Charlotte warns, her breathing heavy, her voice low.

"What are you going to do? I'm in charge here," I remind her as I grip her hips with my hands, my fingertips digging into her curvy body.

"Please, Sir William, please?" She begs with one hand in my hair and the other reaching for my glasses.

"Have you been a good girl?" I ask, handing her my glasses and lowering my face to her warm, sweet cunt.

"So good, so very, very good," she replies.

"Good girls follow directions, don't they?"

"Yes?" She says hesitantly, probably wondering where this is going.

"Excellent. When I tell you to, you're going to touch yourself. Got it?" I smile at her eager nod. "Use your words, Lady Charlotte."

"Yes, Sir William." Her voice trembles with need as she moves her hand to her waist.

"Such a good fucking girl," I praise her before I start lavishing her clit with my tongue. Fuck, she tastes like perfection. No matter how often I eat her out, I can't get over how my body reacts to her scent, her flavor, her delicious little whimpers. Each "OH!" that comes out of her beautiful mouth has my balls tightening with need to be inside of her.

"William!" The way she cries my name tells me she's getting close. I pull my mouth away from her and thrust two fingers in her pussy. She gasps at the sudden intrusion then lifts her hips so I can go deeper.

"Touch yourself, Mrs. Collins." I smile approvingly as she deftly slides her hand down and into her folds. Within seconds, she's screaming my name while her body quakes and squeezes around my fingers. "My wife is so gorgeous when she comes for me." I pull out my fingers and lick them clean for no other reason than I can't help myself.

Her pleased smile and blissed out expression never fail to make me fall in love with her all over again. My wife. My love. For now and forever.

"It's your turn now," she murmurs as she returns to reality and props herself up on her elbows to give me a mischievous yet sexy smile.

"Oh, Lady Charlotte. I've only just begun."

Chapter 25
Charlotte

After spending three days touring museums, historical homes, and ancient churches, both William and I are wiped. Between overcoming jet lag and navigating a whole new country, I'm overwhelmed, but William has been an unexpectedly fabulous tour guide. When he told me he spoke French, I thought he meant he knew enough for a casual conversation. I was pleasantly surprised when he not only ordered our meals but also asked questions to the locals about the best places to see and what to do next in perfect French.

We've seen the Louvre, the Eiffel Tower, Notre-Dame, and all the other touristy places. Today, we're going to the D-Day beaches at Normandy and maybe the Lascaux Caves. There's so much history here I can practically taste it!

As I reflect on where we've been and where we're going, William stretches next to me in bed and pulls me closer to him.

"Good morning, Wife," William murmurs in my ear. I snuggle back against him and sigh contentedly.

"Good morning, Husband." We've been married all of five days, yet adjusting to thinking of William as my husband instead of my fiancé has been extremely easy. It's what he was always meant to be.

"Are you ready for a day full of historical excitement?" He teases me as he kisses my neck.

"That feels like an oxymoron, doesn't it?" I giggle in response. Both Mom and Lizzy thought I was crazy for using my honeymoon this way. They suggested beach trips to exotic locations, sunny places where time slows down and the sun sets into golden horizons. The weather here has been less than ideal with rain pouring down intermittently since we arrived, which is why we've stuck to indoor places. Waking up today, there's not a cloud in the sky, a perfect day for going to the beach and exploring ancient caves.

"I'll order room service while you get ready," William says, releasing me so I can take a shower.

"Sure you don't want to get ready with me?" I ask, standing up and giving him my best come hither look.

"Right after I order breakfast," he says, smiling playfully before reaching over and smacking my ass hard.

"Hurry up!" I grab a fresh, fluffy towel and head to the bathroom. A few minutes go by and, to my dismay, William hasn't joined me in the shower. I decide to go ahead and actually wash my hair and body while I wait for him. Even after I finish, I let the water run a little while longer before giving up entirely. Did he change his mind? That's not like him.

When I walk out of the bathroom, William is sitting on the edge of the bed staring at his phone with an extremely pissed off expression.

"What's wrong?" I ask, sitting down next to him, immediately concerned something terrible has happened.

"It's Cat," he says, looking at me apologetically. "She wants me to come back."

"We're going back in two days. What's the rush?"

"One of the members wants his kid baptized by me and he wants it done ASAP."

"Okay...is the kid dying or something?" I hate to ask such a question, but why else would this guy be in such a rush?

"No, the kid is fine. Apparently, his in-laws are in town and while they're here, he wants it done so they can be there for it."

"Tell Cat no. Mateo can do it, that's why he's there. He's the minister in charge right now." The audacity of Cat to try and end my honeymoon because a church member told her to is infuriating.

"It has to be me. My dad baptized him, so he wants me to be the one to baptize his kid." He runs his hand through his hair. "He's going to donate a lot of money to Hilltop if I do it."

"So that's it, then? Someone waves a lot of cash at Cat and you have to go running?" I stand up and pace back and forth in front of him. "This is our honeymoon, William! We've had this planned for so long! Some rich guy who can't plan his life out correctly isn't our problem!" I can't hide the frustration in my voice even though I know this isn't William's fault.

"I know!" He stands up and shouts, causing me to stop pacing. He reaches out for me and pulls me in for a hug. "I know all of these things, Charlotte. It's my job. If someone is dying at three A.M., I get the call and I go. If someone has just been diagnosed with cancer on a Tuesday afternoon, I get the call and I go. True, this isn't a life-or-death situation, but it's still part of my job."

With his arms around me, I can't deny that he's right and I'm being selfish. Just because it hadn't happened that often yet, didn't mean that his job wouldn't interrupt our lives on occasion. This is the life I signed up for, the life I chose as a preacher's wife. I have to make sacrifices whether I want to or not.

"When are we leaving?" I murmur into his chest, knowing that if I look up at his face I'll start crying.

"There's a flight heading home in four hours. That's enough time for breakfast and packing our things." He pulls back from me and tilts my chin up so I can't hide my watery eyes. "You can stay and finish the trip if you want. I won't make you leave. I know how much you were looking forward to today."

"I'm not going without you. This trip is for both of us. Maybe we can come back later and finish it? I still have most of June and all of July before the new school year begins. It's not like those places are going anywhere." I shrug my shoulders and try to sound nonchalant.

"Thank you," William says, bending his face down to kiss me. He takes his thumb and wipes away a tear that falls down my cheek.

"Room service!" A voice and a knock at the door interrupt our moment. After a quick breakfast, we pack our bags and head to the airport. As our plane flies away, I watch France recede from view and sigh deeply. Hopefully, we will be able to finish our trip later on and Cat won't keep taking William away from me.

***

Finding time for just William and I to spend together has been quite difficult since we got back home. After the impromptu baptism, William has been busy at Hilltop helping Josiah put together the Youth Group Summer Spectacular and I'm stuck working with Cat to finalize all the details of the blood drive next month. Every time I have a moment to myself, Cat finds me and puts me to work.

"How are you ever going to keep up with all of this once school starts back?" Cat asks me one particularly busy Thursday afternoon.

"I'll manage," I retort. I refuse to let her be right about the workload I'm taking on as William's wife.

"It's a good thing you didn't get the spot in the worship band. There's no way you'd have time for that past the summer." Her reminder of my failed audition stings. From time to time, I've wondered if Cat sabotaged my chance at singing for the band. That would be crazy...right?

"Yeah, I suppose so," I reluctantly agree.

"Now, this blood drive of yours is costing Hilltop a pretty penny, so this better even out in the books with member donations and new member applications." Cat's threat is punctuated by her nails tapping quickly on a calculator with huge buttons next to her laptop.

"It's more about helping the community, not about the money," I remind her. It drives me nuts that money seems to be the only thing on her mind, William's too, come to think of it.

"Sure it is," she scoffs. "Did you remember to pay the caterer for the refreshments?"

"Oh, I thought you said you were going to do that." I could have sworn Cat said she would do that last week. I even checked it off my To Do list that she had it covered.

"Do I have to do everything around here?" Cat moans as she pulls out a massive checkbook from her desk drawer. "Did you at least remember to check with Noelia about the decorations for the blood drive?" Cat asks, giving me a condescending smirk.

"No, I'm about to go do that." I pick up my handy dandy clipboard and rise from the table, happy to have an excuse to get away from her. "I'll be right back."

Once I'm out of her sight, I take my time walking down the hall to Noelia's office. I plop down in the chair across from her desk and sigh loudly.

"She lives!" Noelia jokes. "I thought Cat would have killed you with work by now."

"This can't be normal," I bemoan, laying my clipboard on her desk.

"Close my door, would you?" Noelia asks. I eagerly comply. "It's not normal. All the things Cat has you doing are usually done by her or other people. She's putting some of her workload on you."

"I knew it!" I bet that's the real reason why she wanted William to get married, so she could get some free labor.

"Yeah, she's got you running ragged around here. What has William said about it?"

"He doesn't know," I admit. "He's been busy working with Josiah on the youth group thing. I've barely seen him the past two weeks." If Cat hadn't approved of me marrying William, I would think she was overworking me to keep me away from William and mess with our relationship.

"Once that's over, things should calm down around here," Noelia assures me. "Well, then there's your blood drive."

"I so regret planning that right now. I'm so overwhelmed by everything." This is the first moment I've had to breathe all day and my anxiety is starting to catch up to me. My chest is starting to tighten, so I put my head between my knees and take several deep breaths.

"Hey, it's going to be okay," Noelia says as she comes around her desk and sits in the chair next to me. She places her hand on my back to comfort me. "One thing at a time. What's next on your list?"

"Decorations for the drive," I say, sitting back up and grabbing my clipboard. Noelia smiles and draws a big check next to that particular item on my list.

"They arrived this morning."

"Finally! There's still a whole week before the drive, but I was getting nervous." The burden on my shoulders lightens by ten percent.

"You should tell Cat you need a day off. This is your break from your actual job. You need to have some time to enjoy it." Noelia's words sound so nice.

"I don't think Cat would approve." I shake my head and stand up. "Speaking of, I should probably get back to her before she starts looking for me."

"Between you and me, Cat might be in charge of everything, but William is the real boss around here. This is his church. Maybe he should remind her of that."

"Maybe. Thanks, Noelia." I don't have the heart to correct her and explain that Cat's the one pulling the strings; William's just the pretty face bringing in the money. As I take my time walking back to Cat, I take a detour to William's office. There's a good chance he's not even there, but I need to see him.

His door is ajar, so I walk on in. Sadly, he's not here, though it looks like he was here recently. His computer screen is lit up and his chair is pushed back from his desk. I wonder what he's working on.

Sitting down at his desk, I can't help scrolling through his sermon for this week. It's much different than usual, but in a good way. It doesn't read like someone paraphrasing from the Bible while reminding everyone that God loves them. It reads like someone who has a real message for his people, a message they actually need instead of another security blanket.

"Hey, stranger." William's voice pulls me from his sermon.

"William!" I smile broadly and quickly walk over to him. He wraps me in his arms and kisses me deeply. "I'm so glad you're here."

"Me too. I hate how busy I've been."

"Speaking of that," I begin. "Can you ask Cat to give me a break?"

"Sure, but why can't *you* ask her?" He raises his eyebrows questioningly.

"I'm scared of her, you know that," I reply. "I don't want her to think badly of me. She's got me doing so many things and I'm worn out."

"I thought you were just doing the blood drive?"

"That was the plan. According to Noelia, I'm basically doing Cat's work for her. I knew there would be a lot involved once we got married, but this is ridiculous."

"I see." He furrows his brows and frowns. "I'll talk to her. Your role is to support Hilltop, not work for Hilltop. She better not be taking advantage of you because she's pissed you didn't quit teaching."

"I'm supposed to go back and work out the final details of tomorrow night's concert. I just want to go home. A nap would be amazing right now." I step on my tip toes and kiss William again. And while my mind knows I need a nap, my *body* wants me to strip him down right here and now before he mercilessly pounds me into his desk.

"It really would," he admits, placing his hand on the back of my neck and nipping my bottom lip. "You go on home. I'll talk to Cat and wrap things up with Josiah for today."

"Really?" The relief in my voice is palpable. "Thank you!"

"Besides, my wife's needs are way more important than Hilltop's." He smiles suggestively. "We've both been way too busy lately. That stops now."

"I love you so much," I gush.

"And I love you so much." William's smile warms me from the inside out.

Shortly after I arrive home, he texts me to say something came up and he'll be home late. Again. I cuddle with Tony and Cleo in the bed and cry myself to sleep.

Chapter 26
William

I did so well with keeping work at work while we were engaged. However, the dam I built between home and work is now bursting at the seams. To make matters worse, Sierra decided to become a stay at home mom when her maternity leave ended and I haven't had the time to hire a new assistant. Everything I procrastinated is coming due and now poor Charlotte is getting soaked by the leaks I'm running around trying to stop.

Cat is less than pleasant when I ask her to stop putting so much work on Charlotte.

"Well, if she thinks this is bad, it's only going to get harder when she tries to do this and have a job at the same time. I'm just preparing her for later on," Cat retorts, crossing her arms and glaring at me like a disobedient toddler.

"I find it odd that she's so busy when, aside from the blood drive, all of these tasks were already someone else's job. Did you fire someone and give their work to Charlotte?" I'm frustrated by how Cat is treating Charlotte, though I keep my tone polite.

"No, we're just very busy over the summer, you know that," she snaps at me.

"I'm aware of how busy we are," I reply with a sigh. It's impossible to balance Charlotte's needs with Cat's demands.

"She knew what she signed up for, literally." Cat pauses and shakes her head. "I'm tired, too, yet the work must get done. *You* should have prepared her better for her role at Hilltop."

"I see that now," I admit begrudgingly. "She just needs a day to rest. Even God rested after creating the world." My logic falls on deaf ears.

"She can rest after the blood drive. That was her idea, after all." Cat throws up her hands and gives me an aggravated glare. I hate arguing with Cat. She makes me feel like a child with her condescending tone and demanding personality.

"Fine." That's in two weeks. Surely things can't get much worse in two weeks, right? Hopefully Charlotte will understand that I tried.

***

With the sanctuary seats cleared out and replaced with collapsible beds and medical equipment, it looks like one of those makeshift wartime hospitals from WWI. Blood drive nurses and volunteers mill about tending to the donors, checking iron, and filling out online paperwork. I was the first one to donate earlier today. Cat took pictures for the website and made a big fuss about me being a role model and a true Christian. Considering I was initially against the drive, it felt a bit hypocritical to get all that praise.

I should have been more supportive of the idea from the start. Like my father, I'm slow to change; I'd rather keep doing the same thing over and over again. As far as I can tell, Hilltop isn't broken, so why fix it? I can't deny how successful the drive is, however, as the head nurse updates the total number of donors to 458.

Looking at my watch, I realize it's time for Charlotte to donate. I told her I would be there to keep her calm since she was anxious about it. When I reach her, she's already on the table with a needle in her arm.

"That was quick!" I comment, glancing from her arm to the nurse at her side.

"She's got good veins. That made it easy," the nurse explains. "Just keep squeezing that ball, okay? I'll be back to check on you in a bit." She pats Charlotte's shoulder and walks away.

"How are you feeling so far?"

"Okay," she winces for a second. "It feels weird."

"What kind of weird?" I'm immediately concerned. Should I call the nurse back?

"Like I can feel my blood leaving my body. Am I supposed to feel it?" Her weary eyes tug at my heart. Once today is over, she can rest. Or at least that's what Cat told me, and that better be true.

"It's normal the first time you give blood for it to feel weird as it's happening," I smile to reassure her. "I've got a break after you're done. Do you want to go grab lunch?"

"That would be nice," she says, a gentle smile on her tired face. "We haven't eaten together in a while." The reminder of how little time we've spent together lately fills my stomach with guilt. True, Cat's been keeping her busy, but I'm the one whose been working late and leaving early almost every day to catch up on everything from the past few months.

"I know. After today, things will be better. I promise." I kiss her cheek and when I do, I realize how pale she's gotten in the past few minutes. "Hey, are you feeling okay?"

"I'm sort of lightheaded and woozy now, also kind of like I might throw up. Is that normal?"

"No, no it's not. I need a nurse over here right now!" I shout towards the group of nurses huddled around the check in table. One of them runs over and immediately gives Charlotte a bottle of water. A second brings a fan over to cool her down.

Charlotte's hand trembles a little as she sips the water. She looks at me and my heart presses against my rib cage. She's going to faint.

The first nurse lays the back of the bed down so Charlotte is now lying flat. I grab a juice box from the snack table and shove a straw in it.

"Drink this!" I take the water bottle away and give her the juice instead since that's easier to drink while lying down. After a few minutes that seem like a few hours, her color comes back and I can breathe easy again.

"I knew this was a bad idea," I mutter to myself. Unfortunately, Charlotte hears me.

"No, it was a good idea. I'm just bad at giving blood." Her joke doesn't make me feel any better about the situation. She hands me the empty juice box and looks at me with such sincerity. "How can the pastor's wife not donate when the blood drive was her idea in the first place?"

"Have you eaten today?" I answer her question with a question of my own. This is the first time in two weeks I've really gotten a good look at my wife and, aside from being worn down, she's also lost weight.

"Um, I may have forgotten to have breakfast," she admits, avoiding eye contact with me and glancing down at her arm as the nurses remove the needle and pack up her donation.

"How often have you been forgetting to eat?" I place my hand on her wan cheek and force her to look at me.

"I've just been really busy and..." she stops speaking when she sees how livid I am. "I'm sorry."

"You have to eat!" My voice is low and my tone is intimidating. "Is she good to go?" I turn and ask the nurses who are not doing a good job of hiding their interest in our conversation.

"Yes, but she needs to eat something and hydrate immediately." The nurse finishes Charlotte's arm wrap and walks away. I wrap my arm around Charlotte and help her off the table. She's a little weak on her feet, so I support her on the way out.

"Where are you going, William?" Cat's voice screeches from the door-way as we exit the sanctuary.

Without acknowledging Cat, I answer, "Home."

Once we're home, I prop Charlotte up on the living room sofa and order us lunch from her favorite restaurant. Cleo and Tony make themselves at home on her lap and for once I'm grateful for their presence.

"You don't have to treat me like a child," Charlotte complains. "I'm capable of taking care of myself."

"So am I." I lean over the back of the couch and rub her shoulders. "Eat."

After Charlotte begrudgingly eats her lunch, I sit down next to her and hand her a bottle of Gatorade. "Drink."

She rolls her eyes at me then precedes the drain the bottle. "I think I'm good now," she says, leaning against me. "Did you ever talk to Cat and tell her I need a break like I asked you to?" Charlotte asks accusingly.

"I did." I pause. "She explained that as soon as the blood drive was over, things would slow down."

"They better. I can't keep this up and I don't want to quit my job. I miss you."

"I miss you, too." It breaks my heart how little time we've spent together since we got married. "I'm going to do better about working late. I need to delegate more things to Mateo and stop being such a control freak about every little thing."

"This is why being Type B makes everything better," she teases me and kisses the side of my neck. "Being Type A would be so exhausting," she says with a yawn.

"Okay, time for a nap." I stand up from the sofa and scoop her up in my arms. She opens her mouth to protest. "Don't even deny you need it. You donated blood, you're not eating enough, and Cat has worked you nearly to death. Besides," I pause. "I promised you one two weeks ago and I'm overdue."

I carry her to the bedroom and lay her on the bed. She rolls over to her side and flops onto her pillow. I slide under the covers and curl around her body. Within seconds, she's completely passed out.

I feel absolutely awful that she's been working so hard and I've been too busy to notice. Worse than that, I hate myself for letting Cat do this to Charlotte. I need to stand up for her and stop being afraid of the consequences. The worst Cat can do is fire me and she won't fire her number one money maker.

Maybe Josiah is right. Maybe it's time to shake things up.

Chapter 27
Charlotte

"You look so good!" Lizzy gushes.

"Thanks, I feel good!" For the first time in a month, I'm refreshed and pampered. Two days at a really fancy spa with my best friend is just what I needed.

"You should guilt trip William more often about being a workaholic. This is paradise!"

"I'm glad you're enjoying yourself." True, the trip was William's way of alleviating his guilty conscience, though it doesn't replace all the time he's spent working at Hilltop. Thankfully, he has been more attentive and better at letting others take on tasks for him since the blood drive.

"Other people may think William is overpaid, but he really does earn his money," Lizzy says offhandedly.

"Who thinks he's overpaid?" Asking such a question is ridiculous when I'm wearing a luxurious plush robe after receiving a very long hot stone massage and drinking the most expensive smoothie of my life. I've been doing my best to not think about William's ridiculous salary and how much I've been benefitting from it lately. Other couples fight because they don't have enough money; we fight because he has too much.

"The older folks, mainly," Lizzy says, brushing my concern aside. "They still think movie tickets should be fifty cents. Besides, if they don't like it, there are plenty of other churches they can go to."

"I guess." I shrug my shoulders. "Those other churches probably have more exciting sermons, though, and that's why they don't leave."

"I was wondering if you'd noticed that." Lizzy sips her cucumber water and looks at me apprehensively. "If not for my parents, I'd probably go somewhere else."

"I wouldn't blame you if you did." I've thought about bringing that up to William. However, I wouldn't appreciate his feedback on my teaching, so I don't feel right criticizing his work. "Is Cat the reason they're so repetitive and basic?"

"I don't know about that, but she's definitely the reason for the ever so subtle reminders that God favors the generous," Lizzy points out, rolling her eyes.

"You know she called him and scolded him after we left the blood drive? She said she didn't care that I wasn't feeling well. He needed to be at Hilltop. All he was doing was walking around and talking to people!" I don't want to disturb the peaceful atmosphere of the spa, but I can't help getting a little loud when I think about Cat's audacity. That woman is the bane of my existence.

"She's such an awful old bat. I think because she worked with his dad, William is hesitant to speak up for himself."

"I bet Cat would lose her mind if William gave a sermon she hadn't approved. Her face would be priceless." I chuckle to myself as I imagine her reaction. "I read one of his sermons a few weeks ago and I was surprised that it actually had a message. I was looking forward to him giving it; however, when Sunday came, he gave another routine "God is love" and "everything in the world is great" type of sermon. I was so disappointed when William didn't give the sermon I read. It definitely would not have been approved by Cat, so I guess that's why he didn't give it."

"No offense, but your husband needs to grow a pair and stop letting Cat push him around. The congregation would follow him anywhere."

Our conversation is interrupted when one of the employees at the spa comes by to remind us it's time for our facials. I push William, Cat, and all things Hilltop out of my mind. I'm here to relax with Lizzy for the next few hours, not stress over things I can't control.

By the time I return home the next morning, I'm a new person, ready to tackle any problem that comes my way. Unfortunately, I don't have to wait long for one to present itself.

At first, it seems like a typical church service. I'm sitting in my usual seat at the front of the church, my hands resting in my lap while I busy my brain thinking about how to improve my teaching next year. As William is wrapping up his sermon, he pulls out a slip of paper from the folder on the pulpit.

"As we do every year, it's time to reflect on our generosity. On your way out, be sure to stop and grab a tithing chart. Of course, whatever you can give is greatly appreciated. This is simply a reminder of your duty to keep things running here at Hilltop so we can keep doing the Lord's work around the world and in our own community." He smiles politely as he speaks, completely embodying his polished preacher persona.

What is a tithing chart? After I wish thousands of people a good day on their way out the church, I make sure to grab one from Noelia before heading to William's office. While I wait for him, I read over it. What I see has my jaw dropping and my anger boiling. By the time William finds me, I'm overpowered by rage.

"You can't be serious!" I practically shout at him while waving the paper around.

"What are you going on about?" William's confused expression is genuine.

"This chart is insane!" I shove the paper in his face. He grabs it and, without looking at it, places it on his desk.

"Other than adjusting for inflation, it's the same chart I gave out last year and the year before," he replies calmly. "What's the problem?"

"The problem is you expect people who make $25,000 a year to give a hundred dollars a week to Hilltop. That's four hundred dollars a month, a whole car payment! That's absurd!"

"No one is making them give that much. It's a suggestion. I made that clear at the end of my sermon." William remains firm and unemotional.

"To you, it's a suggestion. To them, it's a requirement. There's even a QR code in the corner!" I sigh with exasperation at his cool demeanor. "You don't know what it's like to make just enough money to live. I do. This chart is going to make a lot of your members feel like crap since they can't give the *suggested* minimum each week."

"I've never made any member feel less than because they can't give the suggested minimum and I resent you implying that I have." He's starting to get testy. Good.

"Some of my former students go here. I know for a fact a lot of them are living paycheck to paycheck, with some on welfare and food stamps. They come here for the word of God, not to be reminded that they are less fortunate. You mention giving so often, your sermons are more like begging than preaching," I finally admit. "People probably think they're donating to earn the forgiveness of their sins."

"It's not like that!" William's jaw clenches as his hands clutch into fists at his sides.

"It worked for the Catholic Church for centuries, why not for Hilltop, too?" I can't hide the bitterness on my voice.

"All the money goes to helping others. You know that." His tone is finally sounding as enraged as I feel.

"Do I? For the past few months that I've been going here, I haven't seen a lot of money going towards others. Quite a bit was spent on the Summer Spectacular for the youth group, not to mention repainting the banquet room for our wedding reception, and repaving the perfectly fine parking lot." I pause my rant as an unfortunate and nauseating question enters my mind. "Where does the rest of the money go, William?"

"Well, church upkeep is part of it, and paying Hilltop's employees." He takes a deep breath to help him keep his cool, though I can tell it pains him to keep his frustration inside. We've had a few disagreements before, so I'm familiar with his emotional tells when we fight. This one is different, though, more consequential.

"And how much of that goes towards *your* salary?" I cross my arms and tap my foot impatiently. Even though we're married, he still won't tell me exactly how much he makes. At first, I thought he didn't want me to feel bad about my meager paycheck. Now, it's like he did it so I wouldn't realize how much he was scamming the people of Hilltop.

"Look," he says, glancing down at his fancy watch. "I have a meeting to get to, so can we talk about this later?" I hate that he's still in work mode right now. I want my William, not Reverend Collins.

The split between the two isn't as clear as it used to be since he's been spending all of his time at Hilltop doing Cat's bidding. And the worst part is, he shouldn't have to be two people at all; he should be able to be himself at home and at work. He's ravenous for money the way Cat's ravenous for his presence and service to Hilltop and I'm so sick of it!

"I'm not stupid," I snap at him. "I know you make a lot of money and you like nice things." I nod towards his wrist. "I know Hilltop is a big church with a big need for donations. I just never dreamed you were so...greedy." I ball up the tithing chart paper and throw it on the floor.

"Greedy?" He looks at me like I've slapped him. "You think I'm greedy?"

"There's no other explanation for all the begging and pleading every Sunday for more money. When will it be enough? When will you realize that your job is to bring your people closer to God, not wring their wallets dry? Is that why you never give a meaningful sermon? Are you worried they'll wise up and realize you're using them if you stray from Cat's script?"

"Enough!" William's voice thunders between us. "How dare you accuse me of being greedy! How dare you imply that I'm failing my people! You think you know Hilltop because you've been here for, what, five months? I've been here my whole life. This is my father's church; this is my church. I know them best, not you." The anger in his eyes has me a little scared, yet I can't seem to let this go.

"Then why don't you give them what they need?" My voice is breaking as I fight back my frustrated tears.

"I am! Just because you haven't seen the money going towards others, doesn't mean it isn't. Besides," he pauses and looks at me haughtily. "I didn't hear you complaining about my greed when we were in France for our honeymoon or when you went to that spa for the weekend."

"And I'm a hypocrite for that," I confess. "I'll admit it. Letting you use members' hard-earned money to help me relax was selfish. Flying first class and staying at a five-star hotel with a view of the Eiffel Tower was excessive and wrong. I didn't want to think about the source of my newfound financial frivolity. And that's the whole point. I never could have afforded that trip on a teacher's salary, so what makes you think people who makes less than I do can afford to donate for all this expensive shit?" My skin is crawling with buzzy little tremors that stretch from my fingers to my toes. The world goes blurry and my head throbs like a marching band snare drum. I lean back against William's desk and stare at the floor to try and ground myself before the panic attack gets any worse.

"Frivolity? Is that what you think it is?" He steps closer to me grabs my chin so I have to look up at him. "I work hard for all I have. I earn my paycheck the same as anyone else. You've seen firsthand how much of myself and my time this job takes."

"Is this job worth it?" I ask, staring past his Dolce & Gabbana glasses and into his icy blue eyes. "Why can't you just be content? Getting paid what you're owed is one thing, but that chart is the definition of greed." As the panic takes over and I start hyperventilating, William's expression softens.

"Remember your grounding techniques." His voice transforms from enraged to concerned. "Think about all the animals at a petting zoo. Goats, alpacas, sheep…" He's doing his best to help my anxiety abate, and I appreciate it. I can't remember any words right now, much less the types and names of animals at a petting zoo. He releases my chin and places his hands on my shoulders.

"Breathe, Charlotte. In for two and out for four. In and out." He models deep breathing for me and once I'm able to match it, tears start rolling down my face. "The only thing I'm greedy for in this world is you, *my wife.* I don't give a damn about the money."

"Prove it," I order him once I've calmed down. He uses his tie to wipe my tears away.

"Which part?" He raises his eyebrows and gives me a smirk.

"Both."

The next thing I know, William's whipping his tie from his collar, shoving it in my mouth and bending me over his desk with my skirt rucked up above my waist. Before William, I could easily go months without needing sex. But with him, I'm aching for his cock every day. Even while we were arguing, my pussy was throbbing and dripping with arousal as he got heated with each comeback. My breathing is ragged as he pounds into me, releasing his frustration and desire with each thrust. I grab the other side of his desk to keep myself steady.

"My greed for you consumes me, every waking moment," he growls as the power of his cock fills me completely and I'm lost to a world of pleasure I haven't experienced in so long. Even though William has been better about coming home on time, he's been too tired to do much when he comes home besides eat and sleep. "All I want to do every minute of the day is be with you, be inside you, be part of you, physically, emotionally, mentally. You make my life worth living, truly living." His words cradle my heart yet also send a rush of wetness to my pussy, ramping up the pleasure he's giving me with each thrust.

He bends down and whispers in my ear, "Now, milk my cock, Lady Charlotte. Make me spill inside of you. Feel how greedy I am for you."

Each slide of his cock in and out has me quivering for more. He slaps my ass repeatedly, causing me to scream through his tie. The taste of silk on my tongue has every muscle in my body tensing for release. My orgasm is on the horizon as William's cock grazes my G-spot. His grip on my hips tightens and his sheer need for me sends me over the edge.

My eyes roll back in my head as my cry of pleasure is deliciously muffled by his tie. He pulls out just as his cum starts to spill all over his hand. I guess that does prove how greedy he is for me; he didn't even stop and grab a condom first. I stand up and turn around to face William.

"Open wide." He orders and I comply willingly. After pulling his tie from my mouth, he replaces it with his cum covered fingers. "Clean me." I swirl my tongue around, licking and sucking each individual finger, relishing not only his taste, but also the deep groans that leave his throat each time he removes one from my mouth. "Good girl." He smiles approvingly at me before grabbing my hands and placing them over his chest. "Did I prove myself?"

"Oh, yes," I murmur, my mind and body still reeling from how intensely he fucked me.

"As to the other part," he pauses and sighs deeply. "I'm sorry for getting so wrapped up in my job that I completely lost my way. I," he pauses and looks thoughtful for a moment. "I'm becoming my father." He glances at his father's portrait hanging behind his desk. "I've been blindly following Cat's advice for too long." He stares deeply in my eyes and my heart aches for the pain and hurt in his face. "If you think of me as one of those money hungry, soulless preachers who care more about their bank account than the hearts of their congregants, what must God think of me?"

"God loves you, William. You know that." I assure him. "Money corrupts so easily. Coming into this church to fill your father's footsteps led you down his path, but you don't have to stay there."

"Then I won't." William replies, his tone resolute. "Then Jesus said unto his disciples, a rich man shall hardly enter into the kingdom of heaven. It is easier for a camel to go through the eye of a needle than for a rich man to enter into the kingdom of God."

"That is the kind of message your members need to hear. Cat's opinion be damned." It may be wrong to say such a thing in a church, but it's the truth. I'm sick of her manipulating William and being the one pulling all the strings behind the scenes.

"You know, Josiah said something similar a few months ago and I complete dismissed him." He smiles slightly. "He's going to be so mad I listened to you instead of him."

"He'll have to get over it." I place my hands around William's neck and pull his face down for a kiss. "Thank you for listening to me and taking care of me, especially when I fall apart."

"Taking care of you isn't just my job as your husband. It's my privilege and my honor to be your rock, your steady hand guiding you through the storm of life." William's words warm me inside and out. Just as he is learning to delegate to others, I'm learning to let him help me when I need it.

"As I hope I am to you."

"Always."

Chapter 28
William

I remember the first time Dad let me stand behind the pulpit. I was five years old and small for my age, so he helped me up the step ladder so I could see over it. The church was just beginning to grow at that point and it was in the process of being renovated. Instead of starting over with a whole new church, Dad was determined to just add on to the traditional style church.

I didn't care that the church was a construction disaster zone; it was beautiful to me. As I looked out over the pulpit and stared out at the rainbows of light filtering down onto the pews from the stained-glass windows, I felt the call. I knew that one day, I would be the one giving the sermon from up there. I would be the one the people turned to for advice, for comfort, for God's love.

A lot of people assume I became a preacher because Dad wanted me to. A lot of people assume he and I had a good relationship. People really shouldn't make assumptions.

I never intended to take his job so soon. We all assumed he had many, many more years left and I was happy as his assistant preacher. The way he left this world so suddenly, just like Mom had, rocked my world. However, there was no time to mourn, to grieve, to reflect. I immediately took over as head pastor, beginning with presiding over his funeral and giving every sermon since then except for the Sunday I was traveling to France with Charlotte.

The day after Dad's funeral, Cat came over to me and laid down the rules. I've never strayed from them in four years, no matter how often I've been tempted. Today, that changes.

As soon as I send the email, it's only a matter of time before she storms into my office. While I wait, I give myself a pep talk and remind myself not to let her have her way. I will stand up for myself. For my flock. For my wife.

"What in God's name is wrong with you?" Cat comes storming into my office, slamming the door behind her. Her phone is held high with my email on the screen.

"Nothing's wrong with me. I sent an email. That's in my purview to do as head pastor of Hilltop."

"You know you can't send anything to the members without running it past me first!" Her eyes are practically bulging out of her head. "That's protocol." There's fury in Cat's eyes that normally would have me cowering and surrendering to her will. Not today.

"That's *your* protocol. The one *you* came up with. The one *you've* had in place since Dad was in charge." I stand up and glare down at Cat.

"It works. It prevents problems. This," she points at her phone screen. "is a problem. A PR disaster in the making!" Her face reddens as her voice gets shriller.

"Things need to change around here and that starts today." I tap my finger on my desk calendar.

"And what, may I ask, is the reason for this *change*?" She puts air quotes around the word change. "This is too much. You punched Katie Johnson's poor fiancé last month and now you're telling members not to worry about giving to Hilltop? You're different now." She crosses her arms and glares at my left hand. "Is Mrs. Collins the reason for all of this?"

"The cause is immaterial." I wave away her nosy question.

"Your father would..." she begins. I don't let her finish that thought.

"I don't care what he would think or what he would do. I've been doing what he did for years and I'm tired of it. Charlotte has helped me realize that I've become too greedy, too predictable, to really help my people."

"The irony is unbelievable!" Cat throws up her hands and huffs loudly. "You married a woman who doesn't care about your paycheck when your father married one who cared too much."

"What are you talking about?"

"I know your father was just trying to protect you from the truth; however," she pauses, her expression turning malevolent, "its time you knew that your mom was a gold digger."

"You're lying!" My stomach clenches at her accusation. "I get that you're mad that I didn't get your approval before sending that message. However, that's no reason to make up lies about Mom." Who knew Cat was just one act of disobedience away from having a nervous breakdown? That has to be what this is. Right?

"I'm not lying, William." She steps towards my desk and grins furtively. "Did you really believe she had some good reason for leaving? Did you think she'd had enough of your father's workaholic ways and wanted a different life?" Cat starts cackling and the hair on the back of my neck stands up. "I bet you thought she'd come back one day and apologize, didn't you?"

"Stop!" I slam my hands on the desk, startling Cat and myself. "Are you so much of a control freak that you can't let me do one simple thing without warranting not only a scolding, but also an attack on my mother?

She's not even here to defend herself. Dad would be outraged to hear you talking about her this way!"

"No, William." Cat shakes her head. "He'd be mad I didn't tell you sooner." She looks behind me at Dad's portrait. "I should have told you the day of the funeral and just ripped off the band aid while you were already mourning. Instead, I did the heartless thing of letting you live in your fantasy world where Melanie wasn't a whore and you weren't a love child."

"Look," I say, taking a deep breath to calm myself before I respond to more of Cat's lies. "It doesn't matter what nonsense you make up to get back at me for the email. You need to accept that I'm in charge here and when I make a policy decision, it stands. Got it?"

"It's cute you think you're in charge here," Cat replies, smiling insolently at me. "You forget that I made you who you are today. I paved the way for your acceptance here. I taught you everything you know about how to guide the members."

"I can never forget what you did for me," I admit reluctantly. "However, where you see guidance, I see manipulation. Where you see dollar signs, I see people."

"And that's why you need me, William. You're too soft." Cat places her hands on her hips and shakes her head. "Just like your father."

"My father was a hard man, not a soft one, you know that." Maybe she's going senile after all. She knows better than I do how hard Dad was on me.

"He was hard to *you*. To everyone else, he was kind, caring, friendly. Didn't you ever wonder why he treated you like that? Why a man would treat his only son in such a cruel, almost emotionless manner?"

"A lot of fathers have high expectations for their sons. That's not unusual."

"True, but your case is different. Your father never planned on marrying Melanie. Once she got pregnant, he had to marry her or his good reputation would be ruined. After she attempted to bleed him dry for years, he got fed up and offered her a quiet divorce and a huge lump sum of cash if she would leave him."

"Unless you have proof of that, you will resign immediately." I can handle a lot of verbal abuse from Cat. I have been for years. But slandering my mom's name and defaming her reputation is something I will not stand for. My mind and heart are racing to keep up with all the lies she's spewing.

"You'll have my resignation over my cold, dead body." Her face is fading from tomato red to cotton candy pink, which hopefully means she's calming down. "I'll get your proof and when I do, you'll retract your email and give a proper apology, written by me, at the beginning of your sermon on Sunday."

"We'll see about that," I retort as she turns and stomps out of my office, slamming my door behind her. I drop down into my chair wearily and place my head in my hands. Fighting with Cat has completely drained me of all my energy for the day. For a sixty-year-old woman, Cat is surprisingly feisty. No wonder Dad just let her take control all the time; she's a force to be reckoned with.

What proof can she possibly find to back up her bullshit story? I lean back in my chair and resist the urge to scream. How did a simple email end up becoming a major war between Cat and I?

"You still alive in there?" Josiah's voice comes through my office door.

"Yeah, come in." As much as I want to be alone with my thoughts, it's probably for the best I talk to someone about them, and who better to discuss this crisis with than my best friend?

"I couldn't help overhearing your discussion with Cat," he remarks, a coy smirk on his face.

"I think people in the next town over heard my *discussion* with Cat," I retort, rolling my eyes.

"Did she really call your mom a gold digger? There's no way I heard that correctly." His eyebrows raise as he recalls Cat's less than kind words about Mom.

"Yep." I nod slowly. "She's supposedly getting proof of her allegations right now. When she doesn't find any, its good-bye Cat De Bourgh."

"Good on you for finally standing up for yourself! Sucks that she reacted like that, though." He shakes his head and holds out his hand. "Charlotte was just what you needed to realize the error of your ways."

I stand up and shake his hand. "Jealous you weren't the one to do it?"

"I was the push," he jests. "What you needed was a shove."

"In more ways than one," I respond with a laugh. It's good to joke around with Josiah after such a serious argument with Cat. I hope Charlotte will be proud of me for not giving into Cat's demands. I shouldn't have let her have so much power and control over me for so long. It made sense for the first year while I was getting my bearings. It doesn't make sense anymore.

I should have stood up to her earlier when Charlotte asked me to talk to Cat about her workload. Instead, I caved and Charlotte suffered for it. Neither she nor I will suffer anymore under Cat's thumb. Her rule of tyranny is over.

***

The next morning while I'm making a list of members to visit at the hospital and nursing home, Cat barges into my office and wordlessly hands me a thick envelope.

"What's this?" I take it and hesitantly start opening it.

"Proof." She spits out. "I look forward to reading your sermon for Sunday, apology and all." With a loud *humph*, she turns and leaves me alone to peruse the contents of this mysterious envelope.

I reach in and pull out a hefty pack of papers. My heart sinks when I read the first few lines:

Arthur Collins v. Melanie Collins
Complaint for Divorce

As I flip through the pages hoping for some kind of watermark or weird typing error to show she just made these up online, I realize the awful truth: Cat wasn't lying. It's clear now why Cat was insistent I have Charlotte sign a prenup. Based on the dates throughout the packet, it took two years to fully finalize their divorce, starting when I was fourteen.

Halfway through, I find the document regarding the money Cat referred to yesterday. She had the option of either small payments each month for ten years, or one large lump sum. She picked the pile of cash and never looked back. My parents' signatures at the bottom of each page are rocks through the stained-glass window of my childhood. As the glass shards of memories fall around me, the walls of my office begin closing in on me.

I lay the papers on my desk and place my palms on my bouncing legs. Memories of Mom's bipolar treatment of me now make sense. Some days she would hold me close and pepper me with kisses, others she would completely ignore me and act annoyed when I begged for her attention. Did she ever really love me or was I just a pawn in her scheme to get Dad's money? Based on the fact she left with his money in her bank account and didn't even say good bye, I'm guessing I was the latter.

My breathing becomes shallow and it feels like tiny ants are crawling under my skin. Is this an anxiety attack?

I stand up and stomp my feet to shake off this horrible sensation pervading my body. Instead, the feeling grows stronger as I come face to face with Dad's portrait. His permanent expression of relaxed happiness glowers down at me. The way the world saw him was how he started off. He wasn't always cruel and uncaring. For the first ten years of my life, he was actually a kind and loving father.

"Dad, look at my truck!"

Smile.

"Dad, I drew a picture of you!"

Smile.

"Dad, I want to be a pastor just like you!"

Smile.

"Dad, I love you!"

Smile.

It was only after my tenth birthday that he began to treat me differently, to be less accommodating of my mistakes, to be more critical of my actions, both in school and out of school.

"Dad, I got accepted into the honors program!"

Frown.

"Dad, I'm Valedictorian for my class!"

Frown.

"Dad, I got another scholarship for college!"

Frown.

"Dad, I got accepted to Harvard for seminary!"

Frown.

"Dad, I'm your new assistant pastor!"

Frown.

Perhaps that was when he realized Mom was only with him for his money. Perhaps that was when he began to think of me as a consequence, a mistake, as opposed to his son, his flesh and blood. I was only useful to him as a prop, something to use to fundraise for Hilltop after my accident.

He even managed to make money out of his misery by turning Mom into the bad guy once she left. I see now why that was so easy for him. She was always the bad guy; I was just too naïve to notice. If he had only told me, it would have saved us both so much heartbreak. Maybe he intended to at some point when I was older, never knowing that his life would be taken before he had the chance.

Learning all of my family's secrets like this, through hard copy black and white court documents handed to me vindictively by a woman I trusted for years and thought of as a second mother has me vacillating between anxiety and seething rage.

"You knew!" I scream at his picture. "You knew she never really loved us. You knew I meant nothing to her. You knew I was born to be a pawn! You treated me like shit because of her, because of your own stupid, fucking pride!"

My hands grab the sides of the wooden frame and rip it from the wall. "I refuse to let your shadow hang over me anymore. I'm done with you and your *legacy*!" I slam the portrait over my knee and savor the sound of the canvas ripping into jagged shreds.

I toss the destroyed painting aside and ignore my throbbing knee as I sit back down at my desk. Opening my laptop, I quickly pull up this week's sermon and add a generic apology at the beginning before sending it to Cat. It's the same generic content she likes, nothing problematic, nothing that could potentially offend anyone or draw negative attention to Hilltop. It's the sermon she wants, but its not the sermon she's actually going to get.

I place my hands back on the keyboard and let God's Truth finally speak through me.

Chapter 29
Charlotte

When William told me the truth about his parents, I didn't know how to respond. All I could do was console him and be there for him when the anger devolved into tears. Watching him cry was the most heartbreaking experience of my life. Just when he thought his parents couldn't hurt him anymore, they did.

And as for Cat? She's apparently known for over fifteen years that William's parents split up and only now, after having a hissy fit over not getting her way, she tells him the truth. What a bitch! I was already anti-Cat, but now, I want her gone. Someone that toxic shouldn't be working in a church, much less as the main advisor for the head pastor.

I can't help glaring at her from my pew during the offering. She, Josiah, and Mateo are perched behind William an in their usual seats high above the congregation. Her eyes have been glued to William since he opened today's service. She's fully expecting him to cave and grovel before the church, begging for her imperious forgiveness, flaying himself for her sadistic pleasure. What he doesn't know is that she's in for a nasty surprise.

William assumes the pulpit with a sense of calm confidence. He surveys his flock and smiles broadly at their trusting faces. My heart pounds as my anxiety climbs on his behalf.

"Before I begin today's message, I must first give an apology to you all." He pauses and glances behind him at Cat's wrinkled, gleeful face. "You may be wondering what I could have done to apologize to you about, what could I have done to merit asking for your forgiveness today?"

The members behind me begin to murmur to each other as their curiosity grows. My palms are sweaty as I firmly grasp my hymnal for stability. He's going to do it. He's actually going to do it.

"I have not done my due diligence as your pastor these past few years. I have failed you all." His words cause louder murmuring and whispers around me. I can't hide my smile at Cat's flustered expression.

"While I have been giving you my whole heart when it comes to our personal interactions, community meetings, and overall presence here at Hilltop, I have fallen flat with my weekly sermons. It has come to my attention that my messages are more demanding than rewarding, more begging than giving. Despite what I've been preaching for the past few years, your generosity here at Hilltop in no way guarantees a place for you in Heaven."

The whispers around me have grown to quiet conversations. I glance at Cat's now shocked face as she tries to compose herself behind William. Josiah is grinning like a kid who just learned school got cancelled and Mateo just looks super confused. I'm so focused on their reactions that I don't realize when Lizzy sits down next to me until she pokes my side.

"What's going on?" She whispers.

"You'll see," I whisper back, my eyes never leaving the stage.

"It wasn't until last week's tithing chart was passed out that I realized I'm asking too much of you. The only thing I should ever ask of you is that you love each other as Jesus loves you. With that being said," he stops and glances back at Cat. "Here is the sermon I want to give you, not the one I was told to give you."

If the entire church wasn't staring at her right now, I'm pretty sure Cat would walk off the stage and leave the sanctuary entirely. Her face is bright red and her hands are clenched in her lap as if to stop herself from getting up and strangling William.

"I guess you finally got through to him," Lizzy whispers to me and I nod in response. I can't wait to hear a real sermon from William, perhaps like the one I read on his computer a few weeks ago, one filled with passion, energy, and the Holy Spirit.

"I would like to bring your attention to the book of First Corinthians, chapter ten, verse thirteen, which reads, 'No temptation has overtaken you that is not common to man. God is faithful, and he will not let you be tempted beyond your ability, but with the temptation he will also provide the way of escape, that you may endure it.' In the face of temptation, be it greed or giving in to the will of others because it's easier than doing the right thing, stay strong. God will see you through it. And, if you fail, God will forgive you, for He is a loving, compassionate God. We are merely human; we make mistakes. No man or *woman* is above reproach, but also no one is above God's forgiveness." William glances behind him directly at Cat.

I can't help chuckling under my breath as I watch her flustered reaction to him calling her out. She's been in charge here for so long, it must be infuriating to watch William take control and lay the blame for Hilltop's greediness at her feet.

"I am a sinner in this regard, the same as anyone else. I have given into greed in my own life." He unbuttons his jacket and holds it up for everyone to see. "The suit I'm wearing cost two thousand dollars." He kicks off his shoes and holds them up, too. "These shoes cost four hundred dollars." Dropping his shoes, he pulls back his shirt sleeve and shows off his watch.

"This watch cost seven thousand dollars. I'm too ashamed to tell you how much my car cost." William shakes his head. "It's so easy to let the ways of the world win. It's so easy to replace God with the things Earth has to offer. I know. I've done it. And it took my wife, an underpaid and underappreciated teacher, to show me the error of my ways."

As all the eyes of the church fall on me, my face warms immediately. I wasn't expecting a shoutout in William's sermon. Lizzy taps my leg excitedly, making her bracelets jingle loudly.

"Despite what some may think, God sent Charlotte into my life to be my wake-up call, my voice of reason when I'm lost, my anchor when I wander too far from my purpose. She has shown me that my greed should only extend to her." He smiles charmingly as he makes eye contact with me. Obviously, the congregation has no idea what he's referring to. Since I do, I immediately begin sweating like a whore in church (cliché intended).

"Speaking of sinning, I'm so envious right now!" Lizzy murmurs in my ear, causing my blush to deepen until I'm pretty sure I look sunburnt. Things have been going well with her and Darcy, surprisingly, but what woman wouldn't want a man to proudly proclaim his love for her in front of over two thousand people? Despite my embarrassment, Lizzy's envy feels nice considering that, for the longest time, I was resentful of the fact that William was interested in her first, despite knowing that without that initial interest, I never would have met him.

"The root of greed is selfishness, and God knows I've been selfish. I've been selfish with my work, my time, and my heart. I lost myself through doing what I was told was the best thing for Hilltop. Charlotte pulled me back to the right path, the path of righteousness. And," he pauses to look back at Cat. "I'd like to thank Cat for pushing me to get married in the first place. Without that *push*, nothing would have changed. I would have kept coming up here and giving the same sermon every week, claiming generosity is the way to God's grace when we all know the real way to God's grace is accepting his son, Jesus Christ, as our Lord and Savior."

Cat's face is red as a tomato as she clutches the sides of her chair, probably fighting the urge to get up and make William stop talking. Josiah is practically bouncing in his seat with excitement and Mateo appears highly intrigued. I'm overjoyed by the fact that William is finally expressing himself the way he's always wanted to, the way he always should have been if not for Cat's manipulation and regulation of his sermons.

"None of you should ever feel that your financial circumstances prevent you from having a relationship with God or a sense of community at Hilltop. I've been living in luxury while most of you have been living paycheck to paycheck. Preachers often admonish those who won't give all in reference to the parable of the woman who came to the church and gave all she had even though it wasn't much. Mark twelve, verses 43 and 44 tell us, 'Jesus said, Truly I tell you, this poor widow has put more into the treasury than all the others. They gave out of their wealth; but she, out of her poverty, put in everything, all she had to live on.' This parable is meant to impress upon us the need to give no matter what, and it's a nice idea in theory, but you need your money more than Hilltop does. You give, and give, and give until you have nothing left and we have more than we possibly need or even use. That's not right. The days of greed here are gone. It has played too big of a role in Hilltop's supposed mission and in my own life. It cannot continue." William's expression is intense, though not angry. He exudes a sort of powerful calm, the same sort of calm I imagine Jesus felt when he gave his sermons thousands of years ago.

"I have one announcement as I bring my sermon and today's service to a close. There are many of you who have been members at Hilltop for several years, so you knew my father. He served Hilltop for almost thirty years before the Lord called him home." A strained smile appears on William's face. "If you were fond of him, you may want to leave before you hear what I'm about to say about him." He pauses and glances around the sanctuary to give people time to leave. No one's leaving. Even if they loved Arthur Collins, they still want to know whatever awful thing William is about to reveal about him.

"My father had the misfortune of marrying a greedy woman who loved money more than she loved him. I am the product of their unhappy union." He swallows hard before continuing. "You were led to believe that my mother, Melanie Collins, left him without warning, thereby making him a very sympathetic character. Many of you gave huge donations to Hilltop after that happened. You were deceived."

At this point, Cat stands up and approaches William. My body is completely frozen as little anxious bees buzz under my skin. Lizzy keeps tugging my sleeve to get my attention, but I can't take my eyes off of William. He's telling them everything.

"William, stop, stop right now!" Cat's voice cracks over William's microphone. She actually tries to drag him away from the pulpit, her wrinkled hands creasing his suit jacket.

"No, they deserve to know the truth. They deserve to know how they were used, how Dad only saw them as his personal piggy banks, how he manipulated them after my car accident, how both you and him cared more about the almighty dollar than Almighty God." William's voice booms over the speakers that hang on all corners of the sanctuary.

"William Collins, you're fired!" Cat screams at him, jabbing her index finger in his face, which is a good foot above her head.

"Thank you, Cat," William responds in a surprisingly calm and almost happy tone. The bees under my skin have begun to swarm and breathing is no longer an automatic function. Lizzy squeezes my hand, reminding me to take a deep breath.

"That makes my announcement so much easier." William leans towards the microphone on the pulpit and says, "Anyone who's interested in creating a true church of God, one not focused on the things of this Earth, is welcome to come with me. Right now." He steps around Cat as he makes his way off the stage and towards me.

"Let's go." William approaches me and grabs my hand, releasing me from my anxious prison. I stand up and follow him down the center aisle and out of the church. Once we're in the foyer, I turn to him and exhale slowly.

"I can't believe you did that." I'm in awe of his words and actions. He didn't tell me he was going to air his family's dirty laundry and then walk out of Hilltop altogether.

"Neither can I," he admits. "But it was the right thing to do." He holds me in his arms and looks so sure of himself, so utterly confident in the face of the fire he just set to his career.

"Now what?" I glance between him and the front door.

"We wait." William smiles reassuringly at me and my anxiety abates entirely. His surety fills my heart with hope and excitement for the future.

We don't have to wait long before Josiah bursts through the sanctuary doors like the Kool-Aid Man.

"Let's do this!" Josiah gives William a very enthusiastic high five. "You should see Cat's face right now. She is about to blow." He laughs loudly and looks behind him. "She made a big mistake."

"How so?" Before he can answer my question, the doors open wide and people flood the foyer. Mateo, Noelia, the Bennetts, and countless other members cram into Hilltop's front entrance.

William pulls me toward the doors and we lead everyone out into the parking lot before claustrophobia takes hold of everyone. Once we have more room to spread out, William stands in front of the crowd like Moses must have done when he led the Jewish people out of Egypt.

"Thank you all for your trust in me. I will do my best to not let you down." He takes in his people with a proud smile on his handsome face. "Hilltop is tainted for me now, and I need a new place to faithfully spread the word of God. I don't have a new church for us yet, but God will provide." He beams so brightly, glowing in the late morning sunlight. "The moment I do, you will be the first to know. Assuming Cat takes away access to my Hilltop email account, I won't have a way to reach you all. So," he pulls out his phone. "If you will all put your contact information in my phone, I'll let you know when the first service is." As William's phone makes its way around the group, I start counting each person in the parking lot.

"William," I say, turning to him excitedly, "There are over two hundred people here!"

"God is good," he replies, his eyes shining bright.

"When did you decide to ruin Cat's life?" I joke.

"This morning." He smiles sheepishly. "I was printing out my sermon and I realized that if I'm being honest with everyone, I may as well be honest all the way. If I'm leaving, I'm leaving with a clear conscience."

"I'm so proud of you," I tell him, and I mean it. He's come a long way from the William Collins I met a few months ago. He's no longer stoic all the time, no longer two personas split between work and home, no longer controlled by his father's wishes and disapproval, no longer afraid to step outside of his comfort zone, and no longer held back by a job that told him who to be. He's happy; he's free. He can now have the church he wants and give the message he wants every Sunday. Sure, it will be hard to start fresh elsewhere without an already existing church and congregation to serve as a sort of security blanket, but he can do it, and I'll be by his side to help the whole way, not to mention these supportive people from Hilltop.

"Here you go, William." Mateo hands William his phone with a broad grin. "I can't wait to see the church you create."

"The church *we* create," William corrects him, a welcoming smile on his face. "It will be a church for everyone, one focused on our relationship with God, one not focused on material things. Hilltop started off with good intentions. Over time, Hillltop became corrupted and tainted by greed. Today, we start fresh."

As William and I look at these very trusting people, a summer breeze flows around us and I can sense that the Holy Spirit is with us. When God told me to trust William, he meant to trust him not only with my heart, but with my soul as well. God knew William needed me to help him discover the error of his ways, and He knew I needed William to heal my heart and be my firm foundation when the world gets to be too much.

"I didn't expect so much praise in your sermon today," I admit to William once the crowd has dissipated and we're in his car getting ready to go home.

"I meant every word," he says, starting the car. "And I plan on continue praising you when we get home." He winks at me with a knowing smile as he puts the car in drive.

"Do you now?" I ask with an eager giggle, my center already warming at the thought.

"Oh!" My cheeks color at his compliment as his right hand begins to rove over my thighs. As I lose myself to this moment, I find myself overwhelmed by how surprisingly amazing life can be when you least expect it.

Six months ago, William and I were strangers to each other, completely unaware of how we would grow to love and appreciate each other over time, never knowing that God would use us for both His and our own personal benefit. Who could have known that Cat forcing William to get married would have led to us both finding the person we were meant to be with?

As William races home, the answer comes to my mind loud and clear: God.

Epilogue: One Year Later

William

Shortly after I arrive home from work, I overhear Charlotte talking to someone in the living room. When I enter, she points at the phone glued to her ear and waves me into the room.

"Oh wow! I mean, I knew she was greedy, but this is wholly unexpected." Charlotte says as she sits down on the sofa. Catching my eye, she gestures toward the TV. A reporter is standing in front of Hilltop while two police officers led a very embarrassed looking Cat out of the church and place her in a squad car.

"Cat De Bourgh, CEO of the megachurch Hilltop, has been found guilty of embezzling funds from the church she's worked at for over thirty years. Sources close to De Bourgh say…" The reporter's voice fades away as I process this shocking news.

I mute the TV and rewind the news footage. I pause the screen right as the officers open the car door. I can't help staring at Cat's face, the face that guided me through my first years at Hilltop, the face that comforted me when Dad died, the face that reminded me constantly what my role was as the cash cow of Hilltop, and the face that revealed to me the shocking truth of my parents' miserable marriage. Oh, how the mighty have fallen.

"Lizzy, I have to go. Thanks for letting me know." Charlotte hangs up the phone as I sit down next to her on the couch. "Hey." She looks at me with a soft smile and kisses my cheek. "Can you believe this?" She nods towards the TV where Cat's face is still frozen in time.

"It does explain why she wanted me to beg for money every Sunday. It was all for her in the end." I run a hand through my hair and lay an arm over her shoulders. "I'm so glad we left Hilltop."

"Speaking of not-Hilltop, how was work today?" she asks, snuggling into my chest.

"Really good," I reply, sighing contentedly. I've been so much happier since leaving Hilltop and starting my own church. I no longer spend ten plus hours at work every day, which has been great for our marriage and my overall health. Josiah, Mateo, and Noelia have been working with me and collaborating on church duties as a team. "The Youth Group is volunteering at the food bank this weekend, so Josiah has been on top of coordinating that. Mateo has found a bunch of quality instruments on clearance so we can finally have a worship band now. And Noelia is going to organize a church dinner to raise money for a new roof for the church."

"That sounds wonderful!" She wraps her arms around my shoulders and gives me a tight squeeze. "Don't forget to leave Saturday open for Lizzy's engagement party," she reminds me.

"Still can't believe she's marrying that guy," I groan. "He's so awkward."

"Yeah, but he makes Lizzy happy, so we'll tolerate him. Besides, we're going to support Lizzy."

"Speaking of Lizzy, did you tell her yet?" I place a hand on her lower stomach. She smiles broadly and moves to stand up.

"Not yet. I don't want to steal her thunder." She starts to walk away until I reach out and gently pull her back onto the sofa.

"I'll handle dinner. You rest." I kiss her forehead and make my way to the kitchen.

"I'm not an invalid!" She yells from the living room. "I can still do stuff. What do you think I do at work all day?"

"Work. That's why you need to rest." I return to the living room and prop her feet up on the footstool. Cleo and Tony jump onto her lap and curl into happy purring machines. She's only three months along, so she's not really showing yet. I'm being overprotective, but she's my everything. I want her to be as comfortable as possible during the next few months as her body works overtime to create our child.

"Hey you," she says, reaching her hand out to pull me close. I let her grab my shirt and drag me in for an unexpectedly passionate kiss. "Thank you."

"Careful now," I warn her. "You keep that up and dinner will never get done." I smile mischievously at her and gently wrap my hand around her delicious neck.

"How about we save that for dessert? We're hungry." She pats her stomach and grins sweetly.

"Anything for you, Lady Charlotte." I bow like a knight before his queen and walk to the kitchen to finish preparing dinner. While I stir the pasta, Cat's face invades my thoughts. This time last year, she called me into her office to demand I marry someone or I would lose my job. Now she's being arrested for embezzlement and I'm running an entirely different church totally unconnected to my family's messed up legacy and I'm eagerly anticipating the birth of my first child.

Before Charlotte got pregnant, the happiest day of my life was the day we got married. Now I have so many more happiest days to look forward to as Charlotte and I embark on the terrifying and exhilarating journey of parenthood. I can't wait to be a father, a much, much better father than my own, one who actually loves and supports his son, one who listens and wants to be there for all of his child's good and bad moments, and one who will never, ever make his child feel less than or unworthy of my approval.

I plate dinner and set it on the table before feeding the cats. Once they jump from Charlotte's lap, she joins me at the table.

"Just think, in a few months, it won't just be us at the table." Charlotte says, looking at me with so much love and pride in her eyes I think I'll bust.

"Oh, you mean when Eleanor moves in?" I joke. Eleanor has already planned to take off work and live with us for the first month after little Collins is born.

"That's not what I meant," she laughs and rolls her eyes. "But thanks for the reminder."

"She's going to be a fantastic grandmother," I state.

"I know." She smiles at the thought. "And you're going to be the world's greatest dad. Don't doubt that, ever."

"How could I not be with the world's greatest mother by my side?" I smile tenderly at her.

"Either way, he's going to be a lucky kid."

"He?" Charlotte doesn't usually give our child any type of pronoun.

"I just have a feeling, that's all." She shrugs her shoulders and dabs at her mouth with a napkin. "Now," Charlotte stands up and walks over to me. "I'm ready for dessert."

"Since when are you the one in charge here?" I stand up and grab her chin, forcing her to look up at me with her bright green eyes.

"Since I'm the one carrying our son," she retorts, a devilish grin on her sexy lips.

"Good point." I quickly sweep her up into my arms and carry her to the bedroom. She giggles and kicks her feet the whole way there.

Life is good.

God is good.

Thanks be to God.

Acknowledgements

My first and biggest thank you is to my husband who not only read the first draft and was my first editor, but who also helped me brainstorm and work through plot points along the way. I could not have written or published this without his support and inspiration.

Of course, I would also like to thank my beta readers/friends for reading my book and giving me direct, honest feedback. They are an invaluable part of my writing process and I love them all so much!

I would also like to thank Jane Austen for creating the characters of Charlotte and William within the beloved novel, *Pride & Prejudice*. Without her, this story would not have been possible.

And thank you, the reader, for reading this book and taking a chance on me and my writing! If you liked it, please leave a review online (Amazon, Goodreads, etc.) and follow me on social media: @authorcjowens!

Lastly, as this is a book with Christian characters and I am a Christian, I would like to thank God for not only blessing me with a talent for writing, but also blessing me with a love for reading and analyzing literature, a full time job to support this indie author hobby of mine, and the love of a man who was definitely written by a woman.

About the Author

C.J. Owens lives in the middle of nowhere with her husband and fur babies. She enjoys binge watching Law & Order SVU, reading romance novels, eating too much chocolate, and collecting anything with cats on it. This is the third novel in her Classics Retold Romance series. With a passion for writing deep in her soul, she looks forward to retelling many more love stories between overlooked or unexpected characters from classic literature.

You can follow her @authorcjowens on:
TikTok
Instagram
Facebook
Threads
BlueSky
YouTube

Check out her website:
www.authorcjowens.wordpress.com